Heaven

A Pearl Lake Novel

Book 4

Aquila Thorne

Heaven in the Moonlight
Book 4 Pearl Lake the Series
Copyright © 2021 Aquila Thorne
ISBN: 9798413281826

{Pearl Lake Series}

Reading Order
Moonlit Night (Moonlit Stalker included)
Moonlit Road
Heaven in the Moonlight
The Inn at Pearl Lake
Lane's Destiny
Tim's Bar
Her Christmas Wish
You can find the Pearl Lake Series right here! [1]

{The Blood Moon Series}
The Summons
Heaven and Hell
You can find it here! [2]

Prologue

"What do you mean, I can't get a discount?!" The woman all but screamed across the counter into the young woman's face.

Ava stood, staring at the lady in shock. The last customer of the day and of course she just had to start yelling. Instead of yelling back, Ava mentally cursed out her Aunt Kim. She would need to remember to thank her for sending such a tyrant to her shop.

She inhaled a slow calming breath and counted to ten.

"Ma'am. I'm sorry, but company policy does not allow for a discount on our already discounted promotional packages. Not to mention you did get $50.00 off for the friends and family discount." Ava replied in what she hoped was her sweetest tone.

The melodious tune from the door opening, announced that a new customer had just walked in as the woman continued her rantings.

"I demand to speak to the owner." The woman puffed out her cheeks, making her look like a blowfish that was about to pop.

"Cool your jets there, Claudia." Kim piped up as she sauntered in. Laughing, she asked, "What's got your knickers in a twist now?" She propped her arms on the counter and leaned forward, looking at the woman.

"This..." Claudia looked at Ava with distaste. "...girl refused to get the owner after I had a valid complaint!"

Ava made a small cry of protest at the lie the woman just told.

"Is that so?" Kim arched a brow as she glanced at Ava. She directed her attention back to the crotchety woman. "And what is it you need to speak to the owner about?" Kim couldn't help grinning, knowing that Claudia was about to be in for a rude awakening.

Not that Kim disliked Claudia. She didn't really know her all that well. Aside from her being a patient at the doctor's office where Kim worked as a nurse. A patient that claimed she was in 'desperate need of some pampering' or so Claudia declared to her just last week. The woman did rub people the wrong way with her demanding attitude. Old money ran deep in that family and Kim supposed it was from ordering all her servants around.

"I simply asked for a discount on the package I purchased. $150 is a little steep in my opinion for the services that were rendered." She sniffed.

Apparently, Claudia was cheap too. Kim snorted. She knew there wasn't a finer spa in the city than Ava's.

That remark had Ava seething. Considering it was already half price, the woman was delusional if she thought she was getting it any cheaper.

"Here, let me see the bill." Kim snatched the paper off the counter and noted the smug smile on Claudia's face. She scanned the page and smacked it back down, pointing at it. She looked at Claudia and said, "Seeing how you were already talking to the owner, who happens to be my niece, she can fix this right now."

"Ava, here is your mistake. You gave her a discount for the friends and family... which she is neither." Kim smiled sweetly at Claudia as she walked around the counter to stand beside Ava.

Together, they watched as Claudia turned every color of the rainbow as she dug in her purse for her wallet. "I've never been treated with such disrespect in my life!" Claudia spat, tossing her credit card on the bill.

"Yeah. Well, that's your prob—"

A sharp elbow to her ribs had Kim shutting up. Ava tossed her a dark look as she processed the payment and handed the woman her card back.

Snatching it from Ava, Claudia spun on her heel then stopped. She turned to look back and said, "I will be sure to tell all my friends about this! And Kim, you can be assured I'll be telling Dr. Wellington about your conduct!"

Kim made a face at Claudia's back, mocking her as she exited the building.

"I could have handled that Aunt Kim. What if she tells Dr. Wellington, what will you do?" Ava knew her aunt was already on thin ice with her boss. The thought of all the customers she'd likely lose once word got around, caused Ava's brow to knit with worry as she went to lock the door.

"Oh, I know you could. And I never thought of that to be honest. I just wanted to put that woman in her place once and for all. She treats the world like shit but expects to be treated like she is the Queen of England or something." Kim stifled a yawn. "So where are we going for dinner, I'm starving."

"I thought we would try that new place over on Sunnyside, if that's alright with you?" Ava said, turning the sign in the window to close.

"Sounds good to me."

"Okay, can you give Luke a call? He and Lane are going to meet us wherever we decide on. I just need to do my till and then we can go." Ava pulled the drawer out of the cash register, listening with half an ear, she heard Kim chatting away as she headed to her office.

"OOH THIS IS NICE." Kim looked around in awe as she took her seat. Her eyes settled on the gleaming hardwood of the massive staircase that sat in the center of the dining area of the Edge of the Sea restaurant.

Lane nodded. Grabbing a chair, he pulled it out and sat. "Yeah, it's surprising what they can do to an old riverboat. Just wait till we leave the dock."

Kim's eyes zeroed in on Lane's face. "Wait." Giggling nervously, she gripped his arm like a vise. With a hurried hiss, she asked, "What did you say?" She was glancing around furtively, looking for the closest exit when they felt the smooth rocking of the ship slip forward.

"Oh, hell no. I can't do this." Kim shook her head vehemently while she grabbed her purse and stood up. "Let's go."

Lane pried her hand off his arm and looked up at her. "Aunt Kim it will be fine, it just goes up the river and back. I promise, you'll forget you're on a boat once the food comes."

Ava tugged on Kim's arm and urged her aunt to sit down, once she flopped onto her chair, Ava looked at her brother. "I thought Luke was coming too?"

The waiter's arrival momentarily stopped their conversations. With menus tucked under his arm and a tray full of ice water balanced on the other, he somehow managed to sit a coffee pot on the table without it all toppling over.

"Hey guys." He grinned as handed them each a menu. "I'm Brian and I'll be your gopher tonight. Can I get you folks some drinks before you order?"

Ava smiled. "Water is fine for me."

Kim was fighting the sting of bile that rose in the back of her throat. "Do you have a Gravol margarita by chance?"

The Brian stared at her blankly.

She shook her head. "No? ... water it is." She picked up a glass and chugged half of it before setting it back on the table. A loud burp escaped past her lips.

Ava noticed Brian masked his outburst of laughter pretty quick by faking a cough.

Waving a hand in front of her face, Kim said, "Whoa, s'cuse me, no idea where that came from."

She was oblivious to the staring and snickers from the other patrons, but Lane wasn't. Shielding his face with his hand, he flipped a cup over that was sitting on the table. "Coffee is good enough for me, thanks." He watched as the waiter skillfully poured the piping hot liquid.

"I'll give you a few minutes to decide," Brian said, as he made a quick exit.

Lane glanced at his watch. "Ah... Luke is supposed to be here." He scanned the room for his twin, then jerked his head towards the bar. "There he is."

All eyes turned to look. There stood Luke talking to a striking black-haired beauty. Luke saw them the same instant. Tugging on the woman's hand, they made their way towards the table.

Kim snorted, as she fished an ice cube out of her glass. "Who is that? The new flavor of the week?"

"Kim!" Ava hissed. "What is *wrong* with you?"

"What?! I know you're thinking the same thing. Don't deny it missy." She popped the ice cube in her mouth and grinned as the couple sat down.

"Hey guys." Luke looked around the table. "I want you to meet Cassie, my girlfriend. Cassie, this is my sister Ava, Aunt Kim and you know Lane."

"Nice to meet you." Ava smiled while Kim kept silent, grinning like a fool.

The waiter came back just then and took their order, assuring them the wait wouldn't be too long.

Ava pushed her glass out of the way and laid her arms on the table, leaning forward she looked at Luke. "So. How long have you two been dating?"

Kim giggled. "Oh about—"

Ava shot her aunt a glare. Knowing she was about to say something totally inappropriate, she said, "Aunt Kim, eat more ice." She placed another glass in front of Kim with a thud.

"What?!" Kim said accusingly.

"You know what!" Ava pointed to the glass. "Eat. The. Ice!"

Touching a finger to her temple, Ava said, "Now, where were we? Oh right, how long have you two been dating?"

Cassie looked from Ava to Kim, then Luke. "Is your aunt alright?" She turned her attention back to Ava. "You know I heard that when people need to eat ice it's because they are lacking something. It's called pica... I think. Kim, did you eat paint chips or feces as a child?"

"Sweet baby Jesus. Now look at what you did Ava! The girl thinks I'm a shit eater."

Lane burst out laughing at the same moment Ava kicked Kim under the table, imploring her with her eyes to be nice.

Eyes flashing, Kim didn't say a word. Instead, she stuck her fingers into the water and fished out a nice square cube. Popping it in her mouth she sent a sarcastic smile at her niece. Ava knew her better than anyone at the table.

"Ah, we have been together for a week. I'm bringing her to meet Mom when we go up for May 24," Luke said, gazing into Cassie's eyes.

Kim whipped her head around to look at Luke. *Bring her to meet Abbi... is he nuts?*

All the sudden, she could feel her eyes bug out of her head... the ice cube went down the wrong hole. Clutching her throat all she could think about was the regret of not leaving the restaurant. She should have swam to shore.

"Aunt Kim, are you alright?" Ava cried in alarm. Feeling guilty that she told her to eat the ice in the first place, Ava stood and smacked Kim on the back.

"Jesus Ava, you're going to break her ribs. Here Aunt Kim, take a sip." Lane handed her his coffee cup.

Kim took a gulp of the scalding coffee. It melted the ice cube alright, because it made a searing path down to the pit of her stomach. "Thanks," she gasped as she set the cup on the table, she wiped the tears that sprang to the corners of her eyes on her sleeve.

Concern was etched on Ava's face. "Are you okay?"

"Yeah. I'm good."

"Good." Ava sat back in her chair. "Okay. So, I wanted to know from you two how do we convince mom to move back home?" she asked, looking at her brothers.

She missed their mother more than they did. Having done everything with her, it was a hard pill to swallow, when she upped and moved to Pearl Lake. Ava didn't blame her. After her mom's book hit the number one on the New York Times best sellers list, some crazed fan was after her. Abbi pulled up stakes and was gone in the blink of an eye.

"Oh, would you look at that!" Cassie said, all eyes turned to see the waiter carrying a large tray with their food.

"Ava, you can't, that's how. Your mom is finally happy. You can't expect her to move back here. She's made a home there." Kim reasoned. With a fear of tossing her cookies, she took her plate from the waiter.

"But she's alone, and since the break-in I worry about her constantly." Ava sighed.

"Well, I don't think she's alone. Not anymore." Lane leaned back as the waiter placed a heaping plate of food in front of him.

Luke smiled. "What do you mean she's not anymore?"

"When I called and told her we would be up Thursday, she said she was going to invite a friend over." Lane shrugged his shoulders. "Said his name was Ben."

"Ben? Ben, who?" Kim asked, munching on a fry.

"She didn't say. Nor did she say what kind of friend."

Ava's thoughts turned to the worst scenario. In her mind, she could picture exactly what he looked like. The type that was only after one thing. Money. She pushed her food around with her fork. "Why don't we surprise her and go up early. Beat the traffic?" She was ready to leave this second, the sooner the better as far as she was concerned. She wanted to see what this friend of her mother's was really like. "Well?" she asked, impatiently.

"How soon were you thinking?" Luke asked, checking his phone to see if he had any meetings for the rest of the week.

"Now."

"Are you crazy Ava?" Lane bit out. "We can't just leave now."

"Why not? All of us have the luxury of just picking up and leaving without the worry of being fired. And besides, how long has it been since we've seen mom? Christmas, that's how long. Don't you think that's been long enough?" Ava asked.

"She does have a point." Kim nodded vigorously.

Lane looked at Luke, who then looked at Cassie then back to Luke. Glancing at his sister, he threw his hands in the air. "Sure, why not?"

"Yes!" Ava squealed. Jumping up, she ran around the table to hug her brothers.

"Ahem." Kim cleared her throat.

All sets of eyes turned to Kim. "What about you Kim, do you have any plans for the next week or so?" Luke asked.

"I can't say that I do, I'm off for a month." Her thoughts turned to Claudia and the display she had caused in Ava's shop. She smoothed a hand over her hair and mumbled, "Um, likely indefinitely."

"Then it's settled. Let's get out of here." Ava headed back to her chair to collect her belongings; she grabbed her cellphone to check the time. Tossing three, hundred dollar bills on the table, she said, "We can all meet at our place if you like."

At her brother's nod, she headed towards the exit. "Come on Aunt Kim, let's go home and pack."

Chapter 1

1 *year later*
The sound of paper ripping filled the room as Ava tore off the used sheet on the massage chair. She was tidying up from the last customer of the day and was looking forward to having the weekend off. She couldn't remember the last time she'd had a day off let alone two.

Since selling her spa in Windsor and becoming a permanent resident Pearl Lake, one would think business would be nonexistent in the tiny village. It was the total opposite, not that she was complaining. She was happy that she'd made the move. Nine months ago, she had bought a century old, two storey brick home. It sat atop the hill overlooking the lake in the heart of the village. As soon as she saw it, she knew it was the perfect place to set up her shop, knowing it would offer her clients a relaxing view as well as herself.

She loved living there. She loved it even more for the fact that the two most important people in her life were there too, her mom and Aunt Kim. But something was missing from Ava's life. What – she wasn't entirely sure. Maybe it was a man.

Don't be silly Ava, you don't need no man in your life... she reminded herself gently as she closed the door and headed to the reception area.

She had already traveled down that road once in her life and there was no way she wanted to do so again. There was another reason why she'd moved, there was more to it than just wanting to be close to her mom. She had needed to get away from the town she'd grown up in and Kurt Falconer, her ex. He was an ass... an abusive one that used her as a punching bag more often than naught.

Everyone was shocked when they broke up, her family as well as his. After five years she'd had enough. She never told her mother or her aunt what really happened with their relationship. To do so would have only made things worse... much worse. Many times, he had threatened to go after her mom, knowing she was Ava's weakest link.

Kurt had vowed he would destroy Abbi publicly if Ava told a soul. He had connections in the publishing industry and her book sales would have plummeted. In retrospect Ava knew that would never have happened, but at the time he had her convinced it would. And Aunt Kim, she would have ended up in jail no doubt from beating the shit out of him. No, instead, she'd told them he had cheated. Ava never did have proof and wouldn't be surprised if he had, but in her mind he'd still cheated. He had cheated her out of the life she deserved... what every woman deserved, to be loved and cherished. Just like how Ben, her mother's fiancé, treated Abbi like she was a precious gem in a sea of pink diamonds.

She'd finally gotten rid of Kurt when she threatened to expose him for the scum that he was. With his mother being the mayor and his father considered the best plastic surgeon in Ontario, it was a threat he took very seriously.

A knock on the outside door interrupted Ava's thoughts. Crossing the room, she felt a sense of panic when she saw Ben standing there through the beveled glass.

She yanked the door open. "Oh my gosh is it mom? Is the baby coming?!"

"What? No! No, I just had to stop at Mack's to get a few things and thought I'd stop by to see if you and the others wanted to come over for dinner tonight."

Immediately Ava relaxed. Ever since finding out her mom was pregnant; she was always worried. With Abbi about to have a baby at the age of 46, Ava figured she had a right to be worried.

She smiled. "I don't know about Kim and Mark, but sure, sounds like a plan to me. Let me get my purse and I'll walk with you."

Walking to her office she turned off her computer and closed the blinds. She gathered her things from under her desk and closed the door with a soft thud. She was busy looking in her purse making sure she had the week's deposits as she walked into the reception area. Satisfied, she closed the clasp and slung the strap over her head, holding it securely to her side.

"I'm ready. Can we stop by the bank first or do you have anything that...?" She looked up, her words suddenly coming to a halt. *Where the hell is, he?*

Following the sound of people talking, Ava walked out onto the veranda. There, Ben stood with a man in front of the water fountain in the side garden. It was more of a jungle than it was a garden she was ashamed to admit. She'd had every intention of cleaning it up to reveal the heirloom plants hidden amongst the weeds, she just never had the time.

Maybe this weekend I'll tackle it.

"Here she is." She heard Ben say. "Ava this is Ashton Davenport, he just moved here from..." Ben frowned and squinted at the man. "Where did you say again mate?"

"Texas, southern Texas," he drawled, holding his hand out to her. "And Ash works fine."

"Texas huh? That's quite the distance from here." Ava commented, taking his proffered hand.

"It is. I needed a break from all the sun I guess you could say."

"Ah, Ava." Ben scratched his head and shot her a sidelong glance. "We were just talking about your garden here. Ash does landscape for a living and thinks he could offer some help."

She arched a brow at Ash. "Do you now?"

Ava had her doubts about the man. For one, he didn't look the type to get his hands dirty, his hand was too soft. And for another, he wasn't tanned. For a man working outside daily in the hot Texas sun, one would think he would at least have a slight tan.

"I do." Ash nodded. "For the last ten years or so."

Ben could feel the tension radiating off Ava and it wasn't the good kind either. Taking a step between the two of them to diffuse it, he looked at her. "You might want to think about clearing the area up a bit, you know, to give your clients a calming view."

"Perhaps," she responded. At Ben's look, she added. "Yes. Maybe I should." To appease Ben, she said, "Where might you be staying at Ash? In case I want an estimate."

She had no intention of hiring anyone to clean the garden. She would do it herself.

Ash jerked his thumb over his shoulder. "I'm just over by Mackwell's store, right across from it. Yellow house."

Ava always admired that house. It reminded her of grandparent's home. A cute two storey, cape cod style home, trimmed in white against sherbet yellow siding. A huge weeping willow graced the side yard, covering it in shade for the better part of the day. But the best parts were the massive veranda and the old wooden screen door that softly creaked and banged every time someone passed through it. It was a home that Ava could see herself living in one day... alone of course.

"Okay then I'll be in touch." She turned her attention to Ben. "Um Ben, are you ready to head out, I need to stop at the bank."

"Ah... yes. How about you Ash? Are you ready to head out?"

Ava squinted at Ben; a scowl formed on her brow. *You did not invite him to dinner...*

"Yeah, sure thing. I just need to make a quick stop at home. But you two go on ahead. I can meet you there in say... twenty minutes?"

Ben nodded. "Yup, that will be perfect. See you then."

He all but shoved Ava in the direction of home. He had to get her out of earshot of Ash before the words erupted from her. Any second, she was going to explode.

"Are you serious?!" She spat, as she made her way down the hillside. Thankfully, Ben and her mom had the foresight to build a staircase from the top of the hill down to the road below. "Haven't you learned anything from last year? You don't just invite complete strangers to your house for supper." Ava huffed as she followed the path that would lead them to home.

"Yeah. Well, he kind of put me on the spot."

Ava stepped onto the dirt road and stopped. Frowning, she looked at Ben. "What do you mean, he put you on the spot?"

"He asked what was in the bag I was carrying, and I told him dinner. It just snowballed from there and somehow, I ended up inviting him to join us."

"Ben. It was none of his business what was in the bag." She pointed out.

"I suppose." He nodded as he started walking the short distance to home. "Strange chap he is. He wanted to know all about the owner of the spa."

"Why? What did you tell him?"

"Nothing. You joined us right after."

Ava fell silent. She knew she didn't like the man for a reason. He was attractive enough. But something about him put her on the defensive. Lost in her own thoughts she didn't even realize they passed her house.

"Wait. Didn't you need to stop at the bank?" Ben asked.

"What?" Her brows rose with the question. She stared at Ben, a blank look on her face.

"The bank." Ben pointed. "We are at your house. Didn't you need to stop at the bank?"

Unnerved, she said, "Ah...Yeah, I did. I do." She put a hand to her head. "You know what. I'll do it tomorrow. I'll be over shortly."

Nodding her goodbye, she marched across the yard and up the steps to the front door. With any luck, Kim and Mark would be home and free tonight. She needed her backup team if she was going to have to face Ashton Davenport again.

Rushing into the house, she went directly to the shower, stripping her clothes off as she did. Quickly she washed the tension of the day from her hair and body. She would have loved to have a bath. Soaking her tired muscles in the pulsating jets of the whirlpool tub was the only way she could get a massage. Funny how she continually made others feel their best but always put herself on the back burner.

She sighed as she turned off the taps and reached for a towel. Wrapping it around herself, she tucked it in as she walked to the vanity and wiped the steam from the mirror. Ava looked at herself in the mirror and saw the shadows under her eyes that her makeup always concealed. She was tired. Tired of working herself ragged. Tired of being alone... well, she wasn't alone. But she did envy those who had someone to love. She had Kim and Mark, her two partners in crime whom she knew loved her unconditionally, but it wasn't the same.

Grabbing a brush, she ran it through her hair and smiled as she thought back to the time they had played 'detective'. They really thought they were on to something when they searched the boat that had been hanging around this very house, looking for clues.

Glancing to the wall sized window behind the tub, her gaze drifted down the beach. The very beach Mark and she had walked together the first time they met. She was enthralled with him. No one could blame her really. Him being an actor, one that she had a huge crush on. She had quickly quashed those feelings, knowing he would never be interested in her when he had his pick of celebrities. To this day he still didn't know her feelings for him. *And he never will!* No, he could never know because he would never let her live it down if he did.

A squeaking at the window drew her attention back to the present. Brutus, her mother's Bull Mastiff American Bulldog mix stood there with his nose smooshed up against the glass as he licked the window; something he did often. If Ava didn't know any better, she would think he could see her. But it was impossible. The glass was one way. She herself had checked many times even going as far as checking at night while the room was ablaze with lights.

The chiming of the old grandfather clock echoed through the empty house, reminding her she had better get a move on, she still had no idea what she would wear. Cursing, she quickly braided her long hair and headed for the door that led to Kim's room. Her mom had designed the bathroom in a way that it was hidden from anyone who entered the house. The only way to get to the private paradise was through either bedroom.

She stood with her hands on her hips, biting her lip as her eyes scanned over Kim's clothing. Taking a pantsuit off a hanger she held it up and looked at her reflection in the mirror. She frowned when she saw the large orange hibiscus flower print.

What the hell was Kim thinking when she bought this?!

Tossing it over her head onto the bed, she grabbed the next hanger. A florescent pink sundress that looked like it came straight from the 80's. Being a brunette, Ava could pull anything off, but not that! "Ugh Aunt Kim, we need to go shopping," she muttered in distaste as it sailed over her shoulder. Within minutes the contents of Kim's closet were scattered everywhere in the room. Ava cast a critical eye over the mess, scowling at it.

Oh, why did I tell Ben I would go?

She felt like calling her mom and telling her she couldn't make it. That she was too tired or sick or both. No. She wouldn't do that to her mom. Besides, truth be told, she *was* sick and tired of being alone. She needed to meet new people, starting with Ashton Davenport. Even though he rubbed her the wrong way.

Chapter 2

Mark's pickup had been having a problem with the brakes for the past few weeks and he knew it was time to get them looked at. He was leaning against the counter, waiting for the mechanic to tally up his bill.

Glancing at the clock behind Pete's head, he was hoping to get home before Ava and Kim. Before either of them made plans for the evening. It was their 'date night'. Once a month they would get takeout in the village, stop by the video store, and grab a couple of movies. They would then go home and pig out while watching them. But tonight was different, he thought he would take them to Springbank for an actual night on the town. That was if Pete ever got done with the bill.

"What's the damage Pete?" he asked, pulling out his wallet, in hopes of speeding the process. He tugged his debit card out and tapped it on the counter.

"Well let's see. We had to replace the brakes and calipers on all four wheels. Then there was the brake fluid," he said as he punched some numbers into an old adding machine. "Then we changed the oil, and filters." He added those up too. Pulling off his glasses he looked at Mark. "You know, you ought to change that motor oil a bit more often. That's a mighty fine truck you have there. You don't want the engine blowing smoke, now do you?"

Mark looked at Pete. That was the tenth time the old man told Mark about the oil and just like every time before Mark patiently said, "Yup, I know. You're right, I should have that taken care of more often. So how much do I owe you Pete?" He held his breath, hoping this time he would get an answer.

"That'll be $500.00 with labor and tax. Now, if you can't afford to pay, I'll knock off $200.00." Pete told him as he passed him the debit card machine.

Mark couldn't help but smile. He could pay it, and then some. Even though acting was more like a part time job for him, it paid very well. "That won't be necessary Pete." He smiled as he inserted his card and punched his PIN# in. When prompted, Mark doubled the amount for a tip. He knew Pete's business wasn't booming in such a small village and the old man wouldn't notice right away he'd done it.

"Thank you kindly," Pete said, as he handed Mark his invoice and keys. "Now remember, you come back and see me in about four months, and I'll change that oil for you again. Need to keep that beauty in tip top shape for when you sell it to me." He grinned.

Mark laughed. "Oh, I don't know about that. Maybe one day I'll just give it to you," he said, tossing Pete a wave as he headed out the door.

Jumping into his truck he turned the key. The sound of the engine rumbling to life would never get old to Mark. Checking the time, he saw it was just after 4:00 pm. "Damn." Ava would be done with work and home by now.

He threw the gear shift into drive and headed towards their house. But not before making an impulse buy. He slammed on the brakes when he spied a barrel of flowers sitting outside Mack's store.

"Sonofabitch!" He swore, rubbing his forehead where it hit the steering wheel. He completely forgot that Pete had just replaced the entire braking system.

What the hell is wrong with you man? He wondered to himself as he pulled up to the curb. He knew exactly what was wrong and had been for the past five months. The very reason he'd slammed on the brakes in the first place...Ava. She'd been on his mind ever since they had shared a kiss on Christmas day. Clearly it had been a mistake. But that didn't stop him from thinking about her constantly. Especially when they lived as roommates along with Kim.

Getting out of his truck, he saw a man walk up the sidewalk of the yellow house across the road. *At least it's no longer vacant.* Like he had room to talk. If it weren't for Ben buying up his old property, that house likely would have been taken back by the land. That was one thing he could honestly say he regretted in his life. Selling that property. But then again, he never did take the time to stay there for more than a weekend. He'd been too busy living the Hollywood lifestyle.

Selecting a bouquet of a spring mix, he opened the door to go inside to pay just as Kim was coming out.

"Mark. Wanna give me a lift home?" She asked. Not waiting for an answer, she headed to the passenger side of the truck, opened the door, and plopped down on the seat. Mark shook his head with amusement and walked in the store, up to the counter.

"Hey Mark, how are you doing today?" Mack rambled over to the cash register.

"Not too bad Mack, how about yourself?"

"Better than what you look like."

"Huh? What do you mean?" Mark asked, pulling out his wallet from his back pocket.

Mack swung a finger at his head. "Your forehead. What'd you do, knock it on something?"

Mark grabbed a pair of sunglasses off the rack beside the register. Looking into the mirrored surface he scowled as he rubbed the spot, wincing at the pain it caused when he realized it was a goose egg.

"Damn it. I whacked my head off the steering wheel when I slammed on the brakes," he mumbled, returning the sunglasses to the rack.

"Why did you go and do that?" Mack asked, as he rang up the flowers.

Mark picked up the flowers as he handed Mack the cash. "To get these, I thought Ava might like a little pick me up, she's been down in the dumps lately." Come to think of it, it wasn't just lately. She'd been like that since, well, Christmas. "And Kim too of course," he quickly added. He didn't want Mack getting the wrong impression by thinking he had a thing for Ava. In no time it would spread through the village like a lit matchstick would to a dry wheat field. No thanks. Before he knew it, the talk would be that they were getting hitched next. That was never going to happen to Mark Donovan.

"I need to get these in some water." He waved the flowers as he headed out the door. "I'll see you later Mack."

Back in his truck he started the engine and was getting ready to put it in gear when something caught his eye.

Kim looked at him and scrunched her nose. "What happened to your forehead?"

Across the street, the same man that had walked up the sidewalk to the yellow house was now walking away from it.

Distractedly, he said, "Whacked it off the steering wheel."

Mark found it odd that Mack didn't mention the man. If he was a newcomer to the village, no one escaped Mack's eagle eye. He found it even odder as he watched the guy walk down the road towards the lake seeing how there were only three houses that way. The old Anderson place, long ago abandoned and forgotten on the left at the base of the hill and to the right and about a half of a kilometer away was the house he shared with Kim and Ava and a few hundred feet from it, Ben, and Abbi's. The road at one time went through their property and on the other side. But when Mark had bought the place years ago, he'd checked to see if it could be included in the deal. No one ever used it and so it became part of the land. The old lake road was now known as a dead end.

Looking in her purse, Kim produced a tube of lip balm. Smearing it on her lips she smacked them together. "Why?"

"Huh?" Mark swung his gaze to her. "What?" It dawned on him she wanted to know why he hit his head. "Never mind that." He waved a dismissive hand. "Who is that guy?" He pointed to the man crossing in front of them.

Kim looked to where he was pointing. "No idea." She shrugged. "Likely someone on vacation, going to look at the lake."

Mark eased the truck away from the curb only to slow it down 10 seconds later. Despite Pearl Lake being a vacation destination, he didn't trust any newcomer that hadn't passed Mack's clearance. Not since what happened with Raven Black.

Pulling alongside him, Mark put the passenger window down.

"What are you doing?" Kim asked.

"Shhh." He held out a hand in front of her. "Don't say anything. I mean it." He raised his brows, just as she was about to say something.

"Hey there, are you new in town?" Mark asked by way of greeting.

The man looked at Mark and nodded. "I am." And continued walking.

"Rude much?" Kim muttered.

Mark gave her a warning look.

Kim went through the motions of zipping her mouth shut and tossing the imaginary key out the window.

Mark drove at the pace the man was walking. "Right. I'm Mark by the way. Hey. Do you want a lift somewhere?"

"Nope. I'm just heading up the road aways."

Mark nodded. "See you around then." Without another word, he pulled away from the curb and drove off, intent on not giving it another thought.

Kim leaned forward to look in the side mirror at the man. "What a dick."

"Yup," Mark said, turning down the dirt road that led to home.

Minutes later, pulling into the laneway he was still bothered by the guy. Something about him just rubbed him the wrong way. Mark had no idea what the hell it was, but it was something. No sense letting it ruin his night. He turned the truck off and grabbed the flowers. "What are you doing tonight, any plans?"

"Hmm not sure. I might read a book or something." Kim asked, "Why?"

Slamming the truck door shut, he thumbed the key fob, locking it while they headed across the yard. He loved living here, with the shade trees and the gardens Abbi had so lovingly cared for.

"I was going to see if..." Out of the corner of his eye, Mark caught a movement. "Oh, *shiiiit*!"

He took off at a sprint across the yard, leaving Kim in his dust. He was almost to the house when Brutus came at him like the wind; the mutt thought he still lived here. Mark watched as he took one powerful leap, it was that moment he knew he was a goner.

He tossed the flowers in the air the second before he was tackled to the ground, only to be stared at nose to nose. Mark didn't fight it anymore; it was just one of those things in life that was better not to fight. Every time he came home, and Brutus was out, it happened. He knew the dog would stare him down just as he knew at any second that slobbery wet tongue would slop across his face.

Ah yup...There it is.

Mark squeezed his eyes shut and held his breath for the inevitable ritual. He had even come to name it the daily cleansing. Thank God it would be over soon enough.

"Getting your bath there are you, Mark?"

He cracked one eye open only to see Kim standing there with her hands on her hips, cackling.

"As usual. Call him off me, will ya? I swear to God he gains ten pounds every week."

"Brutus, come on," Kim tugged on his collar. "Go," she said, shoving Brutus in the direction of his home. She shook her head as she watched the dog head for the house, only to climb the steps and plant himself on the porch. She looked down at Mark. "So, you were saying?"

"I thought we would head to Springbank, take in a movie after we eat. Need to see if Ava has any plans first though," he said, bounding to his feet.

"Why would she have any plans, it's not like she's met anyone new."

Mark thought about the man he'd just seen walking not more than five minutes ago. He shot her an exasperated look as he dusted his jeans off. Jokingly, he said, "Who knows, maybe she met Mr. Right." His brows snapped together as those words sunk in.

Was that why the guy was headed this way?

"Come on, let's go and find out." He scowled. Not waiting for Kim, he scooped up the flowers and stalked towards the house.

With Brutus by his side, he took the steps two at a time. Unlocking the door, he turned the knob while the dog nosed it open wide, walking in like he owned the place. Mark cocked his head and Brutus' ears perked up. Both stood stock-still.

Without a word, Kim came plowing over the threshold right into Mark's back.

She hissed. "What the hell is wrong—" she couldn't finish as Mark quickly turned to her and smothered her question with his hand.

Swallowing the rest of her words, she bugged her eyes at him. He mutely held a finger to his lips, the universal signal to shut up. With a quick jerk of his head, he motioned for her to follow him.

Down the hall, Brutus led the way at a leisurely pace as if he were strolling in a garden. He stopped at the second doorway on the left. Now Mark's room but it had been the animal's room when Abbi lived there. He sniffed along the floor, making his way to the bed, and put his paws on the side of it. Brutus raised his head, his nostrils quivering with each sniff.

Excited, Kim jabbed Mark in the ribs. Nodding she grinned at him and mouthed the words. "He's caught a scent." They watched as Brutus leaped onto the bed and circled it, only to lay down with a humph.

Mark rolled his eyes. "Caught a scent, did he? C'mon."

Silently, they passed each empty room, when suddenly they heard what sounded like a cat with its tail caught in a door. Only problem was, they didn't have a cat. Following the hall, they took a short right. Ava's room was on the left and Kim's on the right. Mark held out his arm blocking Kim from going any further.

Kim looked around him at the open doorway. Her eyes took in the scene before them. The room was tossed and left them wondering who would do such a thing. Both froze when a keening sound came from Ava's room. As one, they whipped their heads to the door on the left. Mark reached out and soundlessly turned the doorknob, pushing it open.

There, Ava sat in the middle of the floor with what looked like the entire contents of her closet surrounding her.

Kim rushed in and grabbed her by the shoulders. "Ava, what's wrong?" she asked, searching her face.

"I have nothing to wear for tonight." She sniffed.

Mark came around to face her. "Ava, you don't need to dress up, we are just going to Springbank for dinner."

She looked at him. Her face, tear stained, scrunched in confusion. "What?"

Mark's breath caught in his throat.

God she is beautiful.

He chuckled nervously, trying desperately to gain some control. "Our date night? It's Friday, or did you forget?"

"Oh my gosh! I did! I completely forgot. Ben asked if I wanted to go to dinner at their house tonight, well all of us. And I said yes but wasn't sure if you guys did." She looked between the two of them.

"Ah... well we can still go out Kim if you want." Mark didn't know what to say, he didn't want to disappoint Kim. Ava didn't *have* to come with them, but he was hoping she would.

"Yeah, sure. I could go for a movie."

Mark noted the disappointment flash across Ava's face but said nothing.

Kim looked around at the mess her niece made, getting up, she asked, "Why would that make you cry and why the hell did you destroy my room too?"

"I thought you might have something I could borrow. You didn't. Which reminds me, we need to go clothes shopping for you." She hiccupped. "And because..." Ava took a deep breath. "Because Ben invited some stranger to come. Not that I care, he seems like a total asshole, but I still want to look nice, you know?"

Stranger? Mark felt the hair rise along his neck.

Oh, hell no! ...

No, it couldn't be. Ben would never do such a thing.

Picking up a dress, Kim noticed it was inside out. "I do. So does this stranger have a name?" she asked. Righting the garment, she put it on a hanger and hung it in the closet.

Ava rubbed her temples. She had a god-awful headache ever since meeting the man. "Ashton Davenport. Ash for short," she mumbled. "He lives across from Mack's in that lovely old yellow house that I love so much."

Mark could feel all the colour drain from his face. "Wait. Whoa, whoa." He made 'a time out' motion with his hands. "*Whoa...!* Hey. I've got an idea." He rushed on. "Kim, how about we wait until tomorrow so that we can all go?"

He leaned his sweaty palm on the wall, trying to appear nonchalant. He was everything *but* nonchalant. He was a wreck. He changed his stance and tried to look indifferent by looking at his nails and picking non-existent lint off his shirt, none of it was working. "We can go with Ava over to Ben and Abbi's. How does that sound, does that sound okay to you?" He nodded vigorously. Not waiting for an answer, he continued. "Right? Okay then, it's settled. I'm getting in the shower." He turned and left the woman staring after him, speechless.

Mark felt like a fool, but he had to do something. Ava couldn't go alone to Ben and Abbi's with Ashton Davenport there. If she did, he might never have a snowball's chance in hell at convincing her she had already met her Mr. Right... and he was currently getting in the shower to wash the sweat of embarrassment away.

Chapter 3

The men were out tending the BBQ while Kim and Ava stood in the middle of Abbi's kitchen, slicing, and chopping vegetables.

Ava watched as her mom waddled to the fridge to get the fixings for a spinach dip. Any day now Abbi would give birth to her 4th child and Ava wasn't sure how she felt about that. She of course was happy for Ben and her mom, but she couldn't help feeling sad for herself. Someday she wanted a baby too, but first she had to find a man. Then again, she didn't *need* a man, but she kinda wanted one.

"Are you making soup with those veggies Ava?" Kim giggled. "You're chopping them a mite small, aren't you?"

"What? Shit, I'm sorry," she mumbled. Lifting the cutting board, she shoved the cauliflower with her knife onto the awaiting tray. One thing was for sure, no one would choke on the tiny bite sized pieces.

Ben came into the kitchen and looked around. "What else needs to be taken out?"

"You can take this." Kim handed him the veggie tray and placed the dip in the middle, snagging a couple of carrot sticks as she did.

"I'll take this out." Abbi grabbed the large bowl of potato salad. "Ava, can you get the rolls and cheese?"

"Love, here let me get that."

Ava watched as Ben leaned forward and planted a quick kiss on her mother's hair as he took the bowl out of her hands before going outside.

"What's the matter Ava?" Her mom came over and put an arm around her shoulders. "Are you homesick?"

Homesick? Hell no!

She couldn't be happier about making her move here.

"It's nothing mom." She shrugged her shoulders. "I'm just bored I guess."

"You need a hobby." Kim pointed a carrot at her accusingly.

Ava smiled. "Do I now?"

"Yes. And he's right out there." She flung her hand, carrot stick and all in the direction of the patio.

Amusement flashed in Abbi's eyes. "*Mark?!*"

Ava grinned at the mention of his name but quickly pulled the mask over her face. It was no use to even think about Mark like that. She just wasn't his type.

"No! Ashton," Kim said, in a hushed voice.

"I don't know..." Abbi started to say but was interrupted with the return of Ben with Mark hot on his heels.

"Ladies, are you ready to eat?" Ben asked, rolling his eyes.

All three looked at Ben and all three caught the look he sent their way.

"Yes," they said in unison.

"What the *hell* were you thinking man?" Mark spat, running his hands through his hair. "He's a con, how can you not tell that?"

Ben put his hands on his hips and turned to look at Mark. "I think you're being a bit dramatic mate. Just because you don't like what the man had to say doesn't mean he's a con."

"What did he say?" Abbi asked, concerned over what it was Ash said.

Mark turned to her. "He said all actors were overpaid fakes with no real talent."

Ben sighed. "He isn't wrong. They are overpaid, some at least."

"He's discrediting your profession." Mark flung an accusing hand at Ben. "You are one of the highest paid actors and you think that's okay?"

Ben held up a finger. "Correction. Was my profession, I'm out of it, remember? And yes, the pay was good."

Ava spoke up. "Can you two not have this conversation right now, please?" She just wanted to eat and go home.

"I agree, the food is getting cold... err... hot. Both, you know what I mean. Let's just eat," Abbi said, ushering them towards the patio.

"Fine, but it's..." Mark stopped talking. With one look at Ava's stony face, he decided it wasn't worth it. Truth be told, he didn't like Ash and he was finding every excuse for the others to not like him either.

"Come on Ash. Time to eat," Kim yelled, as they all came out of the house.

He was standing at the water's edge, staring across the calm surface, smoking a cigarette. Tossing it on the ground he stepped on it before he headed towards the house.

"Here." Abbi handed him a paper plate. She smiled gesturing to the table. "Help yourself, there's plenty so don't be shy."

Everyone filled their plates then took a seat and dug into their food. Ava sat silently eating while the others made small talk. Kim and her mom were talking about the pains Abbi had been having lately, Braxton Hicks, she heard them say. And Ben, Ash and surprisingly Mark were talking about the fishing on the lake. She looked at Ash. He was quite nice looking. He was of medium build and if she had to guess, she would say about 5'10", just a few inches taller than her. His hair reminded her of a horse she had as a child, a warm chestnut color that glinted in the sun. His eyes she wasn't entirely sure of, as she had yet to see them. Not that it mattered all that much. After watching him talk to Ben and Mark, she decided he didn't seem all that bad. Even Mark seemed to be getting along with him.

Getting up she went into the house and tossed her plate into the garbage. Looking around she started to tidy up from the meal prep. There was no way she was going to leave this mess for her mom and Ben to clean up. She was just about done and was planning on tackling the table outside when Ash came in, with his hands full of serving bowls.

Turning between the island and the countertop, he asked, "Um. Where should I put these?"

"Here. I'll take them." She took a step towards him just as he took one towards her. Bumping into each other, they watched in horrified unison as a bowl slipped from his hand smashed to the floor below.

"Oh man, I'm sorry. It just slipped from my hand," he said, setting the other bowl safely on the island. "Here, I'll clean it up." He bent down just as Ava did, their heads colliding.

"Ow!" Ava howled, as Ash jerked back. His foot slipped in the mess on the floor, and he was airborne, landing hard on his back.

She rushed to his side. "Oh my gosh are you okay?" she asked, peering into his face. She noticed his chest shaking. *Good lord, is he convulsing?* "Aunt Kim!" she shouted as she knelt by his side.

Kim came running from the patio. "What?!"

"Ash hit his head, I think, and now he's convulsing." Ava looked at him worriedly.

A rumble of laughter came deep from within Ash's chest. He wasn't convulsing as he sat up. "I'm fine." He chuckled. "It's just replaying it in my mind, and I realized how foolish I must have looked."

"Oh, thank God. I thought you might have a concussion or something. Here, let us help you up." Together Kim and Ava each grabbed one of Ash's hands and braced themselves as he hauled himself off the floor.

"Are you sure you're, okay?" Kim asked. "I can give you a lift to the clinic and Doc can check you over."

"No. Really. I'm fine. Thank you."

"What's all the commotion?" Mark asked, setting the veggie tray on the counter.

Carefully picking up the shards of the broken bowl, Ava glanced up at Mark. "Nothing, Ash and I bumped into each other and made a mess."

A dark look passed over his face. *What kind of bump?*

"Let me help you." Ash grabbed an empty box and tossed the glass inside.

"Thanks." Ava looked at him and smiled.

When he smiled back, she was so startled she just about dropped the glass she was holding. He had the cutest grin she ever saw on a person, a little lopsided, with dimples on both cheeks. It transformed him completely. She no longer felt the need to run home but instead she wanted to stay. If he continued to smile at her that way at least.

"Abbi, where is your mop?" Ash asked, as she came into the house.

"Oh, don't worry about that. Ben just lit a fire down by the water. You go and enjoy yourself." She smiled, shooing him towards the door. "Oh wait." She snatched a bag of marshmallows off the counter and tossed them to Ash. "Take these. It's dessert." She grinned.

Kim grabbed a roll of paper towels and squatted beside Ava and started wiping the remnants of the salad off the floor. "Mark, can you wet this?" She unraveled a bunch and passed it to him.

Mark had seen the look that passed between Ava and Ash. Scowling, he was still trying to figure out how they managed to bump into each other. To say he was upset was putting it mildly. Turning on the tap to do Kim's bidding, he said, "Ah Ava..."

"Yeah?"

"How did you two bump into each other?"

She glanced at Mark, frowned. "What do you mean, how?"

"Well." He passed the dripping paper towels back to Kim. "To bump into each other, one of you had to be pretty close."

Just who did Mark think he was? He certainly had no say in who she was near.

Ava stood up. "What the hell are you implying?"

"Me?" Mark had the sense to look ashamed. "I'm not implying anything. I just..." He stopped at the look that crossed over Ava's face. She was mad. No that wasn't it. She was pissed!

"Excuse me." Ava snarled as she grabbed the box with broken glass, and she headed towards the door.

Mark put a hand on her arm as she passed by. "Ava... I'm sorry. I..."

Ava stopped and looked down at the hand on her arm. Slowly she raised her eyes to meet his and stared him down. "Take your hand off me."

Mark snatched it back, then watched as she walked out the door. The coldness in her eyes had matched the tone in her voice. He felt as if he'd been burned by her iciness — like dry ice on bare skin.

"What's up with Ava?" Ben jerked his thumb over his shoulder as he walked through the patio door. "I've never seen her so... so —"

"Pissed?" Mark, Kim, and Abbi all said in unison.

Ben nodded in agreement. "Ah... yeah you could say that."

"Well. Mr. Smooth talker here put his foot in his mouth... again." Kim snorted.

Ben chuckled. "You don't say? Come on mate, what did you say to her?" he asked, raising a brow.

"I didn't say anything." Mark threw his hand in the air. "All I said was that her or Ash had to be pretty close to bump into each other."

Ben groaned.

"What?!" Mark shrugged. "What did I say that was so bad?"

"Mark, it's not what you said but how you said it." Abbi pointed out.

Kim held up a finger. "Ah, I beg to differ, it's what he said."

"Well, really, it was both. What he said and how he said it," Abbi said, looking at Ben.

"I am here you know!" Mark leaned against the counter. "Okay, I screwed up," he said, miserably. "Now how the hell do I fix it?"

Ben cleared his throat. "I got this one. You don't. At least not yet. Let her cool down. She will come around, and once she does, you grovel and ask for her forgiveness."

Taking Abbi's hand in his, Ben brought it to his lips and softly kissed the back of it.

"Must you two always be so... *affectionate?*" Mark spat.

"As a matter of fact, yes." Ben laughed at his friends' discomfort. "Come on love, let's go sit around the fire for a bit." He took her by the hand. "Before I put you to bed," he murmured, as they headed out the door.

"Those two make me sick," Mark grumbled.

Kim grinned. "Yeah, they do have something special, don't they?" She was the teensiest bit jealous of her sister and Ben's relationship.

"If you say so." Mark folded his arms across his chest. *Why the hell am I even staying here?* He could just go home and sulk in the dark at least no one would see him.

Kim sighed. Opening the fridge she grabbed two beers, and as she handed him one, she asked, "Mark, when are you going to tell Ava how you feel?"

"What are you talking about?" He took the bottle, popped the cap, and took a long swallow. Truth be told, Mark knew exactly what she was talking about. He knew he should have told Ava a long time ago how he felt about her but never had the courage to do so. He couldn't blame Ash for being interested in her, hell any guy with eyes in his head would be. But he didn't have to like it nor Ash for that matter. And he wasn't about to spill his guts to Kim. He wasn't that desperate... yet.

"Okay." She chuckled, nodding her head. "I know where you're going with that. Want to play dumb with me? We can do that. But remember one thing. I live with you two and I see everything."

"Fine!" He took another swallow. "I'll admit it. I have... feelings for Ava. There, are you happy?" He sat his beer on the countertop, losing all interest in drinking while his stomach churned.

"Then tell her. She isn't a mind reader you know."

"I can't. I won't. I'm not used to women like her..."

Kim cackled at that. "Of course, you're not. She's not chasing after you down the street screaming your name."

Saluting him with her bottle, she walked past him and said, "Buddy, you have your work cut out for you. I'm heading to the fire, are you coming?"

"No, I don't feel like it. I think I'm heading home."

"You're joking, right?" She stopped at the door and looked back. "You're going to leave now? Why? So, Ash can get to know her better? Suit yourself." With that Kim turned in the direction of the fire pit.

Smiling, she put her arm through his, and gave it a squeeze. "We got this, soon, Ava will be eating out of the palm of your hand."

Together they walked silently along the path to the lake, each lost in their own thoughts. Kim was thinking on how she would get her two roommates together and Mark wondering if he would ever get the chance to talk to Ava again in this lifetime. He thought he had a way of making up to her and was feeling confident that he could make it work. That was until Kim and him approached the fire.

The sickly feeling of panic washed over Mark as his eyes took in the scene before him. Ben and Abbi were nowhere in sight. And sitting no more than a foot from one another, heads together, talking in hushed tones was Ava and Ash. Holding hands...

Without breaking his stride, Mark pivoted on his heel and headed in the direction of home.

AT THE SOUND OF SOMEONE scurrying away. Ava turned in her seat and saw Kim standing there. "Where is Mark off to?" She asked.

Kim didn't know what to say other than the first thing that popped into her head. "Ah he threw up on his shirt?" *What the hell kind of an excuse was that? Just go with it Kim*, she told herself. Joining them at the fire, she sat in a vacant chair. "Yeah, he tossed his cookies all over the front of himself. He won't be back."

"Oh. That's too bad. Ash was just reading my palm. He was going to do Mark's and yours too if you want."

"Hot damn. I'd love for you to read mine," Kim said. Jumping up, she took the chair beside Ash and held out her hand.

While Ash read Kim's palm, Ava sat staring into the flames. She wished Mark hadn't gotten sick. She'd love more than anything to find out exactly what his palm would reveal...

Chapter 4

Mark hated nuking his coffee just as much as he hated drinking it cold. Being pressed for time, he would never make it to his appointment if he made a fresh pot. And it was an appointment he didn't want to miss. But being in dire need of the jolt of java, Mark slammed the microwave door shut and stabbed the beverage button on the display. He leaned against the counter, folded his arms across his chest, and stared off in a daze. His sleep had been troubled ever since the night at Ben and Abbi's, almost a week ago.

Seeing Ava and Ash together so close had shocked him in more ways than one. He was shocked at how he'd felt towards the man. And shocked to realize he was not merely attracted to Ava, but in love with her.

Scowling, he noticed the sour taste in his mouth whenever he thought about it. Ava and Ash had seen each other three times since then and each time she would come sneaking in like a thief in the night at 2 am. He knew because he had stayed up, sitting in the darkness until he heard her key in the lock, the second he did, he would scurry off to his room.

The first night it happened, he'd forgotten Brutus was there. Refusing to go home for the night, the beast had sprawled at Mark's feet, sound asleep. If Mark hadn't been listening so intently for Ava's return, he would have heard the snoring coming from the floor. But no–– he didn't. The second his bare feet had smacked on the tiled floor in a panic, Brutus bolted upright. Looking around in confusion the dog stood on all fours just as Mark took the first step in a hasty retreat. That's as far as he got.

As his legs contacted the dogs' side, he felt himself catapulted through the air. At that moment, all Mark could do was thank his mother silently for putting him in gymnastics as a kid and thank God he was still nimble. He did a diving tuck and roll, but instead of the perfect execution he laid stock still, praying he wasn't found out. Lucky for him Brutus ran to the door to greet Ava. She hurried off to her bedroom dragging Brutus along with her. He'd laid there on the cold tiles longer than he cared to admit.

The sound of the microwave beeping had him pushing away from the counter. "Forget the coffee," he said aloud to himself as he stomped off towards the bathroom. A cold shower is what he needed.

"GOOD MORNING MRS. STANFORD," Ava smiled as she came around the counter to greet her first customer of the day. "How was your weekend?"

"Oh, you know, same thing, different day," the elderly woman smiled.

Ava smiled back. She knew exactly what she meant by that. Mrs. Eleanor Stanford was the village spy. Oh, she was harmless, but she was known to sit by her big bay window with a pair of binoculars in her hand. Watching the coming and going of village life.

Ava didn't blame her one bit. She was all alone in the big house. Coincidently, the one that sat right beside Ash's. A little thrill went up her spine at the thought of him. She really was starting to like Ash and more than just a friend.

Ava made a mental note to mention how lonely Eleanor was this afternoon. They had scheduled a time for an estimate on the garden cleanup and if he knew that his new neighbor was that lonely, he might offer to help her around the house sometime.

"Follow me and we will get you set up in the chair," Ava smiled as she made her way to the back room where the hydro massage chair was.

Ava, took the frail woman's arm, helping her onto what looked like an oversized lounge chair. "Okay Mrs. Stanford, you sit right there and get comfy." She set the controls to a nice gentle relaxing wave of pulsating warm water.

"Here is the control." She positioned the tablet attached to the chair for Eleanor to see. "All you need to do is touch the screen, remember?" At the old woman's nod, Ava continued. "This button is to change the intensity, and this one, if you want it warmer. I have it set to the lowest setting for you."

"Oh, this is lovely on my old bones." Eleanor smiled in delight. "How do I know when I'm done again, dear?"

"It will shut down, it's on a timer." Ava headed to the door, and paused, she turned and looked at Eleanor. "You just call me if you need anything, I will be at the front desk."

Ava headed straight to the lobby, smiling while she went, knowing full well the old woman would fall asleep before the chair shut off. She checked her watch and saw that it was 10:30 am. She had fifteen minutes before her next client showed up. Having no idea who it was as they had booked online, she sat down in the office chair to check the name: *Mr. Marcus, full body massage. New client.*

The door chime announced someone had just walked in. Thinking it was the new client she glanced up with a smile pasted on her lips. Only to see Mark walking up to the desk.

The smile fell from her mouth as she saw the brooding look, he shot her way.

"What is it?" She asked, alarmed.

"What?" Mark looked at her in a daze.

"What's wrong? You look a little upset?"

"Oh. Nothing. I just saw a weasel on the way over."

Getting up, Ava took a stack of folders and turned to the filing cabinet, she pulled the top drawer open, and started to file them away. She glanced at Mark. He was watching every move she made.

What is up with him?

"A weasel? You're that upset over a weasel," she chuckled. "It looks like you're ready to bite someone's head off."

Yes, he was. Especially when the weasel he was referring to was Ash. Mark had passed him on the road not more than five minutes ago heading in the direction of Ben and Abbi's.

"So, what brings you here? Were you out for a walk and thought you'd stop by?" Ava asked. Bending down, she pulled open the bottom drawer and stuck the last folder in its place, slamming it shut a little too hard.

Every move she made had him wanting her more. Even slamming the damn drawer. "Um," he squeaked out. Clearing his throat, he tried again. "I ah. I'm here for my appointment. At 11:00."

Ava spun around in shock as 'full body' massage screamed through her mind.

I can't do that... to HIM ... Of course, you can Ava, you're a professional!

"Mr. Marcus?" she asked, trying to hide her reservations. "You know, all you had to do was ask, we could have just done it at home," she winced, biting her lip at her choice of words.

Mark scratched his head, needing to put some distance between them, he backed away. "Yeah, well, I uh, knew you would never accept payment and I fully intend on paying you."

She nodded, knowing he was right. "Why don't you take a seat? Mrs. Stanford should be just a few minutes more and then we will get started. Excuse me." She desperately needed to get away.

Ava rushed down the hall to the lunchroom. The original fully functional kitchen was never converted. She had decided that if she ever moved locations, it would be best to keep it as original as possible, in case someone wanted to live in it as a home.

She went straight for the fridge. Grabbing the handle, she yanked it open. Her eyes seeking out the one thing that would tame the wild emotions coursing through her body. Her fingers snatched it up the second her eyes spied it... dark chocolate.

She ripped open the package and stuffed a square into her mouth. Closing her eyes, she felt the tension at once wane as the bitterness melted on her tongue and down her throat. She shook her head. Nope. One piece wasn't going to cut it.

She was cramming half the bar into her mouth when she heard a cough behind her. She froze. Horrified at the thought of being caught, she chewed rapidly, desperately trying to force the thick chocolate down her throat. Hoping it would melt as fast as she chewed, she slowly turned around. Unaware that she still clutched the wrapper in her hand, she smiled as the goo dribbled down her chin.

Mark raised his brows. "Wow..." He had never seen Ava in such a state before. He'd never known her as a closet eater. Or maybe she was just hungry? Whatever it was, he needed to play it cool. And saying 'wow' was not playing it cool. He tried again.

"Wow! That Mrs. Stanford sure is a talker. Ah she left her money there at the front desk." He jerked his thumb over his shoulder as he covered his mouth with his other hand. He was trying desperately to stifle the laugh that bubbled in his throat as she swiped her chin with the back of her hand.

Ava whipped the chocolate wrapper into the garbage pail and stalked to the sink as tears filled her eyes from lack of air. Wordlessly she filled a glass with warm water and drank it in one long swallow. When she thought she could communicate without suffocating, she turned to look at Mark.

Nodding her head, she blinked rapidly and said, "Yes, she is. She is a sweet, lonely old woman, is all."

Mark noticed how her eyes looked a little watery and felt guilty for wanting to laugh at her. He wanted nothing more than to take her in his arms but knew he couldn't. No doubt she would think him strange if he did.

"So, are you ready for your massage?" Ava asked. Needing to get this over with she didn't wait for an answer and walked towards the hall.

Mark followed her, wishing now that he never booked the appointment in the first place. Every time he planned to do something, to try to get her to notice him, it always backfired in his face. He knew in his gut that this time wouldn't be any different.

"Okay. Just get undressed and lay on the table. Here is a towel to cover... yourself with." She turned to leave the room but stopped and looked back at him. "Stay here. I will be right back." She closed the door with a soft thud.

Get undressed?

Did he hear her right? Mark had never had a full body massage before, and he certainly didn't know he needed to be naked. For some asinine reason he thought he'd be fully clothed. He couldn't let Ava touch him with only a towel on. That would be a telltale disaster if he ever did see one. He had to think quickly, but it had to be convincing enough, he decided as he took his shirt off.

Kim! Grabbing his phone, he punched her name in as he unzipped his jeans.

"Hey Mark, what's up?"

"I need you to call me in like five minutes. Can you do that?" he shimmied out of his jeans and looked at his socks. Did one take their socks off for a massage? He would leave them on. Less to put back on when he hightailed it outta there. He tossed his clothes onto the chair.

"Why?"

"Don't ask." He yanked his boxers down and stepped out of them. Picking them up he buried them under the rest of his clothes on the chair. He laid face down on the table, taking care to make sure his butt was covered with the towel. "I'll tell you later, I don't have a lot of time right now. Promise me you will do it?"

"Yeah. Sure, I can do that," she said. Then Mark heard her yell. "Hey Doc, room 3." Kim came back on the line and said, "Look Mark, I gotta go."

"Make sure you call me!!" he said, into dead air.

A soft tap at the door had him tossing his phone onto his clothes.

"Ready when you are," he called out.

The door cracked open.

"Are you decent?" Ava asked as she peeked through the crack.

"Yeah. As decent as one can be under a towel," he chuckled.

She walked into the room, hesitantly at first. Mark noticed how she clenched her fists into tiny balls only to relax them, then do it all over again.

"A little tense are you?" he asked with satisfaction.

"What? Oh. No. I'm just stretching my hands. Now, I will do my arms," she said, as she placed them behind the small of her back. Lacing her fingers, she brought them up and held them for a few seconds, only to repeat the process.

He felt like a fool to even suggest that she was tense. She was as usual, her cool as a cucumber, self.

"Do you want some light music on?" Ava asked, looking at him. God, she hoped so, it would help disguise her heavy breathing. She always did breathe heavily during a body massage, it was that strenuous, but she had a feeling she would be breathing a whole lot heavier when she touched Mark.

She had always drooled over him whenever she watched a movie he was in. Her first Hollywood crush, and she had crushed hard, she still did.

"Yeah, sure," he mumbled, waiting on edge for his phone to ring.

"Great." She hurriedly walked out of the room to the closet in the hall and flicked on the switch to the stereo.

"Sonofa..."

Mark bolted upright causing his towel to slip to the floor as Simple Minds, 'Don't you forget about me,' blared through the sound system. Retrieving the towel, he took a favorite word from Ben, and said to the empty room, "Not bloody likely," as he covered his backside.

"Were you talking to someone?" Ava asked, coming back into the room. She walked directly over to a cabinet on the wall.

"Ah, no. I was just a... No," he mumbled as her words reminded him that five minutes were up and no phone call from Kim.

She took a bottle and squeezed a generous amount of lotion on her hands. He watched as she rubbed it between her hands, warming it up.

"Okay, then. Here we go," Ava said, as she laid her hands on his shoulders. Holding her breath, she slowly glided them over his skin, shocked at how soft it was. Sure, she had given him a massage many times while watching tv but not on his bare skin, and never alone. Kim had always been there.

Her hands found a knot around his left scapula. Skillfully she worked at it with her fingertips until the muscle felt somewhat pliable, then made her way down to his lower back. She dropped her gaze to his towel covered butt.

No, I'm not going there... she thought as her heart thumped in her chest. Ava stopped what she was doing. She needed to not touch him for a moment.

Crossing to the cupboard on the wall, she looked over her stash of essential oils. Lavender should do the trick! Ava unscrewed the lid of a jar of jojoba cream, specifically for the use of mixing it with her oils. She carefully added a few drops of the heady fragrance, hoping it would help calm her nerves.

"Where did you go?" Mark muffled into the hole of the massage table.

"I'm here. Just mixing some cream," she answered, sucking in a breath. "I'm going to let your back have a break for a minute and will start working on your neck." She dipped her fingers in the concoction and rubbed it between the palm of her hands.

Moving to stand at the head of the table, she placed her hands on either side of his neck. At once she felt the muscles tighten at her touch. "Relax," she said softly as she ran her fingertips along either side. Slowly she could feel the tension releasing its hold on his neck.

Leaning over him, she made her way down his spine, sweeping outwards with the heels of her hands down to his mid back. So, intent on her work she didn't hear the sound at first. It was a low groan coming from the underside of the table.

Damnit, I pressed too hard... "Is it hurting?" she asked, as she lightened the pressure.

"Not at all," Mark murmured, trying desperately to sound normal. Yeah, it hurt like hell. She was so into working on his back, she likely didn't know that he could feel her breasts pressed against his back. He was rock hard against the table. There was no way he would tell her that though.

She snatched a hand towel off the side table, wiping her hands on it and said, "Okay, well. I think we will call it a day. I don't want to do too much and cause you more pain. As it is, you had some deep knots I was able to work loose."

Mark slowly sat up taking care to keep himself covered.

She turned to a small bar fridge in the corner, opening the door, she took out two bottles of water. As much as she hated to say it, she would need for him to come back. "You're going to be in a bit of pain later today and even more so to-morrow. We can book you in a couple of days... if you want." She passed him a bottle, leaned against the wall, and twisted the cap off the other. Taking a long swallow, she drank until she quenched her thirst. She looked at him then. She felt like grabbing him by the face and kissing him senseless.

"Yeah sure. I feel great by the way."

"Good." Tipping her bottle towards him, she said, "Drink lots of water, your body is going to need it to flush out the toxins."

He nodded. "Okay, I'll do that." If he forgot, once home he was sure she would remind him. Mark raised a brow and looked at her expectantly. "Is it okay if I get dressed now?"

"Oh! Good gravy, yes! I'm sorry!" She sprung away from the wall and hurriedly crossed the room to the door.

"No worries." He waved. "I'll be out in a bit." He chuckled as she closed the door with a soft thud. He felt a little springier when he jumped off the table knowing she seemed just as flustered as he was.

He walked over to the chair and pulled his shirt on followed by his boxers just as his phone rang. Kim. Clearly, she didn't know how to tell time. He grabbed up his phone without looking to confirm who the caller was and pressed the talk button. "Remind me to get you a watch for Christmas."

"*What?!*"

"Hey Benny boy! How's it going?"

"Never mind that."

Mark froze at the tone of Ben's voice. He knew his friend. Something was terribly wrong.

"Abbi is in labor; Kim is with her. I tried calling Ava, but she didn't answer. Grab her and get over to the clinic now."

"What?! Is she okay? Is the baby okay?"

Mark waited for what seemed like an eternity. "Ben?"

His voice thick with emotion, Ben answered, "Doc says it's not good... Mark... I can't lose Abbi." His voice broke when he said her name. "Please just get Ava here as fast as you can." With that Ben hung up the phone.

Grabbing his shoes, he jammed his feet into his jeans and yanked open the door.

"Ava!" He yelled as he ran down the hall. In the reception area, Mark came to a skidding halt when he saw she was talking to someone. It was Ash.

Could this day get any worse?

Startled, Ava turned at his voice.

"What is it? What's wrong?!" She paled at the sight of Mark. His phone in hand, his eyes wild with worry, glistened with tears. Something was wrong. At that moment she knew. Her mom. Something was wrong with her mom.

"We need to get to the clinic now," Mark said, shoving his feet into his shoes.

Ava's world went dark, very dark. She could not lose her mother. Without a word, she grabbed her purse and ran out the door to her car with both men hot on her heels. She stopped, now remembering she had walked to work this morning. Without missing a beat, she bent down to take off her shoes. She would run to the clinic if she had to.

"Ava you're in no condition. Let me drive you." Ash turned to Mark. "Both of you."

Giving Ash a quick nod, Mark ushered her into the truck. From what Ben had said, he prayed they made it in time...

Chapter 5

While Ash parked the truck, Ava and Mark ran into the clinic and headed straight for the front desk. Misty, the co-op student, looked at her with huge eyes.

"Where is my mom?!"

The girl pointed. "She's in the back, first room on the right."

They took off around the desk and hurried through the small waiting room to the door that led back to the examination rooms. Mark grabbed her arm and saw the fear in her eyes. Wanting nothing more than to hold her, he said instead, "Ava, I'll wait here for you."

She silently nodded then turned and went through the door.

Mark made his way to a chair and sat down just as Ash came through the front doors of the clinic.

"How is she?" Ash asked, as he took a seat across from him.

Mark leaned back and stretched his legs in front of him. "No idea." He sighed. "Ava just went to the back."

"I see."

"Yeah." Mark nodded. He didn't want to make small talk. Not when he didn't know the condition of Abbi or the baby and certainly not with Ash either. He still didn't like the guy.

"So how long have you lived here with Ava and Kim?"

Mark looked at him. He would answer that question though, happily. "In a few months it will be a year."

"Huh. Really? That long? Ava, never mentioned it." A dark look crossed Ash's face. One that he quickly concealed. But not quick enough. Mark noticed it instantly. It wasn't jealousy but something else.

Wanting to see how far he could push the guy, Mark stared at him to gauge his reaction. "Oh yeah. It's been the perfect arrangement. Ava gives the best massages I've had in my life." He scratched the stubble on his jaw as he watched for the man's response to that tidbit. When nothing happened, he added. "As a matter of fact, she gave me one this morning... just before you arrived."

That did it. Ash was furious.

Why would a guy get that mad over a woman he met less than a week ago, one that was doing her job?

Mark had to know. "So, what's with —" Ben appearing from the hall had him shutting up. Instead, Mark stood. "How is she? How's the baby?" He took a step back and searched his friend's face.

"I'm glad I got a hold of you when I did. Ava made it in time."

Mark's brows snapped together. "Time? Time for what?"

Ben couldn't stop the grin from spreading across his face. "Time to see her baby sister come into the world." He beamed.

"A girl?!" Mark laughed, then punched Ben on the arm. "You scared the shit out of me! I thought you said there was something wrong, you said it wasn't good."

"Well, it wasn't when I called. The baby was breech. While I was on the phone with you Doc managed to get her turned around. I'm sorry, I should have called you back."

Mark waved his hand. "Pfft... you had more pressing issues at the time. It's all good. I'm happy for you Ben." He smiled and pulled him in for a bear hug.

Ben took a step back and chuckled. "Want to come and meet your 'niece'?" he asked, as he turned towards the hall.

"Hell yeah!"

Ben stopped and glanced over his shoulder. "Ash, would you like to come too?"

Why, Ben, why?! Mark wanted to yell at him, but kept his mouth shut.

"Sure, sounds good." He nodded, rising from his seat.

BEN HELD THE DOOR OPEN for the two men to enter the room. Mark scanned the room, Ava and Kim were standing on either side of Abbi's bed as she held the infant to her chest.

"Aunt Kim, do you know if Doc is keeping them here or sending them to Springbank?" Ava asked, looking at the men as they filed into the room.

"I'll go check. He might just as a precaution," Kim said, heading towards the door.

Ben went to Abbi and after a few soft-spoken words to her, he took the baby from her arms and walked over to Mark.

Mark stood in awe as Ben held the newborn in his arms. He couldn't believe how this tiny human had made his best friend into a father. But there he stood, proud as ever holding the bundle of pink. "She's beautiful you two." He looked at Abbi and Ben. "Congratulations."

"Thank you," Abbi murmured tiredly, trying to stifle a yawn.

Ava came across the room and looped her arm through Mark's. Peeking over the edge of the blanket, she looked at and smiled. "I think she's perfect."

"Yes, she is." He wasn't referring to the baby, but the woman beside him.

Ash suddenly cleared his throat, drawing everyone's attention to him. Ava dropped her arm and made her way back to her mother's side and took hold of her hand. Ava didn't want to leave her mom, but she knew she had to. Her and Ash still needed to go over the garden plans, and she didn't want to take up anymore of his time.

"Mom, Ash, and I are going to head out now. Call me if you need anything?"

"Sure honey. We will be fine."

"I'll check with Aunt Kim on the way out, see if she has heard anything from Doc yet." She leaned over and kissed Abbi on the cheek. "Love you. I'll see you soon."

Ava walked over to Ben, touching his arm she said, "Call me if anything changes, I will keep my phone on me at all times." She leaned over and brushed her lips on the baby's brow. "Let me know asap when you pick out a name." She looked up and smiled at Ben.

He chuckled, and walked over to the bassinet, gently he laid the sleeping infant in it. "Of course. You will be the first to know."

Nodding, Ava looked at Mark. "I'll be late tonight. After Ash and I go over the plans for the garden, we are heading to Springbank for dinner and a movie."

Mark frowned. He rubbed the line he felt forming on his brow. "Ah, okay."

What the hell am I supposed to say to that?

"Don't wait up..." She called as she walked out the door.

Now what was he supposed to do? He stood in the middle of the room like a third wheel. For the first time in his adult life, he felt lost.

He jerked a thumb over his shoulder. "Guys, I guess I will head out too,"

"Mark, why don't you and Ben grab a cup of coffee?" Abbi offered, yawning. "He needs to take a break and I could use a little nap while the baby is sleeping."

"Ah, sure." He shrugged his shoulders. "That is if Ben wants to."

Ben looked at her. "Are you sure Abbi?"

She nodded; a slight smile hovered on her lips. "I insist."

Needing to get out of the cramped space, Mark said, "I'll wait in the hall, Ben."

He quietly left.

BACK AT THE SPA, AVA and Ash had just gotten out of his truck and were heading to the garden.

"Oh, before I forget. I wanted to warn you about your next-door neighbor."

"Oh?" Ash offered her his arm.

Ava took it, and as they walked arm in arm through the gate, she nodded.

"Yeah. Mrs. Stanford. She gets bored and has been known from time to time to sit in the window with a pair of binoculars." Ava chuckled. "I just thought I would tell you in case..." She would let him fill in the blank. She was about to say walk around naked but thought better of it when she felt him tense up.

"Ah good to know," he said, as he moved away from her to inspect a shrub.

Ava cocked her head as she watched Ash make his way around the garden. He seemed cautious for some reason. Almost as if he were expecting a rat to scamper over his foot or something.

"So how long do you think it will take?" she asked, ashamed that it had gotten as bad as it had. Really, in her defense it was like that when she bought the place. Well, sort of. There were more weeds now that was for sure. Growing along the path as well as choking out what flowers that were strong enough to fight for the sun's light.

She had to stifle a chuckle when she caught sight of him. Her brows shot high while she watched Ash jump at the sight of a garden spider, sitting in the middle of a massive round web, unperturbed by the intruder.

That's a bit odd, a landscaper scared of a spider...

He looked at her and gave a shaky laugh. "Scared me for a minute there. I ah, wasn't expecting that."

She sent him a smile that didn't quite reach her eyes. "Right." She nodded her head vigorously. "I mean, yeah. It would have scared me to... in a garden." *Not.*

"Um, so how long did you say you were landscaping for again?" She did have the right to know if she was hiring him for the job. She didn't want to insult him by asking for references.

Ash looked at her and squinted.

Ava wasn't sure if he was trying to remember if he had told her before or if the sun was in his eyes.

"Wait..." She wagged a finger at him, "I know! It was twelve years, right?" she said, studying his face.

Relief was clear on his face, as that lopsided grin spread on his lips. "Yeah, you got it."

Why is he lying? Maybe he forgot or maybe he started earlier and only owned his business for ten years?

Wanting to give him the benefit of the doubt, Ava smiled back and turned away towards the fountain. It was massive, 3 tiered in the middle of a moat styled, round pool. "Can you get this running again? Or is it just plants and shrubs you specialize in?" she asked as she scooped a handful of dead leaves out.

He looked at the murky water and blanched. "Ah. It shouldn't be a problem, most likely will need a new pump. I won't know until I get a closer look at it."

"True." Ava stood up and looked at him. "Do you have an idea on cost?"

Ash took her hand in his and looked into her eyes. "How about we discuss it over dinner? Instead of Springbank, is there another town close by?"

"There is a restaurant out on highway 71, the Northern Pike. It overlooks the water." Ava pointed across the lake to its north shore. "See that big red building? It's right there." She laughed; the big red building was more of a blob from where they were standing.

He followed her finger.

"It's perfect." Ash smiled, putting an arm around her waist, he pulled her close. Lowering his voice, he inched closer and asked, "Does six sound good with you?"

When he sent that smile her way, everything sounded good to Ava.

"Mhm. I will make reservations."

Their lips were mere inches from each other.

"Perfect. Six it is," he breathed, as his lips touched hers. Softly at first then with more urgency. Ava leaned back, breaking off the kiss. She was shocked, but not from his kiss.

She put her hands on his chest. That was the first time they had ever kissed, and she felt... nothing. It was weird. She *thought* she was attracted to him, and she was.

Or maybe it's because he's the first man to show a real interest in me in years? Making him seem attractive?

She shook her head. No sense in trying to figure it out. Sometimes things needed a slow heat before they boiled over. That had to be it.

"I hate to rush you out the door, so to speak. But if we are going at six, I really have to get some paperwork done before then." She smiled, pulling out of his embrace.

"Sure. I will pick you up at home around 5:30?"

"That's perfect." She turned away and walked the path to the house. She could feel him right behind her and had the sudden urge to bolt up the stairs. She had no idea why, but she kept her pace as she made her way to the porch. Starting up the steps she paused and looked back and raised her hand. "I'll see you later."

Not waiting for a response, she hurried up the steps and before he could follow, she opened the door and closed it. Leaning her back against it she peeked over her shoulder making sure he was on his way. As quietly as she could, she turned the lock in the deadbolt. Something she had never done during business hours. On shaky legs she made her way to the front desk and plopped down onto the chair.

"What the hell is wrong with me?" She muttered to the empty room.

Had she been out of the dating scene for so long that she forgot how to act around a man? That wasn't it. She didn't act like that around Mark or Ben. But they were different, she reminded herself, they didn't count. She knew them, and she certainly wasn't going to date them.

So why when Ash kissed her just as her eyes drifted shut, did she see Mark's face?

THE LAST OF THE TOWNSFOLK had just left after stopping by to congratulate Ben on the baby's arrival while he and Mark were sitting at the lunch counter in Mack's store. Both sat in silent thought. Mark wanted to mention

Ash's reaction earlier but wasn't sure how. He didn't want Ben to think he was trying to turn everyone against the guy. But he didn't want Ava getting hurt either.

"So..." Ben took a sip of his coffee.

Mark looked at him, waiting for him to continue. Shaking his head, he raised his hands. "So what?"

Ben swiveled his bar stool towards him, leaned his arm on the counter and lightly clasped his hands together. "So..." He squinted. "Correct me if I'm wrong, but was there a certain vibe going on with Ash... a bad one?"

Relief coursed through Mark. He felt almost giddy with excitement. He was finally being heard. "Yes! I've been telling you all along there's something wrong with that guy."

"Right. I felt that earlier." Ben nodded in agreement.

Mark took a swig from his mug. "What do we do about it then?"

"There isn't much to do. I mean if Ava likes the man, who are we to step in?"

"We are her family, that's who."

"Mhm. Have you thought about telling her how you feel?" Ben raised a brow at him.

"What... what do you mean?" Mark wasn't about to confess to anything.

Ben laughed. "Come on man. I'm not blind. Anyone can see you care about her more than just as a friend. When will you finally admit it?"

Mark looked at a spot over Ben's shoulder. *What harm would it cause to admit it?*

"No, I haven't... thought about telling her that is." He sighed. The very thought of doing so scared him. What if she flat out laughed in his face. That would be a blow to his ego. "Don't you dare tell her either."

Ben held his hands up. "It's not my story to tell. You will need to be doing that my friend."

Pressing his lips together, Mark bugged his eyes. "Yeah. I know." He had no intention of ever telling Ava, he hoped that one day she would just fall in love with him.

Mack came over with the coffee pot, intent on refilling each of their cups.

Ben pushed his mug away. "Not for me Mack. I need to get back to Abbi," he said, standing. Reaching into his back pocket for his wallet, he threw a twenty on the counter. "Mark, think about what we talked about. I'll see you both later." With that Ben hurried out the door.

Mark never felt more alone in his life than he did at that moment.

"He's on cloud 9, isn't he?" Mack remarked, as he watched Ben run towards the clinic.

Taking a sip of his coffee, Mark wallowed in self-pity and didn't hear Mack until the old man smacked the counter causing him to jerk in response. Carefully Mark sat his cup down then yanked his hand away as the scalding liquid splashed on his skin.

"What did you go and do that for?" he hissed, wiping his hand on his jeans.

"To get your attention, why do you think so?"

"Oh. Sorry... For what?"

Mack looked at Mark and noticed the light was gone from his eyes.

"Nothing. So, how have you been Mark? I haven't seen you for a spell, not since you bought the flowers."

Mark looked at his coffee. The black liquid was turning his stomach, likely because he had hardly been eating. Not since Ash came into the picture at least. That gave him an idea.

"I've been good. Say Mack." Mark threw a hand towards the windows. "What do you know about the guy across the street there in the yellow house?"

"Nothing really. He doesn't say much of anything. Not the friendly type that's for sure," he answered as he wiped the counter down. He chuckled. "You could go and talk to Eleanor Stanford. If anyone knows something about him, it would be her."

Mark nodded. "True. I never thought about her to be honest." He stood and said, "I think I'll head over there right now."

As he headed towards the door Mack stopped him. "Hey. While you're there, ask her where my banana bread is. Dang woman promised me a dozen loaves two weeks ago."

Mark chuckled. "Will do Mack. Take care."

Once outside, he scanned the house across the road. He didn't want Ash knowing he was going next door. Not that it was any of his business, but he still didn't want him knowing. With a sigh, he struck out across the street. With every step, like a mantra, he prayed Eleanor would have some information on the guy...

Chapter 6

Helping Doc with a delivery was nerve wracking on a good day. Add a breech baby and your own sister into the mix, well, it was a hell of a day to say the least. Kim was glad to be headed home and planned on getting straight into the tub once she got there.

Leaving the clinic, she stepped out onto the sun dappled sidewalk. It was a beautiful day, and she was happy to finally be outside and relieved she walked to work that morning. Not wanting to miss a second of the beauty before her, she stopped, taking it all in. The main street was littered with a canopy of trees, allowing for people to stroll at their leisure from the hot sun.

Just one of the many perks about living here.

She sent a wave to Pete who was sitting in the open bay door of his garage on an old metal lawn chair that had seen better days. One day she was sure she would see his bottom poking through it as he flailed about, trying to get out of it. His equally old black lab laid at his feet, thumping its tail when he saw her.

Making her way along the sidewalk she was about to pass the post office/bank beside Mack's store when she saw something across the street. Her amateur detective skills hammered into overdrive.

Hurriedly, Kim ducked into the ally beside the post office and flattened herself against the wall. She leaned forward just a smidge, enough so that she could see Ash standing on the porch of Eleanor Stanford's house. "What the hell is he doing there?" she mumbled to herself. After the way he acted earlier in Abbi's room, Kim was inclined to agree with Mark. The guy was up to no good.

She watched as Ash opened the screen door and knocked before he tried the handle. Sure enough, it opened, just like every house door in the village would when someone was home. Kim felt somewhat relieved when she saw Eleanor standing in the opened doorway. At least he didn't break in.

Good Lord, now I'm accusing him like Mark, she thought as she watched the door close behind them. Taking a deep breath, she pushed away from the wall and gingerly made her way along the sidewalk.

She froze in mid step when Mark came walking out of the store and stopped, staring directly at the yellow house across the street. Kim held her breath as she watched him direct his attention to the house next door. Before she knew it, he set off, heading straight for Eleanor's house.

Kim bolted into action. Running as fast as her chubby self could muster, she tackled Mark on the grassy boulevard between the two houses. From the cackling coming from Pete's garage, she knew her stunt was seen by at least one person. Luckily, the bushes in front of Eleanor's house would hide her antics from those within.

"What the *hell* is wrong with you Kim?" Mark hissed. Shoving her aside, he jumped up and brushed at the grass stains on his pant legs.

"I.... oooh." She held up a finger as she sucked in air. Leaning forward she waited a few seconds before whipping her head up. She started tugging on his arm, desperately dragging him down the street.

"Are you deranged? Stop it!"

"Can't. Need to get out of here. He might come out any second."

Mark shook his head, refusing to budge another step. "Who are you talking about?"

By this time, they were way past Ash's house and coming upon the small park on the corner.

Realizing she could pull him no further she dug in her purse and produced a water bottle, quickly slugging some back.

"Ahhh. That hit the spot." She looked at Mark and noticed him glaring at her. Wiping her mouth with the back of her hand, she held the other up defensively. "*Okay*! Anyways, I was just coming out of work and was walking home. I waved to Pete sitting in his bay door and was coming up to the post office, just passing it I noticed... guess who was on Eleanor's porch?" She took another swig from her water bottle watching his reaction.

Frowning Mark shook his head again, clearly not following her.

She rolled her eyes and asked, "Who in this village do you despise?"

"*Despise?* I don't *despise* anybody...." Dawning finally landed on Mark's face. "Oh *my god,* Ass... I mean Ash?"

Kim snorted. "Yes Ash. That's why I had to tackle you and drag you away from there. Come on." She motioned for him to follow.

Neither of them said a word until they made the turn in the road that would take them home.

"Why do you suppose he went to Eleanor's?" Mark wondered aloud as he kicked at a stone.

"Who knows. Maybe she called him over. I mean, she was at the door as if she were waiting for him to show up."

"Yeah. Maybe..." Before he could finish, his phone started ringing. Taking it from his pocket he hit the button and answered it just as they reached their yard.

Kim could hear that it was Ben on the other end but couldn't make out what he was saying. Following the well-worn path, they made their way to the house. Kim took out her keys, unlocked the door and disarmed the alarm as they entered.

"Yeah, sure I can do that," Mark said. "Okay, I will talk to you tomorrow then, bye."

"Are Abbi and the baby okay?" she asked, hanging her purse on the back of a chair.

Mark went straight to the fridge and grabbed a beer. Popping the cap, he stood at the counter and took a long swallow before answering her.

He nodded. "Yeah, mom and baby are fine. Ben asked if I could go over and let the dogs out. Said if I wanted to, I could stay the night."

She looked at him. "Are you?"

The last time he had stayed the night was on Christmas Eve when Abbi wanted everyone to. Mark stood there and thought back to that night. The living room was all decked out for the holidays, a fire was crackling in the fireplace and Ava, and he were sitting there laughing. That was until the quilt she was cocooned in slipped and the bare skin of her shoulder was exposed.

"Mark!" Kim snapped her fingers in front of his face. "Hello?"

He came out of his daze, looked at her and said, "Hello."

"Smart ass. Are you staying the night there? I want to know how much food I should cook," she said, poking her head in the pantry.

Maybe it would do him some good to be away for the night, at least he wouldn't be up all night waiting for Ava to come home. He rounded the counter and made his way to the hallway. He had made up his mind. "Yeah, I am. I'm just gonna grab a few things and head over there."

"Sounds good," Kim mumbled, as she looked in the freezer for a frozen dinner.

AVA GLANCED AT HER watch as she stuffed her laptop in her bag. She had an hour before Ash was stopping by the house to pick her up. Gathering up her purse along with the bag, she headed out the front door, stopping only long enough to check that it was locked.

Setting off to the path, she made her way to the stairs on the hillside. She loved taking this shortcut through the tall pines. It was shaded and smelled like heaven and allowed one to see from the ground up to the first bough, in any direction, about six feet high. From her viewpoint she could see Kim and Mark heading up the porch steps of the house. She missed spending time with them. Ever since Ash came into the picture, she never seemed to be home anymore. And if she was, he was always calling or texting. As she stepped on the road, she decided then and there that the next time he wanted to go out, she would graciously decline the offer. After all, she didn't want to insult him by saying a flat-out no.

Brutus ran to greet her, and she couldn't resist stopping to give him some love. "Did they lock you out of the house? Come on boy. You look like you need to cool down."

Walking up the steps she opened the door wide. Kim was standing at the stove, pressing the buttons on the display.

"Hey, what are you cooking?" Ava asked, sitting her bag and purse on the table.

"A frozen lasagna... want one?" she asked, poking holes in the plastic film of the tray with a fork.

"No." Ava sighed. "Ash is coming by shortly. We are going to the Northern Pike. Haven't been there yet, so I thought it would be a good place to try."

"You don't sound too enthused." Kim studied her face while she took a cookie sheet from the cupboard.

"I'm just tired." Ava pulled a chair out and sat. "Where is Mark?"

"He's getting some things and heading over to Ben and your moms for the night." Kim picked up the box she had thrown on the counter.

"Oh, yeah, I suppose. I never thought about that." She rubbed her tired eyes with her fists, fighting back a yawn, she said, "Brutus must have been locked out when they rushed to the clinic."

"Mhm, more than likely," Kim murmured absently as she read the label on the box. "Did you know there is a shit ton of salt in this?" She tossed it back on the counter and stuck the dinner in the oven.

"Why don't you come with Ash and I to dinner?" Ava asked, just as Mark came into the room with an overnight bag slung over his shoulder.

Kim snorted. "No, I wouldn't want to come between your two love birds."

Mark sent Kim a look of surprise. His brows raised high; he shook his head... *Why would you even suggest that?*

"Mark, would you like to come?"

He whipped his head in Ava's direction not quite believing he heard her right. Blinking rapidly, he said, "Come again?"

"I said, do you want to come to dinner with us? We are just going over the plans for the garden at the spa." *I hope...* she added silently.

Mark was tempted to take her up on her offer. He really was. But something stopped him. "Ahhhh.... No. I need to head over to the house. Abbi was worried." He shoved a hand through his hair and sighed. "And I'm sure the animals need some company. Maybe next time." He nodded, with a grim look on his face.

"Oh. Sure, of course." Ava agreed. Disappointed, she got up and pushed the chair in. "Well, I guess I should go and get ready." She started walking towards the hall, pausing, she looked over her shoulder and said, "See you tomorrow, Mark."

"Bye, Ava," he quietly replied.

Once she was out of earshot Kim looked at him. "Why didn't you take her up on the offer?"

Mark leaned back, looking down the hall. He needed to be sure Ava wasn't coming around the corner at any second. When he felt the coast was clear he looked at Kim.

"Because. I'm heading over to Ben and Abbi's right now. I'll feed the animals, let the dogs out and then beat my ass back over here. When I get back..." He glanced down the hall once again. He then pointed at her and said, "You and I are going to go pay Eleanor a visit. But first, we'll go and look around the yellow house...." He sent her what he hoped was a conspiratorial wink. "...if you know what I mean."

Kim raised a hand and jerked it at her own eye. "You got something in your eye? Because you looked as if you did."

"Was it that bad? I was going for a 'knowing' wink, you know." He waved his hand back and forth between them. "Like a secret between 'us', you know what I mean?"

"Yeah, don't do that." She wrinkled her nose and shook her head. "It was really bad. Just so you know. You know?" she mocked.

Mark groaned. "I'm nervous alright? I have a habit of repeating myself when I am."

"Really?"

"Uh... no. I was just joking. Okay then. Now that we've figured that out, I'm off to go next door." He set off across the room to the door.

Kim just about jumped out of her skin when he bellowed out, "I'LL SEE YOU IN THE MORNING KIM. CALL ME IF YOU HAVE A PROBLEM. COME ON BRUTUS."

He lowered his voice and said, "Now your turn."

If looks could kill, Mark would have been fried on the spot. But seeing how that didn't happen she yelled back. "Yeah! I'll do that. Have fun, see ya later." After all, she was a smidge excited to be sneaking around again.

With that, Mark yanked the door open and there stood Ash with his hand raised, ready to knock on the door.

Quickly, he averted his gaze. "Hey Ash, good to see you." *Not.*

He stepped aside to let Ash in. Just as he did, Brutus let out a deep grumble.

So, the dog hates him too, does he?

No sooner did Mark think of it than Brutus let out an enormous burp. Evidently the dog was just full of gas.

Frowning down at him, Mark whistled. "Let's go, Brutus."

Making their way to the path through the trees, Mark glanced at his companion and muttered, "You could have run him off you know."

Brutus stopped and looked at him as if he were nuts. Without so much as a whimper the dog bolted in the direction of home, leaving Mark wondering what had gotten into him. That was until he heard a familiar screeching. Running through the brush, he broke into the clearing of Ben's yard, coming to an abrupt halt.

His brain simply refused to compute what his eyes so clearly saw. Mark whipped his cell phone out of his pocket and scrolled through his contacts until he found Kim's number.

"Hey Kim, are you busy?" he asked as he tried the doorknob. Locked. "No? Good, I need you to come and give me a hand. All the animals are sitting outside."

He glanced at them. Two cats, three dogs and Bird, a sulfur-crested cockatoo that was currently sitting on a tree branch, screeching, *'Asshole get out of my house'* like a broken record.

No sooner did he hit the end button he heard the door slam next door in the distance and the sound of Kim hoofing it through the bush.

Chapter 7

"Here you go Ava," Ash said, while he held the chair for her to sit down.

"Thanks." She replied as she took her seat. Taking a menu, she opened it. Her brows rose as her eyes took in the prices. Sixty dollars a meal seemed a little steep, but who was she to say. "So, I heard that the pike is very tasty here," she said, looking at him over her menu.

Ash smirked. "Should we try it?"

"Ah... Sure. Why not?"

Ash waved the waiter over to their table and placed their order. "Do you want anything to drink from the bar, Ava?"

She looked up at the waiter. "Can I get a glass of red wine please?"

"Make that two." Ash nodded.

"Certainly, I'll be right back."

"So how is your mom and the baby doing?"

"Good." Ava smiled. "I called her just before you came by. They should be home in a few days."

"Have they picked a name yet?" Ash asked, as the waiter came with their wine.

She laughed, taking her glass she took a small sip and shook her head. "Not yet. Knowing my mom, it will be a week or more before they decide."

They sat and chatted for a bit about everything from the weather to Mrs. Stanford next door. It felt like only ten minutes had passed when the waiter came with their food.

"Wow. That was fast." Ash leaned back as the waiter placed his food before him.

Ava looked down as her plate was thumped onto the table. Her stomach rolled with revulsion as the fish looked at her from the plate. Not wanting to appear like she didn't want to eat, she picked up her fork and dug into the bed of rice it was served on.

Trying desperately to forget that the fish's beady eye was staring at her, she asked, "So, um...did you come up with an estimate for the garden?"

"I did. With the cost of materials, it will roughly be around $4000.00. Mind you that is with labor costs. I did some recalculations, and I was able to get it knocked down to two grand."

Hmm, he said he would need to look at the fountain to see if it needed a pump.

"I see. And what would that all entail?" she asked, watching him closely.

Ash wiped his mouth on his napkin then took a drink from his glass.

He seemed to be stalling.

"Well, that would include clearing the area of all weeds. Laying the path with either gravel or on the higher price range a nice cobblestone patterned brick. And planting some new shrubs and flowers as needed." He took a notebook from his shirt pocket, laying it on the table, he pushed it over to her. "Oh, and possibly a pump for the fountain." A sly smile formed on his lips, almost as if he knew exactly what she was thinking.

"I see." She felt like a fool for even doubting him. "Well, I don't want you to feel you need to cut corners. I don't have a problem with the cost."

He reached across the table and laid his hand over hers. "I insist. I can't charge my girl full price for something that I can do in a couple of days."

My girl?! Where the hell did that come from? She liked him, but he was moving way too fast for her liking.

She faked a smile. Then, not knowing exactly how to remove her hand, she feigned a sneeze. Yanking it free she covered her face and ahcooo'd into it.

"Excuse me, that came out of nowhere! Ah, what were we saying?" She looked at him and squinted. "Oh, that's right, about the garden. When do you think you can start?" She asked, stuffing more rice into her mouth.

Surprised at how much rice she shoved in her mouth; Ash looked at her in disbelief. "How does tomorrow work for you?"

She nodded as she chewed. Tomorrow was Saturday, and thankfully the spa was closed. She could give him a hand. Washing the rice down with the rest of her wine, she said, "Absolutely, I can help too, if you don't mind that is."

"Why would I mind?" He grinned. "It is your yard after all."

"Then it's settled. We can meet at the spa, say around 9:00 in the morning?"

He gave her a quick nod and that lopsided smile that she loved. Motioning to her plate he said, "Seeing how you don't want to touch that fish, shall we order dessert?"

"You noticed." She laughed. "Dessert sounds fantastic."

KIM GULPED IN AIR AS she all but collapsed into Ben and Abbi's yard. "What the hell is going on Mark?"

"Beats me. The door is locked yet all the animals are out here." He scratched his head, looking at each of the windows on the back of the house. Not one of them was opened, not even a crack. "You don't think Ben and Abbi left them outside when they rushed to the clinic do you?"

"Maybe the dogs and cats, but Bird?" Kim shook her head. "No. Abbi would never leave him outside. In fact, the only time he has ever been outside is in his cage."

Mark turned towards the side of the house. "Well, I'm going to walk around the house. See if there are any signs of forced entry."

"Not without me you're not."

"What about Bird, aren't you worried he will fly away?" Mark asked.

"He hasn't yet? Besides, he will come along. Just need to call him like a dog." She chuckled. Tapping her shoulder, she gave the command. "Come Bird."

True to her word, Bird stopped his squawking and flew over to her. He had other ideas of course and landed on her head instead of her shoulder.

"Get the hell off me, you crazy bird!" she yelled, waving her hands about.

Bird stayed put. Proud as a peacock, he sat perched on the clip in her hair.

Mark burst out laughing, leading the way he reasoned. "Hey, at least he's quiet now."

"He better not shit on my head is all I have to say," Kim grumbled, following Mark to the front of the house.

Together they looked at each window and door only to find everything tightly closed and locked.

"Well, it's safe to say no one broke in. They had to have let them out and forgotten to let them back in." Kim sighed and rubbed her neck. She was getting a crick in it from the weight of the bird.

It just didn't make any sense. Mark wasn't convinced that they would leave the animals to fend for themselves outside. And even if they did forget to put them back in, why didn't Ben mention it to him?

"I guess you're right." Mark said, as they made their way to the back door.

Sticking his key in the lock, Mark turned it then opened the door for all to enter. Bird took off from Kim's head and flew to his perch, while the others clamored for food.

Kim walked over to the fridge and opened it. "I don't think it's a good idea to mention this to Ben or Abbi." Taking out two bottles of water, she sat one on the counter for Mark and took a swig from her own.

Mark frowned as he filled the animal's food bowls. "Why not?" he asked, looking up at her.

"Why?" Kim shrugged. "What purpose would it serve for them to know? Other than making them worry?"

"I guess." Mark sat each bowl on the floor, then looked at Kim. "You know what this reminds me of don't you?"

"Don't even say it. I already thought about *him*."

"Yeah." Mark agreed.

No one liked talking about him. Him being Raven Black. The man that had been obsessed with Abbi. He had done subtle things to her in the past. So subtle one wouldn't even notice if they hadn't been paying attention. But Ben had. And those small subtle things had turned into huge things. So huge that Raven had gone as far as trying to kill Ben not once but twice. In the end Ben had been the one to end Raven's life.

Mark decided he would be like Ben and watch for the subtle things... Only one problem. He wouldn't be home tonight to make sure Ava made it there.

Walking to the table Kim pulled out a chair and sat down. "So, what are we doing? Did you still want to go and talk to Mrs. Stanford?"

Mark looked at the clock on the wall. An hour had already gone by since he'd come to the house. Knowing Ava's routine of late, they would have at least another 5 hours before she and Ash were back in the village.

Snatching his keys off the table he nodded. "Sure. The dogs should be fine until we get back. Let's grab my truck." With that, Kim locked the door, stopping to make sure it was closed tight, they headed home.

KIM AND MARK WERE SITTING in his pickup parked in Mack's parking lot, right across from Ash's house. It was starting to get dark and if they didn't hurry up, they wouldn't be seeing anything.

Kim looked at Mark. "Are we just going to sit here staring at the house or are we going to get out and look around?" she asked.

"I'm thinking..." Gripping the steering wheel, he turned in his seat to look at her. "If we go there and he comes home then what?"

She sat still for a second before answering. "I don't know. I guess we come up with an excuse." She reached for the door handle.

Mark grabbed her arm. "Wait! We need to get our stories straight. We can't risk him figuring something out. I mean he could be on his way home right now."

Kim took her cell phone out of her pocket. "If it makes you feel better, I will call Ava and ask."

"No! Don't do that! We will say that we are out for a walk if we run into him. Let's go."

With that they exited the truck and headed across the street. Excited by the second, Kim glanced around making sure no one was a witness to their shenanigans again. That's all they would need. She shot a quick glance to Mrs. Stanford's window. It was empty. Kim was somewhat surprised, normally a set of binoculars would be starting back at her.

They made their way to the back yard. Mark held his breath as he eased the gate open, hoping beyond hope that the hinges didn't need a good oiling. He slowly released it when it opened soundlessly. He jerked his head. "Come on," he whispered, just as Kim bumped into his back.

"What the hell are you doing?" he mouthed the words.

Kim bugged her eyes at him. "You *can* talk, you know," she said. Pushing past him, she continued into the yard. She was surprised how large it was, being in the village she assumed it would be on the smaller side. Barely being able to make out objects, with every step she felt around with her foot.

This is crazy. Can't see a damn thing.

She turned, intending on going back to tell Mark just that when with her next step she met air. She cried out in shock just as she felt herself plummeting downward. "*Oh, shiiiitt*"!!!

Chapter 8

"It's a beautiful night isn't it." Ash nodded in the direction of the pier as they headed towards his truck.

"Did you want to go for a walk along the water?" Ava asked. She really didn't want to, tired as she was, but it was the polite thing to do.

"Maybe a short one. We have an early start tomorrow, remember?" He leaned towards her and nudged her with his arm.

"Nine o'clock is hardly early." She chuckled.

He raised his hands palm up and grinned. "Give me a break princess, I'm on vacation."

Ava raised her chin a notch.

What is with this guy and the pet name? "Of course, it slipped my mind."

Ash crooked his arm towards her. "Shall we?"

Without a word, Ava nodded and looped her arm through his.

"So, tell me, other than the new baby, do you have any brothers and sisters?" He looked at her as they made their way to the water's edge.

Ava bobbed her head. "I do. Twin older brothers... Luke and Lane. What about you?"

Ava noticed a fleeting, pained look on his face. She stopped walking and clutched his arm. "What is it?"

He took her hand in his and gave it a gentle squeeze. "I don't like to talk about it but I'm a twin too. Only my brother died 5 years ago."

Ava covered her mouth with her hand. "Oh my gosh I'm so sorry to hear that!"

Ash sighed. "He was heading home one night during a snowstorm. He never made it."

Standing in the moonlight, he was touched when he looked her in the eyes and saw they glistened with unshed tears.

"That's horrible. I can't imagine how hard that must have been for you, for your family." She found it strange that there would be a snowstorm in southern Texas but who was she to say. Instead, Ava let her guard down. Something she rarely did but she felt a strong need to comfort him. She threw her arms around his waist and gave him a tight squeeze. They never touched before other than the kiss earlier in the day and holding hands a few times, she thought she could trust him...that was a big mistake.

The next thing Ava knew, Ash's mouth was grinding into hers and his hands were like an octopus; blindly grabbing anything and everything.

She wasn't ready for this kind of relationship. She had to stop it, and now.

Putting her hands on his arms, she pushed down as she backed away. Trying for a light mood she giggled. "Um, let's take it down a notch, shall we?"

"Sorry, I guess I read you wrong."

She raised her hand and held her thumb and index finger apart about an inch. "Just a smidge."

"Understood." He nodded. "How bout we finish our walk?"

They walked along the sandy north shore of Pearl Lake and from there Ava could see Ben and her mom's house. Her thought turned to Mark staying the night there. He would miss her coming home tonight. She thought it sweet how every time Ash took her out, he would be waiting in the dark to make sure she made it in the house, only to run down the hall before she could fit her key in the lock. He had no clue that she knew of course. And she wanted to keep it that way. She never would have known he did that if it weren't for the time he tripped over Brutus. She could hear him on the other side of the closed door. Swearing and thanking his mother. She giggled at the memory.

"What's so funny?" Ash looked at her grinning.

"Oh nothing. I was just thinking about Mark. He stays up to make sure I get home okay whenever we go out." Ava looked at him, the scowl he was currently sporting said it all.

"What is this fascination that you have with Mark?" he demanded.

"What do you mean? We are roommates, there is no fascination!"

"Yes, there is, you're always talking about him. If you want to continue what we have, then you're going to need to move in with your mom."

She snickered. "I'm *what*?!" *Just who the hell does he think he is?*

"You heard me. You're going to have to move out. No way is any girlfriend of mine living with another man."

Ava sidestepped out of his reach as he tried to put his arm around her.

"Let's get a few things straight. I'm not your girlfriend. We have gone on a couple of dates that *I* had to pay for," she said, jabbing herself in the chest.

"You know –"

Ava held up her hand, her eyes shooting daggers. "I'm. Not. Done." Her words dripping with ice she continued. "We aren't in a relationship and with that attitude mister, we never will be. No one tells me what I can or can't do, ..." She raised a brow. "... understood?"

Ash gave her a curt nod and slowly backed away. "Perfectly. You can find your own way home."

Head held high, she retorted. "I already planned on it." Without another word she spun around in the direction of home. She would walk along the beach; she'd done it before and in this case would gladly do it again. That was until she heard the first rumble of thunder. Taking her shoes off, she started off at a slow jog, with any luck she'd make it before the first raindrop fell.

MARK JERKED UP AND swung his phone around. He had been looking in one of the basement windows with his cell phone's flashlight when he heard a shriek.

"Kim? Where the hell are you?" he hissed, as he peered into the darkness. About 30 feet away he saw it... a swimming pool.

"Shit!" Running over, he saw that it had a solar blanket on it and in the blanket was a huge hole. Was she trapped under it? He shone his phone over the surface but didn't see anything under it.

"Mark! Get me the hell outta here!!!" Came her screaming voice a few feet behind him.

Shining his light down, he found Kim in a hole. Her body faced a dirt wall while she looked up at him.

"Are you alright?"

"Yes! Will you get that light out of my face and give me a hand?" She griped.

"If you turned around, you'd see there is a set of stairs behind you." He aimed the light for her to see.

"Now how was I to know that? It's pitch dark down here and my phone flew out of my hand when I fell."

Mark made his way down the steps. "I wonder, why this is in the middle of the yard?"

Kim looked at him. "I don't know, it's creepy. You stay here and find out. I'm getting out of here," she said, pushing her way past him.

"Wait, there's a door. It's probably a storm shelter or maybe a cellar."

That stopped Kim in her tracks. There was no way there was a door. She spun around to have a look. Sure enough, there it was. Right where she was standing not more than a few minutes ago.

Mark looked at her, his hand on the doorknob. "Should we go in?"

She shook her head. "No! I'm sure it's locked. And if it isn't locked, I'm sure it wouldn't be a good thing to go in."

Mark shrugged. "What could it hurt?"

"It could hurt a lot of things. Mainly us." Kim's eyes bugged out of her head as she watched him turn the handle. "Stop!! Have you never watched a horror movie? That could be the gate to hell and you're about to unleash the hounds."

"You do realize movies aren't real, don't you?" he chuckled as he cracked open the door.

"No, no, no. Nope!" Kim shook her head so fast she looked like a bobble head in a hurricane. "I'm not going in," she said, peering over his shoulder. "Besides, it's awfully dark in there."

No sooner did the words leave her mouth when a flash of lightning lit the doorway of the room. A figure materialized before them. Mark squealed and slammed the door shut. Together they ran up the stairs screaming, through the back yard and out the gate as a clap of thunder cracked overhead.

Standing in the front yard, hunched over, Kim raised her eyes to look at Mark. Between gasps she said, "Did you see that? Did you *see that*?!I swear there was a vampire standing there looking at us."

Mark held up a shaky hand, one finger raised. "Vampire? What I saw wasn't a vampire. Oh no, no, no. That was Satan in the flesh," he hissed.

"Right," she said doubtfully as she cast her glance at the gate. She was half expecting to see a vampire/Satan dude flying through the night sky.

"We need to come back tomorrow when it's daylight."

Kim stood straight and whipped her head to look at him. "What... are you insane?! Whatever that was doesn't need to see the light of day. Especially by us." Expecting a response, she grew concerned when he didn't answer. He was standing there with his head cocked, as if he were listening to something. She became alarmed when he turned his head and looked down the street. "*Mark?*"

"Shit!" He took off across the yard. "*Run!*"

He was halfway to the truck before Kim could even register his words. Now she saw exactly what made him run... Ash's truck was barrelling down the street, headed right for her.

Kim dove into the bushes as she heard Mark slamming his truck door.

Well, aren't I in a pickle now?

She held her breath as Ash backed into the driveway. It wasn't like he'd hear her, but it made her feel better for some reason.

The seconds ticked by as she waited for him to exit his vehicle. Praying he wouldn't see her, she snuck a glance to see what was taking him so long, maybe Ava was with him. All she could see was the glow of his cell phone lighting up his face. Something about the way the light played over his features jogged her memory and had her staring longer than she needed to.

What the hell was it? She couldn't put her finger on it. Instead of ducking down like any normal person would, Kim popped her head up to get a better look just as Ash moved to open the truck door.

Across the street and in his truck, Mark was ducked down. The top of his head to his eyes was the only thing showing if someone happened to walk by. He watched as

Ash sat in his truck while Kim's white shirt flashed in the bushes. He made note to mention black clothes only on their next excursion. He also needed to order earpieces so they could talk to each other as he muttered to himself, "Duck down Kim."

Ash got out of the truck and stood. He was looking around, almost as if he knew something was out of place.

Maybe he can smell her?

"Don't be an idiot Donovan," Mark mumbled, to himself.

He willed Kim to lay low and breathed a sigh of relief when she managed to, just in the nick of time. But still, Ash stood there. He swung his glance towards Eleanor's dark house and stood for a few seconds more before making his way to the steps and onto his front porch. A few seconds later a light switched on and Ash was in the house.

Mark glanced at his watch. 9:00 pm. One good thing, he didn't need to worry about Ava getting home with him staying the night at Ben's and Abbi's. She would already be there. Mark quickly flashed his lights giving Kim an all clear.

Kim got up from her hiding spot and ran across the road, looking over her shoulder as she did. She was sure Ash was watching her from the windows with every step. Reaching for the truck's door handle she yanked it open and dove into the passenger side. She was shaking from head to toe. "Get me the hell outta here."

Mark didn't need to be told twice. He started the engine and in one rapid motion set it in gear and stomped on the gas pedal. In a flurry of dust, they squealed out of the parking lot and in the opposite direction of home.

"Where the hell are you going?"

"Away from home. I'll double back just in case he was watching."

Kim leaned her head back against the seat. "Ah good idea. I've never been this scared shitless in my life." She laughed.

Mark glanced over at her. "Oh yeah?"

"Yeah. It was fun." She inhaled a deep breath. "Let's not do it again, promise?"

He sent her a wicked smile. "I promise we won't do it again... at least not tonight."

Kim rolled her eyes and looked out her window at the darkness, just as the heavens opened and the rain came down. "Now why did I have a feeling you would say that?"

Chapter 9

With every step, Ava cursed out Ash. She had been halfway home making good time at an easy jog, when something darted out of the bushes to her left, causing her to misjudge her step. She had landed hard on her ankle and wouldn't be surprised if it were broken. She had called both Mark and Kim with no luck. She should have known better. It was Friday night, their date night, they likely made a trip to the video store or Springbank and ended up pigging out in front of the wall screened tv at Ben and her mom's house. She sniffed at the thought of missing out, of missing those days more than she realized.

She was three quarters of the way home when the first fat raindrop splattered on her face. She was now wet, cold, and hurt but she was determined to get home, or at the very least to her mom and Ben's house. Holding her phone out in front of her like a lantern, she hobbled along. Thankfully, it was waterproof otherwise she would be going along blindly, only being able to focus on the house in the distance as a guide. She couldn't risk another mishap. She was walking along the shore where the lake was the deepest. With no gradual decline into the water but a sheer drop, if she slipped, she'd be in big trouble with her ankle. She needed to take a moment and sit down. Once she reached the fallen oak that stretched across the path into the water, she would do just that.

Her phone rang just then, hoping it was Kim or Mark returning her call she quickly glanced at it, and like before she ignored it. It was Ash. He'd sent ten text messages and called five times. She would eventually answer him, but on her terms not his. It wasn't her fault he was so butthurt over her mentioning Mark. She knew she wasn't in the wrong and there was no way she would be telling him she was sorry. If he wanted anything to do with her, he would be the one apologizing.

Finally, the fallen tree lay before her, carefully she sat and pivoted on her butt, throwing her legs on the opposite side, she sat upon it for a bit. It felt wonderful to take the weight off her foot. She peered at it using the light of her phone. It was hard to tell if it was bruised or just dirty. But it was swollen, there was no doubt about that. Tears formed in her eyes as she saw that her ankle was nearly twice the size of the other one.

So much for working this week.

She would need to call her clients and cancel, and prayed it was just for the week.

She was so utterly tired at the thought of continuing but had little choice in the matter if she wanted to get home sometime before dawn. Noticing a dead branch laying on the ground she snatched it up, it would work as a walking stick. She just prayed it held her weight. Carefully standing, she tested it to see if it would work, deciding it would, she took one step and groaned in agony as her brow broke out in a sweat. Clenching her teeth, she grimaced as determination took over and she set off towards home. She had gone no more than five feet when exhaustion won out.

"REMEMBER." MARK JERKED his head at the house. "When you go in there and Ava asks where we were you tell her we went to the movies in Springbank." He raised his brows. "Got it?"

"Yeah, yeah. Stop reminding me. You know I don't like this, and we've been over it how many times now?" Kim replied, as she opened the truck door.

"I know, I know. I don't like lying to her either but, never mind... I'll talk to you tomorrow."

"See you." Kim waved him off as she made her way towards the house. She was hoping Ava was sound asleep, so she didn't have to face her. She had a horrible time lying to the girl as it was. But to not tell her what they saw, in what they could only conclude was an outdoor cellar was something Kim might not be able to hold in.

Letting herself into the house, she looked around for the tell-tale signs that she was home. Ava had a routine whether she cared to admit it or not. Every time she would come home, she would leave her shoes by the door, next she would either throw her purse on the table or sling the strap from a chair. Ava would then go into the kitchen, where she would make herself a cup of tea. Always leaving the spoon alongside the sugar bowl on the counter and the tea bag on the edge of the sink. Every single time... but not tonight.

Kim made her way through the silent house. For some reason despite Raven being killed in the house, she never had an eerie feeling about living there, until this moment. The house felt different as if something were missing.

As if someone was watching, she thought as she felt the hair rise on the back of her neck. She took off down the hall straight for Ava's room. *To hell if she is sleeping, she won't be for long...* she thought as she blasted through the door.

"Oh," she said to the empty room. Ava wasn't home yet. "Well, I will just go make myself a tea and wait for her," she announced, as she made her way back to the kitchen.

MARK GOT OUT OF THE pickup and headed into the house. All three dogs met him at the door. Each one crying with excitement at seeing him before taking off outside. Closing the door, he locked it with the key. He would bring them in through the back when they were done. Following them to the backyard, Mark saw Brutus at the last second take off barking down the shoreline. He cupped his hands around his mouth and called to the dog, it was no use, his voice was lost in the storm.

Taking shelter under the back patio with Lucy and Molly on either side of him, Mark waited for the brute to come back on his own. Abbi would kill him if anything happened to that dog. Now would be a good time to search the web for earpieces he thought. Taking out his cell he ignored the missed call notification and went straight to a search engine. Fifteen minutes later he was satisfied he'd found the perfect ones and placed his order. Now he would check his voicemail. Scrolling through his notifications he saw Ava had called him nearly two hours ago but never left a message. Hitting the connect button, he waited for her to pick up.

"Ava. What's up?" he said, as she answered.

"Mark, thank God... I need you..." Her breathless voice echoed through the earpiece and then nothing.

"Ava?!" he shouted in a surge of panic. "Answer me dammit!"

He immediately called Kim.

"Where is Ava?"

"She's not here."

Mark shoved a hand through his hair and started pacing. "What do you mean she's not there? I just talked to her, and she said she needed me, then the phone went dead."

"She wasn't here when I got home... oh my god, you don't think Ash has her do you? What if she was in the back of the truck tied up?"

"I'm coming to you. Be ready." Mark ended the call and unlocked the back door. He ushered the two dogs in. Before closing the door, he snagged Ben's trench coat from the peg behind the door. It was a little long, ending at mid-calf, but at least it would keep him partially dry. Now to get Brutus.

He let loose an ear-splitting whistle that he hoped the dog would hear. Brutus yip carried to him on the wind, Mark just hoped he wasn't too far away. He called to the animal as he ran to the shoreline. Stopping, he peered into the darkness. It was no use; it was blacker than the hole Kim had fallen into. He took his cell phone out to turn the flashlight on and swore when the low battery warning flashed. Stuffing it in his pocket he ran to the house to get a flashlight only stopping long enough to plug his phone in to charge before heading back to the shore.

Steeling himself, he took a deep breath before venturing forward. He had his share of dark spaces tonight. If it weren't for the dog being Abbi's suck, he would have left him. But he couldn't do that to her or Brutus for that matter. The mutt had grown on him.

Turning the flashlight on he jumped a foot in the air and screamed like a little girl. Brutus was standing before him in the pouring rain looking up at him, waiting.

"You asshole!" He yelled. Grabbing his collar Mark tugged to no avail. Brutus had his feet planted and refused to budge. "Will you come on? I don't have time for this. I have to go and save Ava."

At the mention of her name, Brutus bucked and twisted out of Mark's grasp and took off in the opposite direction from the house. A second later he came back to Mark and barked.

Mark cocked his head. "What the hell has gotten into you?"

Brutus went for his pant leg, biting down and tugging Mark towards the north shore.

"Okay, I get it. You want me to follow you." Mark swallowed hard, desperately trying to swallow the bile that was burning the back of his throat. Casting the beam from the flashlight along the beach, he followed the dog and prayed he wasn't leading him to the vampire/Satan's home away from home...

KIM WAS WEARING A PATH on the porch waiting for Mark to pull up. She wrung her hands as images of Ava, gagged and bound in the back of Ash's pickup flitted through her mind. She stopped her pacing as a horrified thought popped into her head.

Maybe that's what the cellar from hell is for? Snatching young women and hiding them there, is he a trafficker, a rapist, a cannibal?

She had to find out what was taking Mark so long. Searching in her purse for her phone she had an asinine thought. *Does one take their purse to confront a body snatcher? No!!*, her mind screamed in response as her fingers found what she was looking for.

Quickly she went through her contacts and connected the call to Mark. Opening the door, she tossed her purse inside the house and locked it before pulling it closed. Shoving her keys in her back pocket she groaned in frustration when it went to voicemail. Not waiting a second longer she took off down the steps and headed for Ben and Abbi's.

Within minutes she was pounding on their front door. Kim could hear Molly and Lucy barking on the other side but no sign of Mark. Unlocking the door, she let herself in. Looking up the staircase she called out. "Mark? Are you here?" Turning away, the dogs right on her heels, she went to the hall that led to the kitchen, stopping to check each room as she passed.

Walking to the back patio door, she went out onto the back porch. Shivering in the damp she noticed his truck was parked but no sign of him. "Where are you and where is Brutus?" she wondered out loud.

When her teeth started chattering, she decided it was time to go back in. There was no sense staying out in the rain waiting for him. A tea would help warm her up.

Closing the door behind her, she took the kettle and filled it with water. This night was getting weirder by the hour, and she would be glad to go home to bed. The sooner the better she thought, stifling a yawn as she looked at the dogs who sat patiently by her side.

"Want a treat?"

Lucy pawed the air and Molly spun in circles, their way of saying yes. Kim pulled the cookie jar full of treats towards her and grabbed a handful before sliding it back. That's when she saw Mark's cell phone, attached with its cord plugged in the wall socket. A clammy fear struck her at once. Something was dreadfully wrong. Always fearing he would miss a call from his agent, Mark never went anywhere without it. Kim screamed and the dog treats went flying when a thumping sound came from the front of the house.

She smacked the light switch and grabbed a dirty knife from the sink as the room settled into darkness. Lucy began to whine and sure as Kim stood in the dark holding a knife, she knew the little Yorkie piddled on the floor. The puddle would have to wait. She needed to find out what the hell that thump was.

Creeping down the hall, a knife held in front of her, Kim looked in each room again as she passed the open doorways.

Where the hell was Brutus when she needed him? She made it to the staircase. *Should I go up or make a run for home?* The choice was taken out of her hands when the thumping came again... from the front door.

Flattening herself against the wall she desperately tried to calm her racing heart. She held her breath and cocked her head. People were talking. Her first thought was Ava was home and Mark was with her. But that wasn't the case. It was two men. She strained to listen but all she could hear was mumbling.

What should I do? She took a deep steadying breath. She would open the door and see who it was. *Are you crazy? That's how people get killed in the movies...*

Chapter 10

"Hold up buddy," Mark said as he futilely swiped the rain from his face. For the tenth time he felt like he was on a wild goose chase. He was sure Kim was flipping out right about now, not knowing where he was. It had been at least fifteen minutes since he started following Brutus. What would normally take a five-minute hike in the daytime was taking much longer in the rain, riddled darkness. If the dog didn't show him something soon, Mark was heading back to the house, with or without him.

They were coming up to the oak tree that had fallen a year ago in a storm just like this one. The trunk laid across the path and there was no way around it other than scaling over it. Mark was ready to carry on until he heard the waves lapping around its branches that laid in the water. The wind was picking up. One slip, and he would be going for a swim, or his luck, another tree would fall... on him.

"Brutus, come on boy." He flashed the light around looking for the dog. Aiming the beam on the path beyond the tree, there was no sign of him. A feeling of dread came over him.

Did he fall in the lake?

"BRUTUS!!!" Mark shouted into the wind.

He heard a whimper to his right. Whipping his head and the flashlight to the bushes, Mark crouched down and parted the leaves. There inside a cocoon of foliage was Brutus. His soulful eyes stared back at Mark. The gentle giant laid his head on Ava's belly and let out a whimpering sigh.

"KIM. WE CAN SEE YOU. Open the damn door!"

Good lord, they know my name!

She wanted to go and hide but she was sure as shit they were bound to find her.

"It's Dave and Tim. Come on, we're wasting our vacation here standing on the porch. Open the door."

Dave and Tim? Tim, I know but Dave? Was he the US Marshal that helped Ben, wasn't his name Dean? She wondered.

"Dean. She likely doesn't remember me as Dave." Came a muffled response.

Dropping the knife with a clatter, she unlocked the deadbolt and yanked the door open. Thankful that it was two cops and not the thing that was currently festering in Ash's basement.

Flinging herself blindly at one of them, she said, "Thank God you guys are here. Lucy pissed on the floor, Mark and Brutus are missing and a vampire/Satan is roaming around the village. We think it's got Ava..."

"Nice to see you too, Kim." Dean drawled as he untangled her arms from around his neck. "Sounds like things are still batshit crazy around here. How about we go sit in the kitchen. Have a nice cup of something hot and you tell us all about your night." He turned Kim around and guided her down the hall.

"Tim." Dean darted his eyes to the floor where the knife laid. "Grab that will you?"

With a silent nod, Tim bent down and picked up the knife.

Kim was still having a hard time believing what happened in the last six hours. She had just finished telling them in detail the events of the night and evidently, they were too as they were full of questions. Sitting at the table across from the two men she felt like she was being interrogated.

"Okay, let me get this straight," Tim said, trying to figure out in his head exactly what Kim was prattling on about. "You and Mark went and broke into Ava's boyfriend's house because he showed up at his house without her?"

Kim slowly nodded then took a sip of her tea. "But that's not the reason why we went there. We went there to snoop around. It wasn't till everything happened that he came home alone. Thank the lord he hadn't been any sooner; we would have come ripping out of his back gate screaming like a couple of banshees right into him. And we didn't break in."

Dean chuckled as the image played in his mind. "No, that's right, you fell in."

Kim pointed at him. "Yes! But not in the house. I don't know how anyone could fall into a house unless they fell from the sky. No, I fell when we were snooping around his back yard. Like into a dungeon or something." She took another sip of her tea. Even to her ears her story sounded incredibly unbelievable.

"Right. And there was a..." Tim flipped through his notepad that he'd been taking notes in. "Vampire slash Satan looking dude staring at you and Mark, when he opened the door?" He raised his eyebrows at her.

Dean sat there shaking with silent laughter. Coughing, he recovered quickly to ask. "Could it have been a costume do you think?" When he looked at her, Kim could see his eyes watering. She felt like reaching out and smacking that smug face, but she didn't. She didn't need to add a trip to the local jail for striking an officer on her shit list of the evening.

"It wasn't a costume. The thing had glowing eyes and, and fangs... or something." She shuddered at the memory.

"Did you ever think maybe Ava went shopping or something? Or maybe this guy dropped her off to see her mom and the baby. Did you call Abbi?"

Kim darted her eyes around the room, "Well...no."

Why in hell didn't Mark and I think of that?

Tim took his ball cap off and scratched his head. "Well then, that's probably where she is. Give Ben a call, I'm sure he'll confirm."

Dean spoke up. "I'll do it. I'll call him. Need to congratulate him on the bundle of joy anyway."

"Don't you think it's a little late?" Kim pointed to the clock on the wall. It was eleven o'clock.

"Yeah, you're right. I'm sure Ava is home by now. Have you tried calling her?"

"Of course I have. Multiple times. It goes straight to voicemail. And maybe you're right. Maybe she is home sound asleep while everyone worries about her. But that still doesn't explain what happened to Mark."

"Maybe he went for a walk?" Tim offered as a solution.

Dean chuckled at the thought. "Pfft..." Was all he had to say.

Kim on the other hand squinted at Tim and shook her head. "In a storm. No, I don't think so."

Dean leaned forward and put his arms on the table. Stroking the stubble on his chin, he grinned. "Maybe, he's home with Ava right now? You know he could have waited until you were in the house and snuck over there."

"Why would he go and do that? He called me asking where she was. He said she called him asking for help and then the phone went dead."

"Did she call him back?" Tim asked.

"I don't think so." Kim got up and walked to the counter. "His phone is right there. He never leaves without it." She tapped the screen only to discover a lock code on it.

"Maybe she called and like I said, he's over there right now with her." Dean suggested again.

Kim turned around and looked at him. "Or maybe that lunatic Ash has both of them locked up in his basement?"

Tim stood up and pushed in his chair. "Only one way to find out," he said. "Let's go over to your house and see if they are there."

"And if they aren't?" Kim asked.

Dean spoke up as he stood. "Then we go pay Ash a little visit."

As the three made their way through the bush to Kim's house, she couldn't help wondering why they both were there. As far as she knew, Tim had gone back to Windsor. And Dean, well Dean she was never entirely sure where he lived. Were they hot on the tail of some fugitive? Or were they really on vacation like they said. Being her naturally inquisitive self she had to know.

"So why are you two here?" She asked.

"We are on vacation. But Dean has—" An elbow to the ribs, courtesy of Dean, had Tim clamping his mouth shut.

Kim asked, "Dean has what?"

"Dean has nothing but free time on his hands." Dean replied.

Free time as in how...

"What, did you get fired for your mouth?" She chuckled.

"No. I did not get fired."

"Did you quit? I mean you can't be a day over sixty," she said jokingly as they stepped into her yard. He couldn't be much older than her forty-eight years she figured.

Without missing a beat, Dean said, "If I'm sixty, that means you are too." He winked at her. Giving her a sly smile, he added, "Seeing how we're the same age."

Kim's mouth dropped open. "How do you know how old I am?!" Turning to look at Tim she demanded to know. "Did he get you to do a search on me?"

Tim raised a brow at her. "Kim. Do you really have to ask that question? Of course, he did." He chuckled.

She sputtered. "You sneak! You could have told me! Ooof..."

One second, she was in the middle of turning around and the second she was sitting on her ass on the ground. Smacking right into Dean's back would do that to a person. She never in her wildest dreams thought he would be so solid.

Muttering to herself, she stood trying to figure out why both her partners were so silent. She was about to ask just that when she felt Tim's hand cover her mouth and then he dragged her back into the bush.

What the hell is he doing?

Kim darted her eyes around the yard in search of Dean. He was nowhere to be found.

"Don't say a word." Tim whispered next to her ear as he removed his hand. He pointed towards the house. "There is someone sitting in a chair on the porch."

Softly, she asked, "Where is Dean?"

"He's circling around to see who it is."

Kim nodded and watched for any sign of movement; she hoped it was Ava or Mark. She didn't know if she could handle any more weirdness in one night. Finally, after a few minutes she saw Dean. Gun drawn; he was slowly making his way up the steps, then stopped, and turned around.

"Come on. It's just an old coat," he yelled, waving them on with his arm.

"Did you leave a coat outside?" Tim asked as they made their way across the yard to the house.

She shook her head. "No."

Tim scaled the steps. "Maybe it's Marks."

Dean was giving the coat a once over. Feeling the pockets, he noticed a price tag. "Huh. It's brand new." He held it out to Kim. "Was this here when you left earlier?"

She shrugged her shoulders, and she took it from him. Turning it around, she noted it was a dreadfully ugly, fur coat.

"It might have been," Kim said, tossing it back on the chair.

She noticed the look her companions exchanged. "What? I was worried, okay? I didn't think it was necessary to check my surroundings at the time."

"No one is faulting you, Kim. Usually when something is out of place, people tend to notice it is all," Tim said.

"Well, I didn't."

She stuck her key in the lock and turned the handle. All at once the booming of the house alarm echoed along the lake. Kim rushed over to the panel and disarmed it.

"One thing I do know. I didn't set that alarm."

"It shouldn't have gone off even if it was. Don't you have a delay on it?" Dean asked, as he scanned the room.

"Yeah, twenty seconds." She punched a code on the keypad and finally there was silence.

"That means someone must have hit the panic button."

Just as Tim said that Kim's phone started ringing. She looked at the call display. "It's the alarm company." Answering it, she explained that everything was fine while Dean and Tim searched the house.

She was disconnecting the call just as they returned to the dining area.

"It's all clear. And neither of them are here," Dean said.

"You really should get someone in to look at that alarm. It shouldn't be going off like that." Tim tilted his head towards the panel.

Kim nodded. "I will, first thing Monday morning. Shall we head back to Ben's? Hopefully, Marks back by now."

"Sure. Set the alarm this time." Dean walked to the door, opening it he stepped out onto the porch to wait. Tim followed him outside then poked his head back in. "What do you want to do with the coat?"

"Leave it, maybe it will crawl by itself back into the forest." Kim snickered, snapping the alarm panel closed. Joining the men on the porch, she took hold of the door handle and slammed it shut. "All locked up." She looked at them, wondering why they were still standing there. "C'mon. Let's go."

Kim almost crapped her pants when Dean reached a hand around her. For a second, she thought he was going to go in for a hug. That was until she heard him rattle the door handle behind her.

"Just checking to make sure you locked it, sunshine." He grinned and sent her a wink.

To cover her embarrassment, she said, "Got something in your eye do you Dean?"

His grin widened. "Only when you're around, sweetheart."

She gawked at him. That gleam in his eyes when he said it, it was like he always knew what she was thinking.

She pressed her lips in a tight line and sailed down the steps.

When will I learn that as fast as I dish it out, he's as quick with a comeback?

Chapter 11

With a shaky hand, Mark reached out and touched Ava's bare leg. She was still warm, that meant she'd either passed out or had fallen asleep. He had so many questions but waking her up now and asking, was not the time. Instead, he gently nudged her. "Ava?"

She was laying so still that he was worried she'd hit her head.

He ran his hand over her hair, feeling for blood and bumps. There wasn't any. Mark leaned closer, almost covering her body with his, he gently tapped her on the face. "Wake up, Ava. I need you to wake up," he whispered.

Ava snapped her eyes open. "You might get a better response if you talked a little louder."

"Oh, thank god." He gathered her in his arms. Pressing his lips to her forehead he muttered, "I thought you were dead."

"I feel like it." Ava winced as she tried to sit up. "My ankle, I landed on it the wrong way when I was running home. I couldn't bear to walk another step after I sat on the oak tree, so I crawled in here to get out of the rain."

Mark busied himself by taking off his trench coat then draped it around her shoulders. "Ava, what the hell are you doing out here? What happened to Ash?"

She wrinkled her nose as the memory came flooding back. "We got into a fight."

"Like a verbal fight or…" Mark trailed off. If Ash dared to lay a finger on her in anger, he would be dropping Ava off at home and heading straight to Ash's house. Mark would love an excuse to drill his fist in the guy's face.

Ava pushed a strand of hair out of her eyes. "No. He didn't touch me. He was just being an asshole." She sighed heavily. "He's been calling and texting, trying to apologize. Well, he was until my phone died."

Somewhat disappointed, Mark nodded his head, and sat back on his haunches. "So that's what happened." He didn't want to let on he was in a panic thinking she was stuck in Ash's dungeon of doom. She never was to know about that. "How about we get you home?"

"I don't think I'll be able to walk that far, Mark."

He was reluctant to offer up a solution. He knew exactly what he had to do. It wasn't that he didn't want to carry her, he had no issue with that. She was so tiny it would be like carrying a sack of potatoes. It was the fact that they would be touching that he had an issue with. He wasn't entirely sure he could control himself with her so close to him. But there was no other way out of their predicament.

"It's okay. I'll carry you. Brutus will need to lead the way though." He scratched the dog under his chin. "Are you up for the challenge buddy?"

Brutus let out a howl in response.

Ava laughed and gave the brute a hug. "I think that is a yes."

Mark was mesmerized by her. He wanted nothing more than to stay alone with her and the dog until dawn, he knew he had to get her home. Her ankle needed some attention and the sooner the better.

"Okay. If I back out of here, do you think you can wiggle your way out?"

"Yeah, I should be able to scoot on my butt."

The thought of her butt had him growing hard.

What the hell is wrong with you? he asked himself.

"Okay, I'll see you on the outside."

"Wait!" Ava took the coat from her shoulders and tossed it at him. "If you're going to carry me, you should be wearing the coat."

"But you will freeze if you're not covered."

"So will you," she reasoned.

"Tell you what. You wear the coat, and I will piggyback you. You can drape it around me. Alright?"

"Deal," she said. "And I think I can flip the hood over your head."

Dumbstruck, Marks stared at her. "There's a friggin hood?"

Ava giggled. "Yes, it's right here, zipped up in the collar."

Mark threw his hands in the air. "I got soaked for nothing." He bit his tongue; he didn't mean to imply she was nothing. She meant the world to him. Wanting to tell her exactly that he cleared his throat. Instead, like usual he chickened out. "I didn't mean you were nothing, I just meant. Well, you know..."

Ava put her hand on his arm. "I know. Now, can we please get out of here. My leg is throbbing, and I'd really like to get into some dry clothes."

"Yeah, let's get you home. Here, take the flashlight. You're going to have to hold it," he said, backing out into the downpour.

Ava scooted her way out. With Mark on one side and Brutus on the other she managed to stand up. Mark bent down, far enough that she didn't have to jump.

She opened the coat wide and wrapped the sides as best she could around his shoulders. Somehow, she managed to get the hood to stay on his head as she wrapped her arms around his neck.

"Are you ready?" He asked, hiking her up higher.

"Yes."

He felt that spine tingling sensation, that for some reason, only Ava could create in him. Only this time, her warm breath bathed his neck causing an electrifying zing to shiver over his skin too. He needed to get her home asap.

"Brutus, lead the way buddy."

That was all Mark had to say. The dog grabbed the hem of the coat and tugged, heading for home.

THE WIND HAD PICKED up considerably from when they arrived causing the rain to come down in sheets. Even with the umbrella from the trees of the bush, the rain felt like pins and needles on her face. Kim was really starting to worry. First Ava now Mark. What the hell was she going to do if they didn't turn up.

"Do you think we should call search and rescue?" she asked, anxiety creeping into her voice.

"First, let's see if Mark's back, maybe he's heard from Ava by now," Dean told her, as they stumbled into Ben and Abbi's yard.

"Holy crap!" Kim cried out as the wind swept her off her feet, right into Tim's path.

"Whoa!" He helped her off the ground, then wrapped an arm around her shoulders and guided her to the back porch.

Kim took the keys out of her pocket but was shaking so bad she couldn't for the life of her fit the key into the lock.

"Here, let me," Tim said. Taking them from her, he unlocked the door and pushed it wide for her to enter.

"Holy shit!" Dean shoved a hand through his hair as he closed the door. "I'm having second doubts. Is the weather always like this up here?"

"Not usually," Kim said, flinging off her jacket. She hung it on the peg behind the door and looked at him. "Second doubts about what?"

"Ah..." Dean darted his eyes at Tim who raised his hands, palms up and shrugged. Dean rolled his eyes at him before looking at Kim. "Second doubts about vacationing here."

Distracted with her thoughts she mumbled, "Oh. Well, that makes sense I suppose." She could feel her face scrunching up. She felt like she was on the verge of a good cry. Something she never did.

Dean and Tim each grabbed a chair and sat down. Kim went to the fridge and grabbed three bottles of water. Sitting at the table, she pushed one to each of the men. Twisting off the cap she took a long swallow, hoping it would flush the sting of tears back down her throat. She took a steadying breath. "Now what?" She asked. "Do we call the police now or should we go over to Ash's and kick in his dungeon of horrors door?"

Tim pointed at the ceiling. "Before we do either, have you checked upstairs?"

Kim shook her head. "No. I wasn't about to do that alone. I've had enough scares to last me for the next five months." Things were starting to get to her, because for once in her life she was mortified as a loud burp unexpectedly erupted from her lips. She covered her mouth and mumbled, "Excuse me."

Dean stood up, chuckling, but didn't comment. Instead, he took his gun from his holster.

"Let's go."

Kim stood and looked at him wide eyed. "What's with the gun?"

Dean shrugged. "Oh, you know. Just in case we find a vampire or the devil himself." Grinning, he shot her a wink.

As the three headed to the hallway, to the front staircase. It was on the tip of her tongue to comment about his eye problem again, but she wasn't up to it. She was thankful when Tim started with the questions again.

"Who is this Ash guy?"

Kim glanced at Tim as they headed up the staircase. "From what he's told us he's a landscaper from Texas. He has been seeing Ava for like a month now."

"So, it's not out of the ordinary for him and Ava to go out often?" Dean asked, eyes straight ahead.

Kim lifted a shoulder. "Well, no. They seem to be getting serious."

"I bet Mark's pissed about that." He chuckled as Tim nodded in agreement.

"Ah a little bit. I mean it's his own fault. Everyone has told him so, but you know Mark."

"That we do," they said, in unison.

Dean stepped into the first room to the left of the stairs. He called out. "Clear."

Kim got a thrill of excitement. It was like she was right in the middle of searching for a fugitive.

Together they crossed the catwalk with the glass sides. Looking down at the rooms below, Tim checked the left side overlooking the living room while Dean covered the kitchen and dining area. Nothing was out of the ordinary. All animals but Brutus were accounted for.

They continued towards the spare bedrooms and Abbi's office. Clearing the first two rooms they headed straight for '*Abbi's lair*', as the sign stated above the door. Ben had it made when she'd moved in and hung it above the door. Kim thought it was a cornball idea at the time but in retrospect it really was her lair. Her hideout where she created her spin on murders, mayhem, and diabolical themes. Kim snorted at the thought of her sister.

Dean looked over his shoulder at her. "Care to tell us what's so funny?"

"Oh, I was just thinking how Abbi would get a kick out of this. You know, missing persons, vampires, and the devil. She would be right in her glory."

"Yeah. She sure would." Tim agreed. Having been a classmate of Abbi's since kindergarten, next to Ben and her family, Tim knew her the best.

"Except it's her daughter, her dog and a really good friend that's missing." Dean pointed out soberly.

"Right." Kim looked down at her feet, the instant dread returned and smacked her in the face.

Dean went over to the wall of floor to ceiling windows behind Abbi's desk and looked out at the dark skies. "Has anything else happened around here lately?" He asked, looking down at Mark's truck.

Kim scratched her head. So much had happened in the last few hours she couldn't remember if she covered all of it. Bird suddenly squawked from his perch downstairs. "Yes! Brutus had been at our house today. We thought Ben forgot to put him in the house when he had to rush Abbi to the clinic..."

"Get to the point, sunshine," Dean drawled.

"I am! You jerk!" she said, louder than she intended.

Dean's reaction to her outburst was a stupid grin on his face.

Tim cleared his throat. "Kim, you were saying?"

She stuck her tongue out at Dean, before turning her attention to Tim. "When Mark came over here, he discovered that all the animals were outside. Including Bird. We checked all the windows and doors, but everything was closed and locked up tight."

"And you didn't think to call Ben and ask what was up?" Tim asked.

Kim wrung her hands together, "Well... Mark suggested it." Darting her eyes around the room, she mumbled, "But I didn't think it was a good idea to mention it to them, at least not until they get home."

Dean nodded, turning his gaze back to the window. "That makes sense I suppose. And if there is no sign of forced entry, no reason to call the cops."

Kim's brows shot up at Dean's response. She was expecting cynical, instead he was... sensible.

"Guys, come here," he said. Pointing towards the lake, Dean asked, "What the hell is that?"

Kim's mouth fell open as the room started to spin. She felt like she was going to faint on the spot. Unable to tear her eyes away, she saw Brutus tugging something in his jaws. And that something looked exactly what she'd seen only a few hours ago. The cape of Dracula. Suddenly it rushed at the poor dog and before Kim knew it, her world turned black, and she crumpled to the floor in a heap.

Chapter 12

Mark was blinded not only by the hood of the jacket but also from the rain pelting him in the face. Thankfully, he could see the lights of the house growing nearer with every step.

They had been walking no more than a minute when the rain started coming in a torrential downpour. A few times he almost stopped for fear of toppling into the lake. If it hadn't been for Brutus, he would have done just that. The dog was mindful of the shoreline and made sure that Mark kept on track, if he came too close to the water, Brutus would tug him away.

"How are you holding out back there?"

Ava lifted her head from where it was resting on his shoulder. "I'm okay. Am I too heavy for you? I can walk a bit now, I should think."

He rather liked having her pressed up against his back. There was no way he was going to make her walk in this weather, bad ankle or not.

"You heavy? Not at all. I barely even know your back there."

Which was a lie of course. Having her so close did things to his libido that he didn't even know existed. Strange with all the actresses he'd dated over the years, he would have thought someone would have come close in comparison. But no, there wasn't a single one.

"We're almost there, just a few more steps," he said. The shoreline widened and was replaced with grass as they stepped onto Ben's property.

"Brutus, you can let go now buddy," he said. But the dog was determined to take them right to the door it seemed.

As they passed Ben's dock, Mark was trying to push the thought of her breast pressing against his back, out of his mind. "I think I'll buy a boat tomorrow."

"A boat? That would have been so much faster," Ava said. "Thank you for coming and finding me, Mark. I really don't know what I'd do without you." He inwardly groaned as he felt her lips press to the side of his neck. The jolt that went through him almost made him lose his grip on her legs. If it weren't for the fact it was pouring like a bitch and her ankle, he would have dropped her right there and kissed her senseless. Or at least he would like to think he would. His problem was he was too damn chicken to even try.

"Hang on," he yelled, trying to take off at a run. But Brutus hung on for dear life, tugging him in the opposite direction. The damn dog thought he was playing tug of war now.

DEAN AND TIM SPRANG into action. Both rushed to where Kim lay flat out on the floor.

"What the hell did she do, faint?" Tim asked, his eyes wide.

"Looks like it." Dean jerked his chin at the window. "You take watch and I'll see if I can get her to come to."

"Right." Tim went back to the window and stared intently at the scene before him.

"Kim. Wake up." Dean pushed Kim's hair out of her face and tapped her lightly on the cheek.

She was awake, she just didn't want to respond. She was more than happy to stay right there on the floor and not see what the hell was happening out the window.

"Wake up, come on." Dean stared at her face. He had seen his share of fakers in his lifetime. The ones that faked an ailment or something else just so they didn't have to face reality. And he was certain Kim was doing that too. "If you don't open your eyes, I'm gonna have to kiss you," he said to her, then grinned.

She gasped and sat straight up. "I'm awake. I'm fine. I just fainted is all."

She smacked Dean's hand away when he offered a hand to help her stand.

"I said I was fine," she hissed, picking herself up off the floor.

He raised his hands in front of himself and chuckled. "My, oh my. Aren't you a wildcat? I like it!"

Tim started laughing from the window. "Guys, you gotta come see this."

Shooting Dean, a sour look, Kim pointed a finger at him. "Don't you forget it either," she said, making her way to the window to see what all the fuss was about.

Once there, she gazed down only to see the 'cape' was a trench coat that Brutus held firmly in his teeth. Kim couldn't help but giggle as the person twirled around in circles. She started to laugh hysterically when, despite the unrelenting wind, the dog's ears flapped like an airplane propeller as he held on for dear life. That was until she saw an extra leg. Whoever it was they were carrying someone.

A flash of lightning skittered across the sky at the same moment recognition hit her. "Oh my god that's Mark and Ava!" She whirled around and headed straight for the staircase with Dean and Tim hot on her heels. All three raced down the stairs to the back door. Kim flung it open and yelled, "Brutus! Come!"

Dean and Tim sailed past her to help Mark and Ava. The big jerk of a dog came racing at Kim with his tongue hanging out the side of his mouth. The unmistakable grin of a job well done clearly stamped on his face.

Kim went into the house and grabbed an armful of towels from the laundry room. Returning, she saw that they were all sitting on the porch steps.

"Where have you been? Do you know how worried I was?" she said to her niece as she handed her one. Not waiting for a response, she turned to Mark. "And you!" Kim shoved a towel into his hands. Bending down, she vigorously rubbed Brutus' coat with another. "Why the hell didn't you leave me a note?" She glanced at Mark accusingly.

"It's nice to see you too, Kim." Rubbing a tired hand over his eyes, Mark stood. "Ava needs her ankle looked at. Let's get her inside and we'll tell you everything."

Mark denied offers of help from Tim and Dean to get Ava into the house. Instead, he picked her up and carried her into the house, through to the living room. He set her on the couch, while the others hovered nearby.

Mark pushed the coffee table close and stuck a pillow under Ava's leg, propping her foot up. "I'll go and get some of your mom's clothes for you," he said before turning away. Stopping, he looked at Kim. She was already feeling for a pulse in Ava's foot. "Kim. Do you need me to get anything? A tensor bandage or...?" He trailed off, not quite knowing what she would need for Ava's ankle.

She glanced up. "Ah. Yes, a tensor bandage would be good, if you can't find one then I think Ben had some compression socks when he broke his leg."

Nodding he left the room in search of supplies.

"So, Ava, what made you take a nighttime stroll along the lake?" Dean asked.

"I was out with Ash. We had an argument; it was stupid really." Now when she thought about it, she did feel bad. She would need to call him once her phone was charged. "I decided I would rather jog home instead of going with him." She gasped when Kim pressed down on her ankle. "I landed on my foot the wrong way."

"Sorry." Kim glanced at Ava as she stood. "I don't feel anything broken. You really should get an x-ray to rule it out though."

Ava yawned. "Can it wait till tomorrow?"

"No. Not really." Kim answered, glancing at her watch. "But seeing how late it is, I guess it can't hurt."

Mark returned with the clothes, an ice pack and a first aid kit. "I couldn't find a tensor bandage or those socks you were talking about, but I did find these." He held up a pair of black panty hose.

Ava and Kim looked at him like he was nuts.

Tim laughed. "What good will those do?"

"Trust me." He took a pair of scissors and cut one leg off. "When I was on set and one of the stuntmen sprained their ankle, they wrapped it with a pair of these. Works in a pinch," he said, passing it to Kim.

She set to work wrapping Ava's ankle. And sure enough, Ava said it helped.

"I'll help her change. You guys go wait in the kitchen." Kim ordered them out of the room. "And turn on the kettle," she yelled after them. Turning to Ava, her face softened. "I'll make you a nice cup of tea and get you some pain meds."

"Thanks Aunt Kim," Ava said, stripping off her shirt and replacing it with an oversized sweatshirt. Shimmying her jeans over her hips, she stopped when Kim said, "Don't do that, let me help." She sat on the coffee table and carefully pulled the pant leg over Ava's foot. "So, are you and Ash done then?"

Ava looked at her. "I don't know. I was supposed to meet him at the spa tomorrow to get started on the garden. I'll need to call him in the morning and tell him not to."

"That didn't really answer my question, Ava. What was the fight about?" Kim asked, as she slipped a cozy pair of pajama bottoms over Ava's feet and up her legs.

Sighing heavily, Ava bit her lip. "Well for starters. He thinks I talk too much about Mark." Lifting her hips up, she pulled the pj's up to her waist and sat back down. "Which is ludicrous. Yes, I talk about him, but I talk about you just as equally." Shoving a hand through her damp hair, she continued. "The kicker was when he said I would need to move in with Mom and Ben."

"What?!" Kim chuckled. "Are you serious?"

"Yeah, that's what I thought too."

"Why would he even say that to you?"

"For some reason he thinks we are dating, I guess. His exact words were 'No way is any girlfriend of mine living with another man.'"

"Jesus Ava, I hope you set him straight."

"Oh, I did and that's when he said I could find my own way home. Which I had already planned on doing." Ava laid back on the couch and looked at the ceiling.

"Did you tell Mark any of this?"

She glanced at Kim. "No, and I'd rather you didn't either."

Kim snickered to herself. *Me keep this tidbit of info to myself. Yeah, like that's gonna happen...*

"Don't get me wrong, I like Ash, and yes, I will talk to him. But he needs to realize I'm not jumping headfirst into any relationship. I don't care who it is." Stifling another yawn, she closed her eyes.

Kim took the throw blanket from the back of the couch and covered Ava with it. "Okay, well you just rest here for a minute. You hang tight and I'll be right back with the tea and pills."

"SO, WHEN BRUTUS STARTED barking at me, I figured I'd better follow him." Mark was saying, as Kim went into the kitchen.

"Smart dog." Tim wrote something down in his notepad.

Dean jerked his head towards the window. "Yeah, I'll say. Sounds like Ava was damn lucky you two came when you did from the looks of that storm."

Kim rushed over to the kettle and turned it on. Pulling out a chair, she waved her hand in the air. "Forget all that. Guess what Ava told me." She grinned looking from one set of eyes to the other.

Dean scratched the stubble on his chin. Tim shrugged his shoulders and Mark flung his hands wide. "What did she tell you?"

He knew what the look on Kim's face meant. She had a secret to tell and was just waiting to bust at the seams with it.

"Shh!! I didn't tell you this, but the argument they had..." She swung her gaze to Mark. "Was about you! Ha!"

"Me? Why me?"

"He's jealous of you because Ava talks about you... a lot. And he also said, 'no girlfriend of mine is living with another man.'" Kim mimicked as she got up to fix the tea. "Ava set him straight about that. She told him she wasn't his girlfriend." She nodded approvingly.

Mark's mouth dropped open. "What did he mean? He wants her to move in... with *him*?"

"No. He wants her to move in here," Kim snickered. "That will never happen." She poured the boiling water into the waiting cup. "Ava has no intention of moving. Anyway, I need to get this to her. Warm her up before we head home." Taking the cup, she rushed out just as fast as she had rushed in.

Mark sat at the table, staring off into space, lost in his own thoughts. Why hadn't he ever thought about this before? That someday Ava would meet someone, and she would leave. He was a fool to think they all would live together forever.

"Hey, Mark." Dean snapped his fingers.

Mark blinked his eyes. "What?"

"Are you going to tell her how you feel? Or are you going to let her be the one that got away?" Dean asked, leaning back in his chair.

Mark stared at the table. *What the hell am I so afraid of? It's Ava for cripes sake.*

Looking up, he nodded his head as his knee bounced up and down. "You're right. I'm an idiot for not telling her. I'll do it right now."

Getting up, Mark headed towards the living room. Seconds later he heard the scraping of chair legs followed by the rapid slapping of feet on the tiled floor; the two cops were right behind him.

Chapter 13

Ava woke to the sound of birds chirping and the scent of bacon frying. Her eyes sprang open and focused on the first thing in front of them. A cup of cold tea sitting on the coffee table beside her cell phone; in Ben and her mom's living room. Sitting up, she looked at her surroundings. Her eyes zeroed in on Mark as he slept in the recliner by the window, and she wondered how she got there. Swinging her legs to the floor, the memory of last night came flooding back as she felt the pain in her ankle. Once again, she cussed out Ash, but felt bad as she knew it was partly her fault. She should have been a bit more understanding.

Picking up her phone, she checked her notifications and saw Ash had called and texted her throughout the night. Not once were his words overbearing or condescending. If anything, he was blaming himself. That was a good sign as far as she was concerned. His attitude might be different today she thought as she tapped on his name and waited for the call to connect.

"Hi Ash."

Mark woke up instantly. He stayed still, feigning he was asleep so he could listen to the one-sided conversation. He hadn't had a chance to tell Ava how he felt last night. When he'd finally got the nerve to do so, she was sound asleep on the couch. Despite the urging from everyone to wake her up, he let her sleep. Now he wished he would have listened to them from the sounds of her phone call.

Dean came strolling into the room with a pair of crutches in his hand. "Morning you two. Look what I got for you Ava." He, Kim, and Tim had decided in the wee hours of the morning that the walk through the bush was too far and stayed the night.

"I gotta go. Talk to you later Ash." She tossed her phone on the couch and sent Dean a beaming smile. "You are a godsend." She took them from him and stood up.

Mark pushed the leg rest down on the chair. Without a word he stood and marched himself to the kitchen.

KIM LOOKED UP FROM chopping a green pepper. "Morning Mark."

"Yeah," he grumbled as he made his way to the coffeepot.

Kim waited until he poured his coffee and took his first swallow. "What's up? Didn't sleep so well last night?" She looked at him as she dumped the peppers into a big skillet of scrambled eggs.

"Oh nothing." He yanked a chair out from the table and sat down. "I slept fine. Everything is just peachy. Except for... Oh hey, I know! The fact Ava has every intention of meeting Ash at the spa." Glowering, he looked at his watch. "In *two* hours."

Mid stir of the eggs, Kim held the wooden spoon poised. "Did she say that?"

Mark took a sip of his coffee. Nodding repeatedly, he replied, "Yup. To him. She called him as soon as she woke up."

She stood, stunned. "No shit? I never thought for a minute she would call him back."

"I shit you not. She called him so fast she probably still had sleep in her eyes." He chugged back his coffee.

"She can't do that! She needs an x-ray!"

"Yeah, well you can tell her that. I'm going home for a bit." He stood up and walked to the back door and opened it. "I'll see you later Kim. When you guys come home. I'll come back here."

"Mark, stay and eat. We will come up with a plan. With Dean and Tim to help, I'm sure we can figure it out."

A sad smile touched his lips. "Nah. It's fine Kim, I know when to give up and besides, I'm all out of plans."

With that, he walked out the door without a backward glance.

Kim watched as he made his way across the yard and disappeared into the bush. She was pissed that Ava called Ash the rat, back. She should have just let it go and maybe he would leave Pearl Lake altogether. Kim knew it was wishful thinking on her part. There was something she didn't like about the man. And it wasn't just because he'd come in between Mark and Ava. No. There was something almost sinister about him. She just wished Ava could see it too.

"AUNT KIM, I'M FINE!" Ava told her the third time on the way to the clinic. She really needed to meet Ash and give him a deposit for the supplies he needed. She already told him she wasn't staying to help, that she had something more urgent to deal with. He was completely fine with it and was also very apologetic. That didn't matter to her one way or the other. She had already decided she wouldn't be going out with him again. He just didn't know it yet.

If it were up to Kim, she would take Ava right back home after seeing Doc. But she wasn't a young girl anymore for her aunt to be telling her who she could talk to and who she couldn't. Loudly, Kim sighed. "I know you are, and once you get an x-ray to make sure your ankle isn't broken, you can go and meet him."

"Fine. I will text him that I'm going to be late."

Kim pulled into the parking lot of the clinic.

"Didn't you tell Ash what happened to your ankle?" She glanced towards the yellow house. Big mistake. A shudder of apprehension coursed through at the memory of that dark hole in the backyard.

Grabbing the door handle she shoved it open. "Ah... never mind." She slammed her car door and hurried around the front of it to Ava's side and opened her door. "Come on. Let's get you looked at." She didn't waste any time getting the crutches out of the back seat and handed them to Ava. The whole time Kim was ushering her inside, she kept one eye on the house across the street. She didn't feel calm until they were safely inside.

DOC SPENCE TURNED THE screen towards Ava and Kim. "Not broken," he said. Taking his glasses off he looked Ava in the eye. "But it is a bad sprain. You will need to keep your weight off it for at least a week or two. I can give you a prescription for some pain meds if you want." He reached into his shirt pocket for his prescription pad.

Ava shook her head. "No Doc, it's fine. I have some at home. How long before I can get back to work?"

He moved to a cabinet on the wall and opened the glass door. "Two weeks at the least." He took a tensor bandage from the shelf and ripped the packaging open. "Depends how you're feeling. I'm going to wrap it for you. As good as that nylon worked, it can't stay."

Kim snickered. "Yeah, that was Mark's idea."

Doc nodded as he wrapped her foot. "And a hell of a good idea it was."

Ava needed to change the subject. Ever since Mark had carried her home last night, her thoughts were constantly on him. Not that it was a bad thing, on the contrary, it was a good thing. But he clearly didn't want anything more than a platonic relationship with her. She wasn't going to get all lovesick over him again. It was a waste of time and Ava was not into wasting time any longer.

"So, how's mom and the baby doing?" she asked.

Doc smiled widely. Putting the last tensor clip in place, he said, "They are doing great! I want to keep them for a few more days."

Kim looked at Ava and handed her the crutches. "We should go visit them while we're here."

Ava took them from her and carefully got down from the table. Nodding, she said, "I was going to suggest the same thing."

"Let's go then." Kim ushered her out of the room and down the hall.

MARK WAS SITTING ON the dock with Dean and Tim, each with a fishing pole in their hands. They sat silently waiting for that tug on the line that a fish was on the hook.

Dean looked around Tim at Mark. "You know what I don't get?"

Mark really didn't want to go over this again. He rubbed a hand over his eyes and sighed. "No. I don't. Enlighten me."

"Why are we sitting here instead of searching Ash's cellar?"

Mark cast a wide-eyed gaze at Dean. "You're joking, right? You're a cop are you proposing we break in?"

Dean shrugged. "Pfft, minor detail," he said, as he waved a dismissive hand.

Tim cleared his throat. "Do you know who owns the property? If Ash is renting it, all we would need to do is see if it is included in the lease. If it's not, then we can proceed."

Dean sniffed. "Yeah... I like my idea better."

Mark stood and started reeling in his line. "I think we will go with Tim's plan."

They packed it in and headed to the shed to put the fishing gear away. Mark was lost in his thoughts as the other two men chatted away. If they waited to talk to the owner that might give away the element of surprise to Ash. Something Mark didn't want to happen. He opened the shed door. "So, how are we going to do this?"

"Do what?" Tim asked.

Dean raised his brows. "You mean Ash's?"

Mark nodded. "Yeah." He took the poles and propped them in a corner inside. Placing the tackle box on the floor, he backed out of the shed and closed the door, securing it with a padlock. He turned to look at the two cops he considered friends. First Dean then Tim. "If we wait to talk to the landlord, Ash is going to find out —"

"And if he finds out, he will clear it out is what you're saying." Tim finished for him.

Dean stroked the stubble on his chin. "What you're saying is you want us…" He waved his hand between Tim and himself. "Two cops, to break in?" He threw Mark's own words back at him.

Mark shook his head. "Nah, forget it. It was a stupid idea. I'll do it myself, at least you two won't get into any trouble." He started off towards the house.

"Whoa. On the contrary." Dean put an arm around Mark's shoulder. "It's an excellent idea. We just won't call it that. No. We need to come up with a plan. I didn't work undercover for the past 10 years without learning a thing or two. We can't do it today; the timing is all wrong. Not to mention Ava needs to be on better speaking terms with Ash."

"Are you crazy?!" Mark whipped his head around and looked at Dean. "Why the hell would we want that?"

"Because if she is talking to him, it gives us some working room." Tim supplied. "He doesn't really talk to anyone else, does he?" He pushed open the back door of the house and chuckled. "Unless you want to take him for a beer?"

Beer sounded good right about now. But not with Ash. Mark stalked to the fridge. Pulling the door open, he looked in only to discover there was none. He would need to get to Mack's and replace them for Ben. Grabbing the can of coffee, he set out to make a pot. Gathering cups and spoons, he slapped them onto the table and went back to the fridge for the cream.

Straddling the chair, Mark sat down with a thump. Carefully he sat the creamer in the center of the table. He hated the thought of Ava being in the company of that man. Yes, she was meeting him today. Something that he'd come to terms with. He was foolishly hoping that would be the last time. He should have known better.

Tim snapped his fingers in front of Mark's face. "Can you do that Mark?"

Shaking himself out of his daze, Mark sourly said, "Do what?"

Dean rolled his eyes. "Can you text Ash?"

"Why the hell would I do that?"

"Bonehead, if you were listening, you would know I said, from Ava's phone..."

Mark blinked rapidly. "How the hell am I going to get close enough to Ava to get her phone?"

Dean winked. "Leave that up to me." He had the perfect plan. Now to set it into motion.

Chapter 14

Ava gasped as Ben settled the baby in her arms. "Oh, she's beautiful, guys."

She marveled as the teeny hand clutched her finger. A protective fierceness came over Ava of being the big sister. Something she had never really thought of until that moment. She trailed a gentle finger along a satiny cheek and was in awe as the tiny bow of her mouth formed into a perfect 'O'. She directed her attention to her mom. "Doc says he's keeping you for a few more days?"

"Yeah." Abbi laughed. "I told him it was okay, that we are perfectly fine to go home, but you know Doc."

"I think he likes us here." Ben smiled, sitting on the bed beside Abbi.

"Have you finally decided on a name?" Kim asked, sitting in a chair by the window.

Ben looked at Abbi. With a slight nod and a smile, she encouraged him to tell them.

"Abbi wanted a traditional British name... and so we decided on Annabelle Fern." Ben leaned over and kissed Abbi's hair. "Poppet for short."

Kim closed her eyes and shook her head. "How do you get Poppet out of Annabelle?" she asked, opening her eyes, she looked at Ben.

Abbi smiled. "You don't, it's just an endearment that he likes to call her."

"Well either name fits her perfectly. Do you want to hold her Aunt Kim?" Ava asked. At Kim's nod, Ava moved to hand Annabelle over. The ringing of her phone had Kim pausing a moment as she looked at the display. *Dean?*

Her first thought was to ignore it. But he was with Mark. What if he had done something stupid? "Ah, I need to take this call first. I'll be right back." She excused herself. While she made her way into the hall, she could hear Abbi asking what Ava did to her ankle.

"Dean. What's up?" She leaned her back against the wall.

"Just a plan that we have cooked up is all. I need you to convince Ava to stay the night at Ben and Abbi's... alone with Mark."

"Why?"

"I'll tell you the details later. Where are you two?"

"Right now, we are visiting Abbi, Ben and the baby." Kim peeked into the room to make sure Ava was still in the chair. She lowered her voice. "When we leave Ava wants me to take her over to the spa to meet Ash. I don't want to, but she's giving him a down payment for the work on the garden."

"Oh, is she now? Okay well, just make sure you take her back to Ben's when you're through."

Kim sighed. "There's no way she will go for that. I mean, why would she stay there when she can just be in her own bed?"

"Because Tim will be sleeping in it, and I will be in Mark's room. Trust me. It's all part of a bigger plan," Dean answered smoothly.

"Okay. But won't she think it odd when I drop her off and go home?"

"Jeez woman. Will you just not worry about that?"

"Fine. But if you and Tim are going to Ash's I'm coming with you guys." Kim warned.

Dean chuckled into the phone. "Lady, I didn't doubt it for a minute. When you're on your way to the spa, text me just before you leave."

"Why?" Kim hissed. She didn't want to miss anything.

"Because we need to head to Mack's, and I want to make sure we are back before you guys."

Ben looked out of the room. "Sorry to interrupt but Abbi needs to feed the baby soon." He jerked his thumb over his shoulder. "If you want to hold her you better hurry."

Kim nodded to Ben. "I'll be right there." To Dean, she said, "Fine, but don't you dare do a thing without me. I gotta go, they are calling for me."

As she hung up, she could see concern in his eyes. "Is everything alright?"

She smiled. "Everything is perfect."

Ben raised a brow. "Are you sure? Ava told us what happened last night. That was a dick move on Ash's part."

"Yeah? Well, you know not all guys are like you Ben," she said, patting him on the back as they walked back into the room.

"SO, THE PLAN IS SET." Dean hit the end button on his phone and looked at Mark, "All you need to do is get her phone from her. When you do, text Ash that 'you' need to meet him tomorrow at the Northern Pike at 3 pm."

Dean looked at Tim. "You sit in Mack's and let me know when he leaves. Kim and I will move in and search the cellar."

Mark raised his brows. "What about me?" he asked, as Brutus came into the room and laid his head on his leg.

Dean took a swig of his cold coffee. "You wait here with Ava. We don't want her trying to leave and if Ash should happen to show up, we don't want her alone either."

"I can do that. What do I do if he shows up?" As he stroked the big dog's head, he let out a sharp whistle calling Lucy and Molly into the room.

Dean smiled. "You stall him."

Mark blew out a breath. "Great." He stood, walked to the door, and let the dogs out.

Tim went to the coffee pot and refilled his cup. "Anyone else?" he asked, holding the pot up.

Mark nodded his head and sat down in his chair. Grabbing the sugar bowl, he waited for Tim to fill his cup before he dunked a heaping spoonful into the hot brew. "Now what?"

"Dean?" Tim held the pot, poised above his cup.

"Yeah sure." He leaned back in his chair as the coffee was poured. "Now we wait for Kim to text me. When she does, we will head into the village. Talk to Mack and the next-door neighbor too. We will see if they saw anything unusual."

Mark just remembered, he never did go over and see Eleanor and ask her about the banana bread she was baking for Mack. Everything seemed to have snowballed from the second Kim had tackled him. "Hey, how long does Kim figure before they leave to go meet Ash?" He looked at the clock on the wall. It was 12:00 pm.

"She didn't say." Dean shrugged his shoulders. "Probably another twenty minutes or so. Why?"

"I was thinking of running to Mack's to get some beer. We drank all of it on Ben. Besides, I might need one tonight." He stood up. "You guys want to come?"

Tim raised a finger. "Count me in."

"Sure, beats sitting here waiting for Kim," Dean said.

"Tim, can you check the front door? I don't know if it's locked," Mark asked, letting the dogs into the house.

Tim headed to the front of the house to do his bidding.

"Are you going to be fine here with Ava?" Dean asked.

"Yeah. It'll be fine." He nodded. It had to be.

"Why don't you just tell her how you feel, man? You being a ladies' man and all shouldn't have a problem with that." Dean grinned.

Mark's brow wrinkled. "That's the problem. She doesn't want someone like me. Would you if you were her?"

Dean shrugged a shoulder. "Well, I can't speak from a woman's perspective seeing how I'm not one. But sure, why not?"

"You're a guy, of course you'd think that."

"Everything is locked up tight," Tim said, coming back into the room.

Mark grabbed up his keys as the other two headed outside. Setting the alarm, he locked the door and pulled it closed.

The three of them piled into Mark's pickup and headed down the road towards the village. Less than 3 minutes later the truck pulled up to the curb in front of the store.

Dean jerked forward and pulled his phone from the back pocket of his jeans. "It's Kim. They are just leaving the clinic now."

All eyes looked out the windshield towards the clinic. Sure enough, Kim appeared from the building just down the road followed by Ava, hobbling along on her crutches.

"Have you guys had a chance to see the baby yet?" Mark asked, watching Ava make her way to the car.

"Not yet," Tim said. "We didn't have time last night getting here so late."

"Why don't you two go now while I grab the beer?" Mark suggested. "I'll meet you down there when I'm done."

"Sounds like a helluva idea," Dean said, pulling on the door handle. As he and Tim got out of the truck, Kim pulled alongside them. "What are you three up to?" she asked, leaning across Ava.

Tim bent down and peered into the open window. "We are heading to see Abbi and Ben's baby and Marks getting some beer."

Mark sat looking across the front seat out the open door, staring right at Ava. She sent him a small smile and said, "You look tired."

"I am. After we're done, I think I'll take a nap in the hammock when we get back to Ben's."

Kim patted Ava's arm. "Okay, well we better get you to the spa so you can pay Ash. Then you're going home for a nap yourself."

Mark didn't catch what Ava said in return because Kim stomped on the gas pedal and drove off.

"Right." Dean closed the truck door and through the open window, he looked at Mark. "We'll see you in a bit."

Mark sat in his truck and watched them walk down the street. Pulling the key out of the ignition, he opened his door, got out and slammed it shut. Keeping an eye on them, he headed towards the store. The second they went into the clinic he pivoted on his heel. He had every intention of meeting them at the clinic like he said, after he got the beer. But first, he made a beeline to the house across the street. He needed to pay Eleanor a visit to see about the banana bread.

THEY WERE DRIVING ALONG the road to the spa at an excruciatingly slow pace. Ava looked over at Kim and saw that she was happily taking her sweet ass time.

"Can you not speed it up please?" She groaned, looking at her watch, Ava said, "Ash has been waiting twenty minutes already."

"Why can't I just take you home?" Kim asked sourly. "Pay Ash tomorrow or better yet, send him an etransfer or something. It's not like he's going to even start it yet."

"He needs the money to get the supplies. I can't expect him to pay for everything up front when he's on his vacation." Ava breathed a sigh of relief as her place of work came into view, with his pickup parked in the driveway.

"After what he did to you last night you shouldn't be hiring him to do anything," Kim grumbled as she pulled in behind his truck and threw the gear shift in park.

"It wasn't entirely his fault, you know." Ava opened the car door and swung her legs out.

Kim muttered under her breath as she exited the vehicle. "I will understand that when he gets the hell out of here and goes home to Texas."

"What did you say?" Ava squinted at her.

Shit!

Kim never could keep her thoughts to herself. She didn't want Ava to start feeling bad for the guy. If she realized everyone around her didn't like Ash, she would do exactly that. "I said hurry the hell up so I can get your ass back home."

Ava shook her head. "That's not what you said."

Thankfully, Ash came walking up at that very moment.

"Hey Ash." Kim raised a hand in greeting. Looking at him made her think of what was in his cellar. Before she could think, the words popped out of her mouth again. "How's the cape business going?" She bit tongue. *What the hell is wrong with me?*

"The *what?*"

"Ah... nothing. I'm tired. Was a long night last night." Knowing she stuck her foot in her mouth again, Kim pointed. "Imma... just going to go over there." She stalked off towards the edge of the property to look at the lake below.

Ava watched as Kim walked away. "Sorry about that. With the baby and all the excitement of the last couple of days, everyone's a little tired." She smiled.

Ash brushed the hair out of her eyes. "No, it's fine. I can't help but blame myself for what happened to you. I'd like to make it up to you if you'll let me?"

Ava nodded. "I'd like that."

Relief was clear on his face when that lopsided grin appeared on his lips. "Great. Would you want to come with me tomorrow to pick up the parts for the water fountain in Springbank? We can go for lunch afterwards if you feel up to it."

"That would be nice."

"Hold your crutches together would you."

Skeptical, Ava looked at him. "Why?"

"I want to show you something. And the fastest way to do so is to carry you."

Ava laughed and did as he asked.

KIM HEARD A SQUEAL. Turning around she discovered that Ash and Ava were nowhere to be found. She took off at a run towards the side of the spa. Anxiety rose in her throat as an image of Ash tossing her down the hillside ran through her mind. She skidded to a stop when she reached the garden. Her panic simmered down, only to be replaced with disappointment... Ash was walking through the garden gate–

carrying Ava. Clearly, they made amends and were back to their 'lovey dovey' selves.

"What was that?" Ava peeked over his shoulder.

Ash turned, still holding her in his arms to see Kim standing there with a sour look on her face.

"Are you feeling okay Kim?" He asked. Not waiting for an answer, he continued. "You can go if you like. I can bring Ava home later."

She swallowed hard. Dean was going to string her up. She couldn't let that happen. It would ruin the entire plan if Ash took Ava home.

She waved off his concern. "I'm good." Jerking a thumb over her shoulder, she said, "I swallowed a bug back there." She tapped her stomach. "It's just wiggling its way to my belly at the moment." She noticed a disgusted look flash across his face as the picture she painted sunk into his brain. *Good!*

"It's fine Aunt Kim, go home. We won't be that long."

"But..."

"Seriously. Ava is in good hands. I'll take care of her."

Damnit.

What the hell was she supposed to do now? She couldn't insist on taking her home. Well, she could but what was she supposed to do, wrestle Ava out of Ash's arms? Like that would happen.

"Okay. If, you're sure?" She tried, stalling for time.

Ash laughed. "I insist."

Kim didn't care if he insisted or offered her a million dollars. It was Ava she was asking.

She looked pointedly at her niece, completely ignoring that Ash said anything. "Ava. Are you sure?"

"Yeah, I'm fine, Aunt Kim." She nodded. "I promise. We won't be long."

"Fine. I'll see you home shortly then." She turned to head back to her car. Stopping, she spun around and zeroed in on Ash's eyes. "If you do what you did to her last night ever again... you will have her whole family to answer to." Kim then stalked off to her car.

"I'm really sorry about that," Ava muttered, as she moved to be put down.

Ash waved off her concern. "It's fine. I deserved it. I never should have left you like I did."

Ava tucked the crutches under her arms and turned her eyes on the garden. She couldn't believe the transformation so far. Ash had told her he'd been clearing it since daybreak, and it showed.

Taking a step forward, she glanced over her shoulder. "Let's just forget about it okay?"

At Ash's nod, she smiled. "Now show me what you've done. I can't wait to see all the flowers you've unearthed from the jungle."

Chapter 15

Mark stood at the bottom of the steps to Eleanor Stanford's porch. For some inane reason he felt like he was being watched. Not by Eleanor, with her binoculars in hand but from the house next door. Ash's house. It was crazy because Mark knew he wasn't home. He was most likely canoodling with Ava at this very second over at the spa. Mark glowered at the thought as he placed his foot on the bottom step. Slowly he made his way up to the porch, glancing around as he did. The feeling was still there, to the point that the hairs on his neck were standing at attention.

He walked straight into a spider's web. Suppressing the urge to scream he did a shuddering side jig to the big window overlooking the porch. Peering through the glass he saw no signs of Eleanor. He could see the big bay window in the dining room that faced the house next door; her favorite spot to see the comings and goings of the village. It sat empty.

"Well, only one way to find out if she's home," he muttered. Walking to the front door Mark pushed the doorbell and listened as its chime echoed through the house. The only response was the barking of her Doberman pup, Mouse.

He tried the doorknob to see if it was unlocked. Of course it was, most people in Pearl Lake never locked their doors for some strange reason. He was tempted to go in but with the vibe of being watched and it being simply wrong to enter someone's home uninvited; he changed his mind. He would check over at Mack's first to see if she were there. He took two steps and paused. Mouse's barking turned into a mournful howl. Shutting out the sound, Mark hurried down the steps and across to Mack's store. The bell tinkled above the door when he went in. Scanning the lunch counter for Eleanor, an uneasy feeling creeped over his scalp.

The old man was coming out of the kitchen when Mark sat himself down on a stool at the lunch counter. "Hey Mack. Has Eleanor come in today?"

Mack came over to the counter with a coffeepot in his hand. "Want one?" he asked. Flipping the cup over he didn't wait for a response.

"Ah, sure. So, has she?"

"No. I haven't seen her for a few days now. Did you ever get a chance to ask her about the banana bread?"

"I... No, I didn't. I just came from over there to see about it, and she isn't home. I thought she might be here," Mark said, adding sugar to his coffee.

Mack glanced out the window to the house across the street. "Is she over at Ava's getting a massage?"

Mark never thought about that. Ava might not have had time to cancel appointments. "She could be, I suppose. But Ava sprained her ankle last night so she can't work for a bit."

"She could be over at the hall too. You know those old ladies have their quilting bee or baking days. I can't keep up with them." Mack laughed and turned, setting the coffee pot on the hot plate.

"Yeah, I guess you're right." But it didn't feel right. Not the way the dog was howling it didn't.

"So how is the baby doing?"

"Ah, she's good. I'm heading there right now to meet Dean and Tim. Can I take this to go, Mack?" He pointed to the cup as he stood.

"Yeah sure."

"Great, I'm just going to grab some beer," he said, before heading towards the refrigerator section of the grocery area.

"SHIT, SHIT SHIT!!" Kim chanted, racing to her car. She had to get a hold of Dean, the plan was now screwed, royally. Flinging the car door open she shoved herself into the driver's seat and grabbed up her phone.

She was panting from her excursion when he answered the phone. "Dean!"

"Kim. What's up?"

"I was sent on my way that's what's up. Ash is bringing Ava home. He ruined our plan." She sighed, starting the engine.

"Hmm, maybe. Did they say how long they will be?" Dean's voice boomed as she hit the speaker on her cell phone.

Kim put the car into gear. "No. I don't think too long. But he's going to take her home and not to Ben and Abbi's house. How will we get her over there?"

"I'll think of something. In the meantime, call Ava right now and tell her you are running to Springbank. Then, park your car down the road, make sure you're well-hidden but can see the house. I'll call Mark and get him to meet us over at Ash's place."

She frowned as she pulled onto the road, setting her pace at her usual ten-kilometer crawl. "Why would I hide?"

"Because. You're going to be the lookout. If you see Ash leave, call me right away."

"Got it," she said, hanging up. She hit the speed dial for Ava's number. Once she was done filling her in on her 'trip' to Springbank, Kim stepped on the gas. Nelly, as she liked to call her old car, must have had the crap scared out of her. She backfired and took off like a rocket, headed directly for the lake. Kim knew the perfect spot. The old Anderson place. More specifically the lane way. Level with the road, it had a hill on both sides of it. She could pull her car right up to the abandoned house and lay flat on the hill near the road. She could watch as Ash drove his truck along the bend to their house. No one would see her unless they were in the lake.

Turning onto the lake road, she hung a left towards her destination. She was mildly shocked to see a 'for sale' sign in the front yard with a sold sticker on it. Slowly she pulled into the driveway and wondered who in their right mind would buy such a place. Apprehension replaced the excitement from a second ago when her eyes took in the old house. It was an old mansion that looked like it was from a gothic horror movie with its blackened stones and spires. At one time, it was spectacular, but years of neglect had taken its toll.

She let out a scream when out of the corner of her eye she saw a rat skitter across the weed filled lane.

"Oh, hell no!" As visions of all things creepy crawly ran through her mind Kim threw the car into reverse. She would drive to Ben and Abbi's and park her car behind the house and hide in the bush between the two houses. If she were spotted which she highly doubted, she would come up with an excuse.

MARK PULLED THE DOOR open of the clinic just as Dean and Tim were coming out.

"Perfect timing, buddy. We have to do a little walk-through," Dean drawled, as he put an arm across Mark's shoulders. He guided him towards the yellow house on the other side of the road.

"What's going on?" Mark looked at him skeptically.

"Change of plans. Ash is taking Ava home. Kim is on watch somewhere to let us know when they show up and for how long," Tim told him.

Mark stopped walking. Running a hand through his hair, he said, "I think we should forget going there."

Dean sighed.

"Why?" Tim asked.

Mark held out a hand. "Don't get me wrong. I still want to see what is in that cellar but..." What he was about to say made him think he was going nuts. He could only imagine what his friends would think.

"But what?" Dean urged.

Mark pointed across the street to Eleanor's house. "But I think we should be checking on Eleanor. I went over there before going into the store and she didn't answer."

"Maybe she's gone," Tim said.

Mark shook his head. "No. I don't think she is. I think something is wrong. The door is unlocked, and the dog was howling like something was wrong and she's not in her usual spot in the window."

"That's fine." Dean nodded. "It's probably better that we wait when we have more time to search anyway. Let's go."

The three of them walked across the street and along the path to the porch steps. Climbing them, Mark noticed the feeling of being watched was still as strong as ever. He couldn't resist the need to ask, "Do you feel that?"

Dean was looking up at the ceiling of the covered porch. "The feeling that eyes are boring into the back of your head, feel? Yup."

Tim walked along the porch and looked over the railing. He stopped at the side nearest Ash's house. To the untrained eye, one would think he was simply looking between the houses. Out of the corner of his eye, he spied the culprit. "Twelve o'clock," he said, just above a whisper.

Dean made his way over, looking directly at the house across the way, he saw exactly what was at 'twelve o'clock'. He let out a low whistle, looking at Mark he jerked his head towards the yellow house. "There's your culprit."

Mark swung his gaze around. A security camera was staring back at him.

"*Sonofabitch!* That means he knows Kim and I were here the other night."

Tim shrugged his shoulders. "Possibly. It could just be a decoy."

"What were you wearing?" Dean asked as he walked to Eleanor's front door.

"Ahh. God, I don't ever remember to be honest."

"Black. You always wear black. Unless of course you want to get caught." Dean shot him a sly smile as he rang the doorbell.

Not satisfied when he didn't get an answer, he turned the doorknob and pushed the door wide. There stood Mouse, happy to see them the Doberman pup ran over, whining.

Three things assaulted the men as they entered the house. 1. The smell of dog urine and feces. 2. Flies buzzing around and 3. The smell of something rotting...

Dean could hear someone gagging. Knowing it had to be Mark he swung his gaze in his direction. Only to see Mark had pulled his t-shirt over his face to the bottom of his eyes. "You okay buddy?"

"What the hell is that god awful smell?"

Dean walked further into the house. "Well. Considering there is dog shit and the flies along with the smell, I would say something dead."

"Oh God... you don't think..." Mark couldn't finish saying what he was thinking.

Tim held up his hand. "Not necessarily. That smell and flies could be from several things." He headed towards the dining room. "It could be garbage that wasn't thrown out. Or..." With one finger, he moved the sheer curtain aside and looked out the window directly at Ash's house, then back at Mark. "A dead mouse."

Mark felt somewhat reassured as he headed straight for the kitchen. Tim was right, it could be several things. He pushed on the swinging door and froze. "Guys it's not garbage or a mouse... It's Eleanor." He rushed into the kitchen and out the back door. With a second to spare, he hurled the contents of his stomach all over Eleanor's pink geraniums.

Tim and Dean rushed in after him. There, laying on the floor was the old woman. Dried blood had pooled under her from a gash on her forehead. Dean squatted down beside her and laid his fingers alongside her throat.

"He's right." Dean jerked his head toward the door Mark had exited through. "The smell could gag a maggot."

Tim looked around for any clues. There was a steak rotting in a frying pan on the stove. It appeared to be half cooked, before the flies had gotten to it. "Speaking of maggots..." he murmured, poking at it with a knife. If he had to take a guess at how long it was in the pan, he would say no more than two days, three at tops.

Dean pulled out his cell phone to call 911. Looking at Mark, he said, "Go get Doc, will you?"

Tim's brows snapped together. "What for?"

"She's alive."

Chapter 16

Mark couldn't believe all that had happened in the eight hours since waking up. It had been a brutal day from the second he'd heard Ava talking on the phone that morning. Before he even had a chance to open his eyes and it snowballed from there.

After they had found Eleanor, he was certain that Ash had something to do with her demise. He remembered while rinsing off the geraniums he fertilized so generously, that Kim saw Ash go into her house. He had been shocked to learn that she was still alive. He felt like an ass when Eleanor awoke after Doc used smelling salts on her and told them she'd fallen and hit her head. Doc called in the air ambulance that had to land on the beach and she was rushed to Springbank.

It was now 7:00 pm and he was sitting in the kitchen at his house with everyone... including Ash. Ava had been oblivious to everything going on because she had been with Ash, doing God knew what and now the others were filling them in.

Now would be a good time to search his house... Mark thought, as he sat there glowering. He could use the excuse that he was going to Ben and Abbi's house. No one would be the wiser. But did he really want to check it out alone was the question. No. He couldn't do it alone. Getting up, he looked directly at Kim and jerked his head towards the living room, hoping she caught the drift and would follow.

She did.

With a raised brow, she asked, "What's up? You look like you stepped in dog crap or something."

He looked at her, his eyes large. "Do you really have to ask?"

She sighed. "Yeah, forget I did. So, what's the plan Stan? Are we going to go break in or what?"

"Yeah. That's exactly what I was thinking." He glanced towards the kitchen, making sure no one was coming. "I'm going to tell them I'm heading over to Ben's. I will call your cell, come up with an excuse as to why you need to leave, and I'll meet you on the stairs on the hill." He glanced at his watch then raised expectant eyes to her. "In twenty minutes?"

Kim leaned a hip against the couch and nodded. "That will work. But why the hill? Aren't we driving?"

"No. The car is a dead giveaway that one of us is nearby. Plus, it's easier to slip in and out of places."

"Okay, you go in there and tell them and I'll come in after you leave."

Mark took a step, but she stopped him by grabbing his sleeve.

"*Wait!*" She uttered softly. "What about Dean and Tim, don't we want them to come with?"

Mark looked at her for a second before answering. He shook his head. "No. They need to keep those two distracted as long as possible, besides, I don't want them to get in trouble. Oh, and wear black."

"Right. Will do," she muttered, as he walked away. She just hoped they didn't stumble on another Eleanor Stanford scenario.

"MARK?!" KIM HISSED. To say it was scary in the darkness on the hillside was an understatement. The moon was out in all its glory, allowing for some light to filter through the canopy of pines, but every step she took and every row of tree trunks she passed, she could swear she saw someone standing there... looking at her.

"Why the hell isn't he answering me?" She asked aloud, simply just to hear something in the stillness of the night. She was halfway up the stairs when she bumped into him. She jumped a foot in the air and was setting out to let loose the mother of all screams when she felt him cover her mouth with his hand.

"Shhh," he whispered, close to her ear. "They might hear you."

Fearing the worst, Kim looked to where his outstretched hand was pointing to; a family of racoons ten feet away.

He laughed at the look on her face.

She smacked his hand away and punched him on the arm for good measure. "What the hell is wrong with you?" She spat. "I seriously just pissed myself!"

"You're joking right?" he asked soberly, as he gagged.

"No. Well... maybe a little dribble." It was her turn to laugh at him. "Yes, I'm joking." She cackled. "I swear you have the stomach of a newborn."

"Yeah, I know. Let's get moving."

Together they climbed the rest of the stairs to Ava's spa. Crossing the yard, they headed straight for the road. They passed house after house with the lights gleaming through the windows as the families within settled down to watch tv or eat dinner. Coming up on Mack's store from the back, Mark slinked along the wall to the front of it and held up his hand.

Grinning, she asked, "What are you doing? You're acting like we are on a high stakes op."

Mark looked at her and pushed her flat against the wall with his arm. "Will you get back and stay quiet?"

"What... Why?"

"Because I didn't want to tell you this, but Ash has a camera on his front porch." He peered across the road at the yellow house, hoping to see the flicker of red lights that would show the location of more.

"You're just telling me this *now*?!"

Mark shrugged. "Yeah well. It's a minor detail. Hence why I told you to wear black." He pointed to the house. "So here is the plan. We go along the other side of the house because the camera is facing Eleanor's place. We scale the fence and head to the hole from hell. Remember the swimming pool, don't fall in the damn thing. Sound good?"

Kim laughed in his face. "You expect me to scale my fat ass over a fence?"

"Sure, you can do it. I have faith in you."

"Yeah, okay. Well, I'm going over it first so you can push me over. Got it?"

Mark gave her a nod. "Got it. Let's go."

He took hold of her arm and together they set off towards the road. Halfway across, a car came up the street. Together they raced the rest of the way and dove into a stand of bushes.

"Oh my god, I thought that was Ash," Mark panted.

Kim started giggling uncontrollably. Mark looked at her as if she were insane.

"I'm sorry." She waved a hand in front of her face. "I'm picturing what we look like in my head, and I just can't stop." She started to squeal.

"If you don't stop, you will piss yourself and then I'll leave you here."

That set her off even more, in between moments of breathing and laughing, she clutched her stomach and managed to say, "You're right."

After a minute she finally composed herself long enough to get on with the mission.

Stumbling together, they made their way to the far side of Ash's house and headed straight for the fence around the backyard.

Kim looked up at the height of it and pointed. "There is no way in hell I'm going to be able to climb that."

"Don't worry, I'll boost you up. Put your foot in my hands." Lacing his fingers together, Mark leaned forward in front of Kim and waited.

She put a hand on his shoulder to steady herself as he slowly stood up. Suddenly, Kim could feel herself starting to sway. Quickly she wrapped her arms around his head and hung on for dear life.

"I can't see! Grab the damn fence!" He yelled into her bosom.

"I can't, you're like five feet away from it!" She cried in alarm. "Just put me down before I'm kissing the ground, will you?" She felt his hands fall from her foot and grab her waist.

"Now will you let go of my head?"

Kim at once dropped her hands to his shoulders and felt herself being deposited on the ground.

"Okay. That isn't going to work." Mark sighed looking at the fence.

Kim smacked herself in the face. The damn mosquitoes were out in full force.

"Why can't we just sneak around to the other side? If we stick close to the house, we should be able to avoid all cameras, don't you think?"

Mark looked at her and blinked. "Why didn't you suggest that ten minutes ago?"

"I figured you were the one calling the shots." She turned and retraced their steps from a few moments before. "Come on."

Once again, together they snuck in the darkness, sticking close to the side of the house like bugs on fly paper. Before long, they were crouched down, in between Eleanor's house and Ash's.

"What the hell are you out of breath for?" Kim asked, as she watched Mark bend over and suck in air.

"I've been holding it since the other side."

"Why?" Shaking her head, she said, "Never mind. Come on. If we don't hurry up, Ash will be home before we find out what the hell is in there."

"Right."

Mark creeped up the gate and pushed it open and cringed when the squeaky sound of rusty hinges echoed between the house.

Kim clapped her hands to her ears. "The gate never made that sound before," she said, as they quickly entered the yard, leaving the gate ajar.

She grabbed Mark's sleeve. "Wait. Shouldn't we close it? What if Ash comes home?"

"No. We will be down there. If he does come, we will more than likely miss him and if—"

"He comes home, and we open it, he will hear it." She finished. "Good thinking Sherlock!"

Mark pulled a flashlight out of his pocket.

"Yeah, occasionally I have a good idea. Now. Let's go see what the hell is in that cellar."

THEY WERE STANDING silently at the top of the stairs looking down into the darkness. Both asking themselves if they really wanted to do this. Mark was the first to make up his mind and took the first step.

"Turn the damn flashlight on," Kim hissed, in his ear while grabbing the back of his shirt.

"I will. Once we get closer to the door. If you haven't noticed, we are still above ground level." Within a second Mark switched the light on. There, before them stood the door to Hell.

Without a word, Mark reached out a hand and grabbed the doorknob just as a voice behind them boomed. "And just what the hell do you two think you're doing?"

Kim screamed and Mark kicked the door open in response. The flashlight fell to the cement pad with a thud as Dean and Tim howled with laughter.

"You *assholes!!*" Kim shouted looking up at them.

"You should have seen your faces." Tim laughed, coming down the steps followed by Dean.

"Why are you two here?" She asked. "And where the hell is Ash?"

Dean cleared his throat. "Ava and he are watching a movie. We figured you two would be here. So, we followed you." He put an arm around Kim's shoulder. "You know, it helps if you don't yell when you're out staking a place." He smirked and winked at her.

The flashlights beam illuminated the room within. Mark stared straight ahead, his brain not quite registering what his eyes were seeing.

"Ah, Guys... What the hell is that?" he asked, backing up. There stood what appeared to be a watchman at the door. Kim's vampire and Mark's Satan. A bald mannequin wearing a cape stared at them with golden eyes.

Dean grabbed the flashlight and pushed past Mark further into the room, the others followed closely behind. There in front of them stood row after row of mannequins. It was all so bizarre. But even more so was that each one wore a fur coat in varying lengths. Their unseeing eyes all staring at a photo on the wall as if paying homage to the lady smiling back at them. A chill ran down Mark's back as his eyes took in the photo of the woman. Her beauty was undeniable and one he knew well. It was a photo of Ava.

Chapter 17

Doc Spence took his glasses off and wiped a tired hand over his eyes. He was staring at his tablet, going over Eleanor's MRI results while waiting for a taxi to take him back to Pearl Lake. She was one lucky lady, if she'd hit her head a hair's width to the left, she wouldn't be resting peacefully in a hospital bed now. What Doc couldn't come to terms with was the fact that there was nothing near where she was found to hit her head on. But she was adamant that she fell.

A nurse on the other side of the desk interrupted his musings. "Doc Spence, your taxi is waiting for you outside the emergency department."

"Thank you, Melissa," he said, stuffing his tablet into his bag. He slung it to his shoulder and made his way to the ER department's exit.

The night air was crisp as he left the building and headed towards the awaiting taxi. Opening the door, he looked in and saw that it was Pete. The man had safely gotten him home to Pearl Lake on many such occasions. "Hey Pete. How's it going?" He asked, plopping down on the seat beside him.

"Not too bad Doc, not too ba—"

Both men looked at Melissa who was tapping on the driver's side window.

Pete rolled his window down. "Hey Melissa, how are you?"

"I'm good, thanks," she answered. Ducking down, she looked at Doc. "I'm sorry Dr. Spence. But Eleanor is calling for you."

"Oh?"

"Yes. She said she has something she needs to tell you and refuses to speak to anyone else."

"Alright," Doc said, climbing out of the car. "Pete, will you wait for me?"

"Sure thing, Doc, I'm looking forward to getting out for a nice drive." He smiled, waving him off.

Doc followed the nurse into the hospital and asked, "Is she still in room C?"

"No. She's been moved to the second floor, room 206," she told him.

"Thank you, Melissa."

Doc made his way down the hall to a wall of elevators and walked into the first one that opened. He couldn't help wondering on the ride up what was so important that Eleanor had to tell him.

When the doors opened with a soft swoosh, Doc wasted no time in finding room 206. He went into the room to see Eleanor laying in a bed, her head wrapped in a white bandage. She looked so frail, as if she'd aged 10 years since the last time, he saw her, not more than an hour ago. He crept slowly towards the bed, afraid that if she were sleeping, he would awaken her.

"I'm awake Doc." Eleanor turned her head towards him.

"How are you feeling?" he asked, checking the machines that beeped at the head of the bed.

"I've been better. I wanted to tell you something. Something I should have told you earlier... but didn't."

Doc looked at her and nodded. In his most soothing voice, he said, "Go ahead, Eleanor. I'm listening..."

IF IT HAD BEEN SOMEONE else that was with her right now, she would be enjoying herself. But she wasn't, she was with Ash. Sighing, Ava pushed the thought of Mark right out of her head. It didn't help when Ash persisted on going to Springbank tonight to get the parts for the fountain. He'd finally caved-in to a night at home when she told him to go himself if he couldn't wait until morning.

"Are you okay?" he asked her, as he covered her with a blanket.

Silently, Ava nodded.

"Okay. Well, the popcorn is almost ready. What do you want to drink?"

"Ginger ale is fine, thanks."

She smiled at Eleanor's pup Mouse and hugged him. It had been decided the dog would be better to stay with them, rather than leave him alone in an empty house.

"Be right back."

Ava watched as he went to the kitchen and wished that he would just leave. Her foot was throbbing and all she wanted to do was go to bed. Ash, to be frank, was driving her up a wall. She didn't know if he was feeling guilty about what he did or if he was lonely, but she had enough of him for the day.

"Here we are," he said. Setting the bowl of popcorn on the table, he handed her a can of pop.

She looked down at it and noticed it was open. It was on the tip of her tongue to ask why, when the one he had for himself, was not. But instead, she grumbled her thanks and took a sip.

DEAN LET OUT A LOW whistle. "This guy has a serious problem," he said, looking at the coat hanging on the mannequin nearest to him.

Mark stood transfixed, his eyes on the photo of Ava. There was something about it he couldn't quite put his finger on.

Tim snagged the arm of the coat next to him, the price tag was still on it. "I'll say. This one is $5 grand."

Kim was standing in front of a counter, littered with papers. She picked up one and looked at it. It was a newspaper clipping from years ago on how to care for fur. "Why would Ash have so many fur coats?" Dropping it back onto a pile Kim made her way over to one of the coats.

"How do we even know if these are his? We don't," Dean said, giving him the benefit of the doubt.

"True." Mark nodded. "But if they aren't, what's with Ava's picture?"

"That's right!" Tim agreed. Coming to stand by Mark, he too now stared at the photo.

"Holy shit! Did any of you check the pockets?" Kim asked, holding up a fist full of money. "This one has at least five hundred bucks in it."

Mark inclined his head toward the cash. "What should we do with it?"

"Leave it. Whoever these belong to, they know it's there," Dean answered. He looked at Kim. "Record how much we find, will you? Also, write down if there is a custom name and description of the coat beside each amount."

"Okay." She nodded and snatched up a pen and paper from the counter.

The guys got to work, calling out the total amount of money they found in each coat before stuffing it back into the pockets. Mark was working on the last one while Tim and Dean searched the room for more clues.

"Anything in that one Mark?" Kim asked.

"Fifty in this pocket." He answered as he felt around to the other pocket. He frowned. Shoving his hand in it was just what he thought it was. A jewelry box for a ring. Flipping it open, he looked at the diamond twinkling back at him. He held his hand out for the others to see. "And this."

Kim's eyes bugged out of their sockets. "Holy crap! That must be at least 2 carats."

"Worth around 10 grand?" Tim estimated.

Mark nodded. If he knew one thing it was the value of a diamond. "Yeah, give or take a few thousand."

"Let's see," Kim said, adding up the totals. "So, with the ring plus the cash, there is over $20,000.00. That's not including the price of the coats."

Mark's brows inched towards his hairline. "What kind of landscaper has that kind of money?" he asked.

"None. Come on, let's get the hell out of here before Ash catches us in the act," Tim said, heading towards the door, Mark and Kim followed closely behind.

Dean surveyed the room one last time making sure all was as they found it. "I agree. We need to run a background check on Ash too." Satisfied, he closed the door behind him and followed the others to ground level.

"Already did, just waiting on the results," Tim answered, as Kim's phone started ringing.

A memory flashed in Kim's brain. One from long ago. She didn't have time for that now.

She looked at her phone. "It's Doc." She answered, listening as they walked towards the front of the house. A horrified look replaced the worrisome one. Without a word she took off running.

"What the hell are you doing Kim?" Mark shouted, as all three men shot after her.

"It's Ava," she said, never breaking stride. "We need to get to her now. Eleanor didn't fall. Ash bashed her over the head."

AVA HIT THE PLAY BUTTON on the remote. Together they ate popcorn and watched the movie in silence. That was until Ash excused himself to use the washroom.

She sat waiting for him to return, cuddling moose while staring at the frozen image on the screen, her eyes growing increasingly heavy with every second that ticked by.

"Did you get your gift I left for you?"

Ava jumped at his voice. "Wha... What?" She was having such a hard time concentrating on what he was even saying.

"Your gift. I left it on the front step last night. A coat for you," he said, sitting down.

What the hell is he even talking about and why would he give me a coat?

"Aww you're tired I see. Come here." He pulled her close to him.

Ava didn't want him holding her, but she had no strength to stop him. The next thing she knew was darkness. Sleep had claimed her.

Ash sat holding her in his arms. He stared down at her lovingly. He had waited for this moment for years. Of course, she never accepted him the way he was before. No. He had to change, not only did he have to change his lifestyle but his very life. He wanted nothing more than to stay with Ava and hold her all night long, but he had some business to take care of in Springbank first.

Setting the pup aside, he gently picked Ava up and carried her through the house out to his truck. He couldn't just leave her in it though, even though she would be asleep for hours. Plenty of time for him to do his business and be back before she awoke. He would put her in the one spot no one would ever think to look. The old Anderson place...

Chapter 18

They rounded the corner and were met with Ash's truck barrelling down on them. Scattering into the bushes they watched as he took the road out of the village that would lead to Springbank.

"Where the hell do you suppose he's going?" Dean asked, dusting himself off.

Mark wasn't wasting any time by standing around, he turned and headed towards the house. He could see the lights were on still. Was that a good sign? "Did anyone see if he was alone?"

"Yeah," Tim nodded. "He was alone."

That didn't ease the anxiety that Mark was feeling one bit. Something told him that Ava was still in harm's way. He took off running towards the house and in no time, he was scaling the porch steps and entered the front door.

He could see through to the living room and saw the TV was on, paused on a movie. "Ava?" he called, heading straight for the couch. She wasn't there.

Walking in the house, Kim asked, "Any sign of her?"

Mark shook his head as he went to the hallway, opening doors as he passed them. "She's not here."

"Maybe she was laying down in the truck when he went by us?" Tim offered.

"Why would she be laying down? Unless..." Dean trailed off. "We need to call the cops, have them intercept him on the highway."

"On it," Tim answered, with his phone to his ear.

"I'm taking my truck and going after him," Mark said, storming through the house.

Dean shook his head. "No. You stay here. Tim and I will go." When Mark started to protest, he said, "You need to stay here with Kim and let the cops handle this. We don't know if he even has her."

Mark raised his chin defiantly.

"I mean it." Dean pushed a finger into his chest. "You and Kim check out Ben's place. She might be over there."

Kim looked at Dean. "Fine. Kim, come on," Mark barked and stalked off outside.

"You know he's gonna be pissed at you."

"Yeah. He'll get over it."

"Kim!" Mark yelled from the middle of the laneway.

Kim poked her head out the door. "I'm coming!" She shrieked back. "Hold your damn horses!"

She turned to Dean and Tim. "You two better find her and quick," she said, sailing down the steps.

Kim ran to catch up with Mark. "Hold up." She panted. "I swear to all that is holy I've lost ten pounds with all this running around."

Mark ignored her as he tramped through the bush. They came to the clearing of Ben's yard, and he said, "Something doesn't sit well with me Kim."

"What do you mean?"

Mark walked up the back steps of the covered porch. "I don't know. I just have a feeling she isn't with him."

All three dogs jumped at the door. Mark unlocked it and shoved it wide, just barely getting out of the way of the stampede.

"Maybe not. But I think we should check the house out to make sure. What do you think?" Kim asked, walking into the kitchen.

"She isn't here. He took her home; she wouldn't walk here by herself. Besides, the dogs wouldn't have been waiting at the door if she were here." Mark pointed out.

Shoving a hand through his hair, he pulled out his cell phone and tried calling her. "Voicemail." He sighed. "Let's call the dogs in. Then we will go for a walk."

"To where?" Kim frowned. "Maybe I should have said something sooner. But this all seems too familiar to me."

"What part?" Mark let out a sharp whistle and all three dogs came running but refused to come in.

"The furs, the money. It reminds me of Ava's ex. But Ash isn't her ex. He doesn't act like him; he doesn't talk like him, and he certainly doesn't look like him. And Kurt would never get his hands dirty by being a gardener. It just doesn't make sense." She finally stopped prattling on to notice the dogs. "What's wrong with them?"

Mark glanced down at them and shrugged "Hell if I know. They won't come in."

She moved the door and grabbed the leashes from the peg behind it. "We'll take them with us," Kim said and handed Mark a leash.

AVA SLOWLY WOKE TO sunlight streaming right in her face. She cracked an eye open and groaned, not only from the brightness but also from the splitting pain, searing through her brain. She shielded her eyes and turned to discover it wasn't sunlight, but a lamp directly overhead.

She was lying covered with a blanket on the floor. A floor that she didn't recognize. "Where am I?" She whispered to herself, knowing somehow, that wherever she was, she was alone. Her eyes focused on a dusty old couch less than five feet from her. Sitting up, she pulled the blanket around her and looked around for Ash. He was nowhere to be found and neither were her crutches. She shimmied over to the couch and leaned on it then hoisted herself onto the cushions as a cloud of dust filled the air.

Coughing, she searched her pockets for her cell phone and couldn't help but wonder how she got here. The last thing she remembered was sitting on the couch watching a movie with Ash. He'd gotten up to use the washroom and had come back into the room...

Ava frowned. He'd asked her about a gift. Movement caught her eye. A dark shape, scuttered across the room. She jumped and screamed then felt like a fool when she realized it was only a raccoon.

It didn't care that she was there. Intent on finding some food, it made its merry way out of the room without a care in the world.

THE DOGS WERE LEADING the way. At times, Mark and Kim had a hard time keeping up with them. They would go through the bush then back towards Ben and Abbi's, only to turn around and dart off in the opposite direction.

"Do you suppose we should just leave them at our house?" Kim asked, as they made their way towards it.

Mark shook his head. "I don't know. It's like they are tracking something."

Kim chuckled. "Bloodhounds they are not."

"You're right. But I didn't think Brutus would take me to Ava the first time either. Especially in a thunderstorm."

"True. Okay, so we follow them," Kim said as they headed towards the road.

"Sounds like a plan."

"If we find her—"

"You mean when we find her." Mark corrected.

Despite the darkness, Kim stuck her tongue out at him. "When we find Ava are you finally going to tell her how you feel?"

Mark wasn't sure. He would like to, he just needed to gauge her first. He didn't want to spew out his feelings if they weren't reciprocated. It would be extremely awkward living in the same house if she wanted nothing to do with him romantically.

"Well?" Kim hedged.

He looked up ahead. "I'll see." They were at the turn in the road that would take them over the hill and into the village. "Why are there lights on at the Anderson place?"

"Huh." Kim shuddered at the memory of the rat. "I don't know. I was there earlier and there weren't any on."

"I'd think the hydro would be off. The place should be condemned. It's been empty for close to five years now, for good reason too." Mark muttered as they got closer. "Let's go check it out," he said and headed towards the laneway.

No way in hell did Kim want to go back there. "I don't think so. There are rats in the grass. God knows what's inside."

Mark led the way. "Come on. We don't even have to go in. We can just peek in the windows."

"Fine. But if something jumps out at me, I'm throwing it at your head. Just so you know."

He laughed and took out his cell phone. Turning the flashlight on they made their way through the tall grass.

"Stop!"

Not watching where she was going, Kim walked right into his back. The dog's leashes tangled around her legs causing her to almost fall face first, but lucky for her Brutus caught her fall with his back.

"Help me, you fool!" She hissed at a laughing Mark. He helped her stand upright and removed the leashes from her legs.

"Why do you do that, stop so suddenly all the time! I swear to god you do it on purpose."

Mark pointed to the ground. "I was going to point out the tire tracks. Are they yours?"

She looked where the beam of light shone revealing tracks in the matted down grass and shook her head. "No, I didn't pull in this far. Someone's been here since."

Kim turned towards the road. "The place was up for sale." She pointed to the sign. "It's sold. Maybe the new owner stopped in and forgot to turn the lights off."

"Maybe. Let's go look in the window." Mark shut the light off and together they forged on in the dark.

"Light on, light on." Kim chanted as images of snakes, bats and rats entered her mind.

"No. We will make our way in the moonlight. If someone is there, we don't want to be seen. Shhh!" He shushed her as she started her chanting again. "Hold my hand. Besides, the dogs will eat whatever comes at us."

"Oh, that's really reassuring. Not!" she said, her voice shaking.

"Just. Be. Quiet." Mark looked at her and took her hand. As he pulled her through the tall grass, he had to admit he felt uneasy about the situation himself.

They both breathed a sigh of relief as their feet touched the flagstone sidewalk. At least on it the weeds weren't thigh high.

Together they crossed the stone porch and squatted in front of a window. All that was visible was the top of their heads and eyes.

"I don't see anything do you?" Kim whispered.

"No. But it looks like it's trashed in there."

"Just like the outside. I can't believe someone would buy this place. Why did you say earlier 'for a good reason too?'" Kim cocked her head and searched his face.

Mark looked at her as if she needed her medication adjusted.

"You said, this place should be condemned and for a good reason too. What's the reason?"

"Oh." He waved a vague hand. "It's haunted."

Kim snorted. "Yeah right."

"I'm serious." He quickly looked at her before turning his attention back to the window. "This place is well over 160 years old. The original owner was like the 'town mayor' or something."

"Do you mean the Andersons?"

"Yeah. But like way back when. The house was passed down from generation to generation or something. I don't know how he was considered a mayor, seeing how it isn't a town but a village." Mark popped his head up higher, scanning the room as he did so. "Anyway, he was gunned down right there." He pointed. "Right beside the fireplace."

Kim's eyes grew large as she looked towards the hearth. It was huge, now empty, and black, she could picture the man standing there. She swallowed trying desperately to moisten her now dry throat. "What happened?" she asked breathlessly.

"A land deal gone bad. Back in the day rumor had it that there was a gold mine right here on this land. Him and a buddy, George McCrae, purchased it for a dollar in hopes that they would hit the mother lode." Mark ducked back down and looked her in the eyes. "When that didn't happen, old man Anderson decided to buy out his buddy for ten dollars." He sat himself down on the stone porch. "All of the sudden, he starts building this mansion."

Kim was entranced with the tale; she'd never heard anything of it before. "Then what happened?"

"Well, McCrae got suspicious. Neither one had any money when they had come over from Scotland and all the sudden, Anderson started building this." Mark waved at hand at the house. "Wouldn't it make you wonder?"

Slack-jawed, Kim nodded.

"Right. Me too." He stood up.

"Wait! Don't leave. Finish the story. What happened next?"

"We need to go look in the other windows. Clearly there is nothing here."

"Okay but tell me the rest while we do."

They gathered the dog's leashes and started off to the next window. Peeking in as they passed each one.

Kim was itching for him to finish. "Okay, spill the beans for heaven's sake... I need to know the rest of the story."

"Why are you so fascinated by this?" Mark asked, chuckling.

"Because... I have a love-hate relationship with ghost stories. Do I believe in them? Sometimes and sometimes I don't. Usually there is an explanation for all ghost sightings."

"Yeah, well be that as it may, there have been many sightings over the years."

"Will you just get on with it?" She demanded.

"Fine. Where was I?" He asked as he peered into a dusty window.

"McCrae got suspicious because Anderson started to build the mansion."

"Oh, that's right. Anyway, as the construction was nearly complete, accidents started happening around the mansion. One guy broke his leg, another fell off the roof and died. Landed right in the back yard or so I was told." Not seeing anything in that room, Mark moved along the outer wall to the next one.

"Then when it was all done a few years later, someone stood outside the very first window we looked in and shot Anderson dead on the spot."

Kim gulped. "Why the hell are you just telling me that *now?*"

"I did. I told you he was killed."

"No. You said he was gunned down. That doesn't mean he was killed!"

Mark shook his head and looked at her like she was nuts. "Does it really matter?"

Chapter 19

That was it. Ash had asked her if she'd gotten his gift. A coat... *Why would he get me a coat? Why would he get me anything for that matter...?* She needed to get out of here and fast.

Standing up, Ava flipped the blanket over her hair, hoping to avoid any spiders that decided she looked like a nice cushy place to drop on to. She hopped on one foot looking for anything that she could use as a crutch, heck even a piece of wood would work. As the blanket started to slip, she wrapped it around her like a cloak, there was no way she was giving up her only shield of protection.

She came to the archway leading into a foyer. It was hard to judge in the darkened room until she saw the staircase. She felt around the corner for a light switch. She was not inclined to go any further without the lights on. That raccoon got in somehow, she wouldn't be a bit surprised if there were other critters in the house as well. With her luck she'd run into a black bear. Finally, her hand found what she was looking for. Flipping the switch, the room filled with light from a crystal chandelier.

She was right, it was a foyer. Ava scanned the room from wall to wall. She continued through another archway into a hall. Flicking on light switches as she did only to discover the bulbs burnt out. Finally, she came to what appeared to be a kitchen, she found nothing of use in there either. She felt a thrill of excitement as she went into a room off it. A dining room, with an adult walker behind a sheer curtain that hung over a set of French doors. Despite taking her a good two minutes to make her way across, she let out a little, "Yay" as she took the handles in hand. Now all she had to do was get it out from behind the damn curtains.

"YOU DIDN'T TELL ME it was from that window!! I was standing where a killer was, and you didn't think that wasn't an important 'FYI'?!" Kim spat.

Mark thought a minute and finally said, "No," with a shake of his head.

"Whatever. Go on."

He continued walking to a set of French doors that led onto a back patio area, he supposed back in the day it was called a courtyard. It curved around what looked like a glass turret. He stood watching for Kim to come around the corner to join him. When she finally did, he didn't wait for her to ask him again to continue, he started where he left off.

"Now I don't know if this part is true, but legend says that his wife lived to a ripe old age of 93, she would walk around the grounds with her walker every night, mourning the loss of her one true love." He turned back towards the house and started to walk, intent on getting to the French doors. "She died right here in the house on the couch in the living room... next to the firepla..."

Mark could feel something grab the back of his shirt. Turning around, he saw that it was Kim tugging on it. He blinked. "What?"

Kim pointed and opened her mouth. All that came out was a squeak.

Mark squinted and turned his head to the side. "*What?!*"

"Ggggg... *Ghost*!" she shrieked and took off running for the corner of the house they had just come from; the dogs gave chase thinking it was a game and tackled her in the tall grass.

Mark turned. His eyes grew large as he saw what caused Kim to run away in fear. There, walking away from the French doors was a ghostly figure hunched over a walker, the gauzy curtain caressed its form as she hobbled away from the doors. It was the wife of old man Anderson.

Mark tried so hard to contain himself. He vowed he would never in his life do what he was about to do. Unable to take his eyes off the sight before him, he opened his mouth and screamed like a little girl. He screamed even louder, if that was possible, when the ghostly figured jumped and swung their gaze at him.

He swore he could hear her call his name as it carried on the wind. No. That was impossible. There was no way she could know his name. But there it was again, only louder because she changed direction and came at him.

Run you fool, he told himself, but his feet refused to budge. He was unable to move, waiting for the very second, she would come through the glass pane and beat him over the head with her walker.

Instead of coming through the window she opened the door. "Mark, are you okay?"

"Ava?"

He rushed to her side and hugged her. He was so tempted to plant a kiss on her soft lips but instead he set her at arm's length. "Wait, what are you doing here?"

"I have no idea. I don't even know where 'here' is, or how I got here."

"It's the old Anderson place. Thank God you're okay." Wanting to make sure not one scratch marred her beauty, he scanned every inch of her face. Not that it would matter to him there as, he just wanted to know if he would need to kick Ash's ass.

She shook her head as if to clear her thoughts. "I woke up on the floor covered with a blanket. You don't suppose I sleepwalked, do you?"

"No honey." He smoothed her hair away from her face. "Not with your ankle wrapped. I'm sorry to tell you this but Ash brought you here, for whatever reason."

She shook her head in denial. True there was something creepy about him, but this? "No, he wouldn't do that." *Or would he,* she thought.

"He had to be the one. Dean and Tim left the two of you alone. Don't you remember?"

She leaned out of his arms. Looking up at him she shook her head. "The only thing I remember was being so incredibly tired..."

The open can of pop he gave me.

Her face took on a horrified look and she started to shake. "That bastard drugged me. He gave me a can of pop that was already opened. I thought it odd because his wasn't, but I didn't say anything."

"I think you need to sit down before you fall down." Mark guided her onto the patio and grabbed a lawn chair that had seen better days. Bringing it over to Ava, he helped her sit down.

Her chin started to tremble as she looked at him. "How did you find me?"

Mark felt like his heart was being ripped from his chest when he saw her eyes glisten with tears. He squatted down. "Aww, come here," he murmured and pulled her close.

She collapsed on his chest; her hot tears soaked through his shirt to his skin. Mark rubbed her back soothingly as he held her in his arms.

He felt that familiar tightening of his jeans whenever Ava was near him. He needed to set her aside and take a step back but couldn't bring himself to do that to her. Not this time. This time he decided he would wait for her tears to subside before he moved.

She leaned back and looked him in the eyes. "Why are you so nice to me all of the time?"

It was on the tip of his tongue to tell her he was in love with her but all that he could manage to do was shrug.

Ava took his face in her hands. "Mark. Will you do me a favor?"

He bobbed his head up and down. "Sure, anything"

"Will you kiss me?" She asked, softly.

Silly as it sounded, she wanted to compare it with Ash's. And she also wanted to see if the spark was still there like it was last Christmas or if that had been a fluke.

His first thought was that it was a trick question, his second was that she was still feeling the effects of the drug and his third thought was, hell yes! He couldn't answer her for the life of him and instead, he placed his hand at the back of her head and brought her closer to him. They bent their heads in the same direction and bumped noses. *No, this was all wrong!*

He jumped back as if he was burned. "I'm sorry Ava, I can't kiss you. I mean... I *want* to kiss you; believe me I do. But it's just... It's just too... too...." For the life of him he couldn't think of a word.

She couldn't help but laugh at the look on his face. He almost looked like he was going to run off. "Unspontaneous?" she asked.

He snapped his fingers. "Yes! That's it... too unspontaneous!"

She smiled at him. "That's okay. Another time maybe." She yawned and stretched. "Can we go home now? I just want to go to bed."

He groaned low in his throat as he watched her breasts strained against her shirt.

"Ah...To hell with it." He had waited long enough for this moment. Mark lifted her from the chair, and before he had time to think he held her face in the palm of his hand.

"Ohhh!" Ava uttered in disbelief as his lips swooped down to catch hers in a titillating kiss.

There was no comparison of Ash to Mark. Mark made her feel things with only a look. Whereas Ash, he only made her feel annoyed. But this? This had her melting like a chocolate bar on a hot summer's day.

A moan started low in her throat as he deepened the kiss. This was so much more than the one they had shared last Christmas. Ava needed to stop it now before she tore his clothes off. If they ever made it to more than just friends, she didn't want their first time together in a rundown house.

Slowly she raised her hands and pushed against his chest. Despite her best efforts their lips clung together, neither one of them wanting this moment to end. She caved and wrapped her arms around his neck drawing him closer.

"MARK?" KIM HISSED. Staring bug eyed into the darkness she held tight to Lucy. After getting up from the dogs tackling her, she managed to untangle the leashes that had somehow found themselves wrapped around her legs, waist, and boobs. She had a hell of a time trying to untangle the mess. Only problem with Lucy being the tiny Yorkie that she was, she couldn't navigate through the tall grass, she was currently getting a ride, tucked safely in her bra. Which was fine by Kim, she felt somewhat safer having a second pair of eyes that would bark at anything threatening.

She thought Mark had been right behind her when she'd heard him scream like a banshee but to her surprise he was nowhere to be found. She looked at Lucy and in her most baby talk voice she said, "Maybe it wasn't Mark screaming, maybe it was Medusa, and he is now statue." Good lord she hoped not. She had no choice but to head back to the French doors in search of him.

"Come on you two." She tugged on the leashes. "That's right Brutus, you lead the way," she muttered, hoping that whatever crossed their path would be scared in the other direction.

They were twenty feet away when Kim's eyes finally focused in the darkness. She looked up towards the barn and saw a man standing there watching. It had to be Anderson's ghost. She dared not make a peep. That was until a flutter of movement caught the corner of her eye. She turned towards it and all bets were off.

"AAAAAAAAH!!!" she screamed in a frenzied panic as her eyes took in the scene before her. Mark was getting his breath sucked out of him from old man Anderson's wife no wonder the ghoul by the barn was watching.

She was shocked to see her scream worked, for they jumped apart. The wife nearly lost her balance. *Wait, don't ghosts hover?*

"Jesus, Kim, what the hell is wrong with you?" Mark bit out.

"Aunt Kim! Am I glad to see you!"

"Ava?! *Ava*!" Kim scooped Lucy out of her bra and rushed over. Handing the little dog off to Mark she gathered her niece in her arms. She was so happy at seeing her alive that she didn't even mention the kiss she had just seen between the two. "My god, hunny, I thought you were old man Anderson's wife."

Mark started laughing so hard his whole body started to shake.

Ava's brows snapped together. "Who?"

Kim waved a hand. "Never mind that. Let's get you home. I'm sure you're just exhausted and hungry. I know I am." She cast a wary eye on the mansion before setting off. With a nod she started leading the way through the tall grass. "Follow me. I know this trail like the back of my hand now."

Mark looked at Ava and smiled. "Piggyback or in my arms?"

She grinned back. "For old times sake... piggyback."

He bent down so she could climb onto his back. He hoisted her up just a notch as Kim called back to him.

"And you were right, Mark. This place does need to be condemned."

"Why do you say that?"

"Because. While looking for you. I think I saw Anderson's ghost."

Ava was comforted by the rumble of his laughter against her chest.

"It was Ava," he said, catching up to Kim just as they made the final turn towards the front of the house.

"Uh uh. This was by the barn. Old man Anderson must have thought Ava was his wife too." Kim said, making a beeline for the road.

"I think you're more tired than you realize Aunt Kim." Ava giggled.

Mark felt a feeling of dread, trying to brush it off he snickered. "Are you sure Kim?"

"Yeah. He was standing by the barn watching you two."

Mark hiked Ava closer as they stepped onto the road. He had a feeling it wasn't Anderson because no one had seen the apparition in close to forty years. He had a feeling it might have been Ash.

Chapter 20

The pickup truck barreled down the road eating mile after mile as it neared ever closer to Springbank.

"I think we should turn around. The local cops haven't found anything either," Tim said, glancing at Dean across the front seat. Watching his expression in the dash lights, Tim could tell that he was pissed. "It looks like we lost him." He added. They had been on the road for twenty minutes and had yet to see a set of taillights in the distance.

"Yeah, I think you're right, damnit." Dean fumed. Checking the rear-view mirror, he pulled off to the side of the road and made a U-turn. "I wonder if the asshole double backed on us?"

Bracing a hand on the dashboard, Tim nodded. "Probably."

"What do you think of all of this?" Dean asked as he stepped on the gas.

"Truthfully? The guy seems whacked. I mean it's one thing to have the coats and money... but that photo of Ava is a classic obsession if you ask me."

"Almost like a shrine wouldn't you say?"

"Exactly. But why? I mean they just met. How can you be obsessed with someone you just met?"

"Stranger things have happened." Dean pointed out. "Did you get that background check back yet?"

Tim shook his head. "No, Gil, my contact, told me a minimum of three days."

They were heading into the bend in the road that would take them directly to Pearl Lake. Easing off the gas, Dean said, "Well, then we need to do a little digging ourselves I'd say."

"Agreed. But how?"

Dean squinted. "We start with Ava."

MARK WAS WATCHING TV, waiting for Ava and Kim to join him in the living room. Ava had insisted on showering the second they got in the house and Kim was helping her. He had already thrown the popcorn, bowl and all in the garbage and collected the half empty pop where he'd sat them on the counter, he was just about to dump them down the drain when the dogs started barking. Sitting the cans down, he walked over to the door calling for Mouse to come with them. It wasn't a shocker that Abbi and Ben's trio of dogs had taken to the pup as if he were always one of the pack. Figuring twenty minutes was long enough for the dogs to do their business, Mark bent down to pick the pup up just as a truck came over the hill. An uneasy feeling sunk to the pit of his stomach until it came closer and saw that it was Dean's truck. He stood waiting as they pulled into the laneway. They didn't look happy as they exited the vehicle. That could only mean one thing. They didn't find Ash.

"Hey," he said. "No luck I take it?"

"Nope," Dean answered, slamming the driver's door shut.

"We think he must have double backed." Tim explained. "Or he was speeding like the devil was on his ass."

Mark nodded, running his hand over Mouse's back. His mouth set in a grim line, he looked at the two cops. "I think he was at the old Anderson place by the barn."

Tim looked at Dean. "What? Dean I thought you—"

One look from Dean and Tim stopped talking.

"What makes you think that?" Dean queried; his brows drawn together.

"We found Ava there. Kim said she saw a man standing by the barn watching."

Dean frowned as he folded his arms across his chest. "Oh? Do tell."

"Yeah. Kim and I went for a walk with the dogs down the road to look for Ava. We noticed lights on and thought we'd better check it out. So, we looked in the windows, eventually making our way to the back yard. Ava was in what looked to be a dining room." Mark shrugged, "I didn't see him. To be fair, I was telling her about the ghosts."

Dean's brows shot skyward. "Ghosts? As in plural?"

Tim chuckled, which at that moment, Mark thought was incredibly strange. He scratched his head. "Ah, yeah. There's an old myth around the village that the mansion is haunted by multiple ghosts."

Dean had a faraway look in his eyes as he rubbed his chin. "You don't say," he mumbled, staring off towards the house in question.

At that moment, the puppy started to fidget in Mark's arms. "Let's go inside, I don't want to set this little guy down and he gets lost or something." Walking towards the house, he let out a sharp whistle for the other dogs to follow. Brutus flew past them and up the porch steps and shoved the door wide that Mark had left ajar, allowing the rest to step right in the house.

Dean walked straight to the fridge and grabbed three beers. Twisting the cap off one, he took a long swig and sat on a stool at the counter.

Mark carried Mouse in and sat him on the floor. He looked around the corner to see if Ava and Kim were sitting in the living room. They were and as soon as Ava spied the pup, she called him excitedly to her.

"Hey Mark." Tim called from the doorway. "Do you want me to bring this coat in?"

Mark looked at the coat he held in his hand. It was a fur coat, just like the ones in Ash's cellar.

Dean motioned with his hand. "Bring that here," he said.

Closing the door behind him, Tim brought the coat to Dean while Mark stood and watched him turn the pockets out.

Nothing was in the pockets of the fur coat. Which proved nothing. If there was, they would have known it possibly was left by Ash, or whoever had made the shrine. Without a word, Dean got off the stool and took the coat into the living room.

"Ava. Do you know anything about this?" he asked, holding the coat up by the shoulders.

Ava looked up from petting the puppy. Her eyes took in the fact that it was fur and her blood started to pound through her veins. Yes, it was a fur coat, which did upset her but that wasn't the only reason. "Wher... ahem." She cleared her throat from the sudden sting of tears she felt. "Where did you find it?"

"It has been on the porch since last night," Kim answered. Not quite knowing where Dean was going with this, Kim got off the couch and gave the coat a once over. Turning to Ava, she said, "It was sitting outside on a chair, we didn't know whose it was. Do you?"

Ava shook her head as tears clouded her eyes and memories from long ago flitted through her mind. She was being silly of course for thinking such thoughts but that damn coat reminded her so much of the first one she'd ever buried from her ex, Kurt. Just like the one she'd gotten not too long ago...

In that second when he saw her reaction, Mark knew exactly who Ash Davenport was. Did Ava know too? His own mind flashed back to Christmas at Ben and Abbi's when she had shared her deepest darkest secret with him. Going to her side he squatted down in front of the couch and took her hands in his. "Do you remember what you told me at Christmas?" he asked her softly.

She nodded as she bit her lower lip, trying desperately to stop it from trembling. The fear of what might be, had her feeling unbelievably vulnerable. She shook her head as the tears flowed from her eyes. She knew she needed to tell everyone what Mark and she were talking about, but she just couldn't bring herself to.

Ava looked into his caring eyes. "I can't tell them Mark, please, can you?"

He hugged her to him as he rubbed her back, then murmured. "Of course I will, sweetheart." And then he did something he never thought he would be able to do. He kissed her on the lips for all the room to see.

Tim and Dean gawked at Kim. Silently Dean mouthed the words. "What the *hell*?!" at her. Her response of. "I don't *knooow*!!!" was equally silent.

Mark set her back and gave her one last reassuring squeeze. He got up from the floor and sat on the couch beside Ava, her hand safely tucked into his. "Guys. Ava needs to tell you something, but she can't." He looked at her and sent a reassuring smile her way. "So, I will," he said, turning back to them.

In detail, Mark started from the beginning, that whole night replayed in his mind although, some of it he would keep to himself...

It was 6 months ago Christmas Day and the whole family had gathered at Ben and Abbi's.

A delivery truck was backing into the driveway... He'd thought it odd as he walked to the door and opened it.

"Merry Christmas. I have a special delivery for a..." the man looked at the package. "Ava Petersen. I need a signature, sir."

"Of course." Mark scribbled his name and took the package. Setting it on the floor, he held up a finger and said, "One second." He'd opened the hall closet and grabbed up his wallet from his coat pocket. Taking a one-hundred-dollar bill from it he'd

returned to the front door, passing it to the man. "Here you are, Merry Christmas."

The man looked at Mark, stunned. "Are you sure?"

"Absolutely. No one should have to work on Christmas day."

Holding up the bill the driver grinned. "Thanks man! I really appreciate this. Merry Christmas."

"Merry Christmas to you too. Drive safe out there."

Grabbing the package, he went to the empty living room and put it under the tree before he'd joined the others in the dining room and taken his seat beside Kim.

She looked at him and asked, "Is everything alright?"

"Yeah" he murmured. "There was a special delivery for Ava is all it was."

"Oh?" she looked at him, with an odd expression on her face.

"Yeah. I don't know." He shrugged as he scooped a heaping spoon of scrambled eggs onto his plate. "Some package wrapped with a Partridge in a pear tree wrapping paper. Ugly as sin," he laughed and stabbed his fork into a slice of ham.

Kim smiled at him, but after living with her for the past few months, he knew when she was concerned. And right at that moment in time her concern was through the roof.

"What is it?"

"Nothing. Don't worry about it." But Kim was worried.

After the table had been cleared, the dishes put in the dishwasher and the kitchen tidied up, everyone gathered around the Christmas tree in the living room to open presents.

"Here Ben," Lane said, sliding a huge gift in his direction.

"Wow! Abbi, you didn't!" he murmured with a grin.

"Open it," Abbi smiled.

Ben carefully unwrapped the gift.

"What the hell kind of present is that for a man?" Kim asked. She gestured to the box and said, *"It's a dollhouse..."*

"Yes, it is. And I'll tell you what kind it is." Ben chuckled as he looked at the box. A Victorian style dollhouse, with lots of intricate little pieces no doubt. *"It's the kind I want to give our daughter or son that I can build."*

"He or she will love it I'm sure," Ava smiled as Lane handed her the package. She was still smiling as she tore at the paper and then froze.

"What's wrong dear?" Nancy, Ben's mother asked.

"Um. Nothing. I just..." Ava didn't finish her words. In a hurry she got up and ran out of the room.

Abbi jumped up and opened the box. There within it was a fur coat. Taking it by the shoulders, she pulled it out and held it at arm's length, biting her lip with worry.

Abbi dropped the coat back into the box as Ava came back into the room, fully clothed in her winter gear.

"Where are you going?" Mark asked.

She never said a word as she snatched up the box and hugged it to her chest as she stalked out of the room with tears streaming down her face.

"Where is she going?!" he asked again in disbelief, not quite trusting what he saw.

Luke spoke up. "She's gone to bury the box."

"Oh okay. Wait...What?!"

"Ava hates fur," Kim supplied. *"She's gone to bury it."*

"Is she nuts? That was a Russian sable, it's at least $20 grand. She can't just... just... bury it." He sputtered and hissed.

"She can and she has in the past." Kim cackled. "Her dumbass ex used to buy them for her all the time. And every time she'd bury it."

Mark jumped up and took off in the direction of the hall closet. "I can't let her do that. I gotta stop her."

Kim snorted. "Ha! Good luck with that!"

He slid to a stop in front of the hall closet, grabbing his coat, he threw it on and slapped a toque on his head. He tugged on his boots going out the front door. "Ava!" he ran yelling her name.

"What?" came her muffled response from behind him.

He spun around. His panic at the thought of her burying $20,000.00 came to a crashing halt when he saw her face. There she was, kneeling on the ground in front of a hole underneath the canopy of a Douglas fir. Tears streamed down her face as she tenderly placed the box inside the shallow hole.

He hunkered down beside her. "Ava why are you doing this?" Gently he took hold of her chin and raised it enough to look at her face. She was not the same person he sat with before the fireplace the previous night. The sadness he'd seen in her eyes tore at his heart.

She shook her head. Unable to talk.

"Ava honey. You can tell me; you know that right? I swear I won't say a thing to anyone, including Ben," he coaxed softly.

Ava looked him in the eyes.

"Go ahead," he said.

"My last relationship ended badly." He could tell she was so reluctant to talk about it. "My ex. Would buy me 'forgiveness gifts' he liked to call them." She looked down and pushed the earth around the box covering it with the dirt. "Every time we

got into a fight, and more often than naught, not even a fight, he would leave and return with something stupidly expensive." She mechanically continued to cover the box, staring straight ahead as if in a trance.

He could tell she was reliving it as if it was happening in the now.

"Eight years ago, the first time Kurt punched me for burning dinner. He had come home the next day with a pair of diamond earrings." She sniffed and wiped her nose. "I remember crying my eyes out while I flushed them down the toilet. I felt guilty doing that, like it was my fault that he punched me, because I burnt the dinner. He had asked me days later why I wasn't wearing them and smacked me when I told him I'd lost them."

"Come here." He put an arm around her and pulled her to him.

"The very next day had been the hottest day that summer, that time he returned with a fur coat, knowing full well I despised the killing of any animal for its fur." She took a deep breath as a tear slipped down her cheek. "I buried it a few days later. He didn't ask where the coat was until Fall. Now for the life of me, I can't remember the excuse I'd told him for the missing coat. Likely because I had suffered a concussion after he repeatedly smashed my head into the wall. Every time he thought I did something wrong, or I wasn't good enough, he would hit me and every time he would bring a fur coat home." She snickered and looked up at him. "You would think one of us would have learned huh?"

A blinding rage took over him, he dared not to let on, afraid if he did, she would have clammed up. Instead, he'd said,

"My god Ava, I'm so sorry that happened to you. Who the hell is this guy?" he asked, as he put the last bit of earth on the box.

"His family is very well off. His mother is the mayor and his father a plastic surgeon, one of the top ones in his field."

"Did you mention any of this to your mom? To Kim?"

"No! And don't you dare breathe a word of this to them or Ben. No one knows, only you," she whispered. "Promise me you won't say anything."

"I promise. Scout's honor." He smiled.

"Thank you, I mean that." She leaned over and placed a soft kiss on his cheek.

He was surprised when he'd felt the immediate rush of blood through his veins when her lips touched his face. He'd been shocked, really. Seeing her the way he did the night before, sure he'd been aroused, any man with blood in his veins would have been. But it didn't compare to the electrifying jolt he'd felt.

Living with her for the past few months always felt like they were just roommates. There was an attraction that neither could deny but they'd never acted on it. Never touched. Until that moment. He'd leaned back and searched her face. She felt it too, he could tell. Without a word, he closed the distance between them and softly touched his lips to hers. When he felt her arms reach around his neck he groaned. Hungry for the taste of her, he deepened the kiss.

A twig snapped in the brush, and they sprung apart, only to discover a doe staring at them with curious eyes before it turned and wandered away.

"I'm sorry, that shouldn't have happened," he said, whipping his toque off, he ran his hand through his hair.

"Right. You're right." Ava nodded.

"It will just make things really awkward don't you think?"
He looked at her, in a way, hoping she would disagree.

"Yes, you're right."

She cleared her throat and stood up. Looking down at him,
she said, "Um, I think we should maybe go back inside now."

"Absolutely, I'm sure they are wondering what happened to
us by now," he giggled, nervously and jumped up.

"Right. I just need to put the shovel away and I'll be inside,"
she told him.

"Sure thing." He said and started to walk away. But he
stopped. He turned to look at her, really look at her and asked,
"One thing. Um you don't have to tell me if you don't want to..."

"No, go ahead, ask."

"Okay. I'm curious. How many times have you done that
Ava?" He jerked his chin at the earth covered box.

She bent down and picked up the shovel. Chin held high;
Ava looked him in the eyes.

He saw the tears glisten for only a second before the mask
appeared and she answered. "Forty. I've done it forty times."

In that moment he knew that out of all the women he'd
known over the years, Ava Petersen was the strongest one he
ever met. And he was in love with her...

Chapter 21

"Oh my God, Ava, why didn't you tell us?!" Kim jabbed a finger at her own chest. "Why didn't you tell *me*?"

"Now take it easy Kim," Dean said. "She had her reasons."

Kim ignored his voice of reason. "I would have kicked his ass!" she roared, as she paced like a locked-up lioness.

"And that's exactly why I couldn't tell you Aunt Kim. Don't you see? Living with him was hard enough. I didn't need my family going to war for me. I just needed to get out and I did. Besides, it ended five years ago." Ava sighed. She really didn't have it in her to talk about it. She had long ago forgiven him because she had to... for herself. But she would never forget. No. She would never forget.

When Kim started going off again, Mark took one look at Ava and saw her shaking. "Kim. That's enough," he said, shooting her a warning look. "I don't think it's necessary to bring up the past."

"I agree." Tim chimed in. "One thing I don't understand though is what does this have to do with the ex, other than the furs?"

Still not knowing if Ava figured it out yet, Mark started to speak. "Because Ash is –"

A sudden pounding on the door had them all freezing in place and the dogs barking their heads off. Dean was the first to speak. "You expecting someone?" He raised his brows, looking at each of them.

Mark shook his head. "No." He answered while Kim closed the curtains and Ava stared wide eyed.

Pulling his gun from the back of his waistband, he went into cop mode and soundlessly made his way to the door just as the pounding came again.

"I know you're in there, open the bloody door!" It was Ben.

Relief flooded Dean as he put the safety back on his gun and tucked it away as he unlocked the door. Pulling it open, he grinned. "Ben! How the hell are you?"

"It's about time." Ben chuckled entering the house. "I stopped by the house and saw all the lights on, but no one was there. I thought I heard the dogs barking, am I right?" He asked, looking around.

"Sure are," Dean said, closing the door, nodding his head towards the back of the house. "They are all in the living room."

Ava looked over the back of the couch and saw Ben coming with Dean close behind. "Are mom and Annabelle, okay?"

"They are perfect." Ben beamed. He headed straight for the dogs and got down on all fours to greet them. While giving each a rubdown, he couldn't help but feel that something was off with the people in the room. He stood straight and looked from one to the other.

"So, how has everything been here?" Noticing the puppy on Ava's lap for the first time, he asked, "Whose puppy is that?" Bending over the back of the couch he gave the dog a scratch on the head. When no one answered he looked around at everyone again. Something *was* off. He could feel it the second he stepped into the house. "Come on guys. I know there is something wrong. Tell me."

They had all agreed it was best to keep everything from Abbi and Ben, but Kim couldn't. This was too big not to tell. Being the nurse that she was, she had to warn him to make sure he kept his mouth shut.

"Don't you dare tell Abbi; it will stop her milk supply. Ash whacked Eleanor over the head, the dog is hers and there is a shrine of Ava in the cellar of his house."

Ben squinted and shook his head. "Wait. *What?*"

Ava shrieked. "A *shrine?!* No one told me about a shrine!"

Oh shit.

There she went and did it again. Saying something before thinking it through. "It's not really a shrine per say," Kim said, trying to backpedal.

Tim spoke up. "Yeah, it is. Well in a psycho sort of way."

"What is wrong with you people?" Mark asked, shaking his head in disbelief. "You're not helping any." He sat beside Ava and put a protective arm around her.

Ben held up his hand. "Whoa. Start at the beginning,"

Everyone took their turn telling him all that had happened since that afternoon. When they were finished, Ben folded his arms across his chest. "Okay. So, what you're all saying, indirectly, is that Ash is really Kurt Falconer?"

"What? No–" Kim snickered.

"Ben. Have you ever thought of becoming a cop?" Dean asked.

"Huh, that is a possibility. But wouldn't Ava recognize him?" Tim questioned.

"*YES!*" Mark answered.

And Ava just sat in stunned silence. Ever since meeting Ash she knew there was always something that bugged her about him. It wasn't just what he said or how he treated her. Of course, those were all red flags, but it was something different. It was his mannerisms. Something people can't change no matter how hard they try. She was mad at herself for not realizing it sooner. For not connecting the dots. It took Ben looking at it from a different angle to see it. To see what was so blatantly in front of all their eyes the whole time.

She swallowed hard. Licking her suddenly dry lips Ava spoke. "Tim. To answer your question." She took a steadying breath as the tears fell from her eyes. "Kurt's father is a plastic surgeon. One of the best in the province. That's how I didn't recognize him I guess."

Tim shook his head in disbelief. "Who in hell would do *that*?"

"Kurt would. He's that much of a dick," Kim said over her shoulder while she checked the lock on the French doors that lead to the backyard. "He likely has been sulking ever since Ava ended it."

Ben rubbed his jaw. "But the question is *why* did he change his appearance? Was there a reason other than to come here?"

"You mean an accident? Right. I'm on it." Tim took his cell out of his pocket and left the room to make some calls.

"I don't give a shit what his intentions were. The point is he's here now and knows who Ava is," Mark said, swinging his gaze to her. He could tell she was not in a good spot mentally right now. He also knew that she was likely reliving every unwarranted attack from her monster of an ex. He reached out and took her hand in his, giving it a gentle squeeze, he brought it to his mouth and kissed her soft skin.

"Okay." Kim waved her hands in the air. "We know who he is, but he doesn't know that we know, am I right?"

Nodding, Dean answered. "Probably. Yes, that is if Ash is Kurt. At this point its all just speculation that it's him. We need to prove it's him."

"How? How are we going to do that?" Ava asked.

"DNA sample?" Kim offered.

Snickering, Mark looked at her. "And how are we going to do that?"

Kim shrugged as she sat on a lazy-boy recliner. "I don't know... ask for it? "

Mark rolled his eyes and sighed. "Don't you think that's a little suspicious?"

Before she could answer Tim came back into the room. All eyes turned, waiting for him to fill them in.

"I've got good news and bad news. The good news is the background check came back. There is no Ashton Davenport from Texas." He sighed and looked at Ava. "The bad news is... Kurt Falconer was in a car accident a year ago."

Kim jumped up. "See! So, it is Kurt!"

"Don't get too excited Kim," Tim cautioned. "Kurt Falconer is dead."

Kim crumpled back onto the chair, her mouth agape. "What do you mean, he's dead?!"

"His car crashed six months ago, and he was pronounced dead at the scene," Tim said. "I made a call to the OPP in the area of the accident, and they confirmed it."

Mark looked at Ava. Expecting to see a look of shock on her face he was surprised to see the ice queen mask in place. The wall was back up and there was no way anyone would be tearing that down.

Truth be told, Ava was wracking her brain, trying to figure out who it was. If indeed Kurt was dead, who else could it be? She never dated anyone other than him, so it wasn't a past boyfriend. She was dumbfounded as to who it could be.

"Ava," Ben came to stand before her. Squatting down, he took her hands in his. "Is there anyone you can think of who it might be? Someone you worked with in the past or a relative of Kurt's maybe?"

She shook her head. "I don't have a clue who it might be. He doesn't have any brothers, and his friends, I knew all of them at the time we dated. Ash isn't any of them."

"What about a co-worker of his?" Tim asked.

"Kurt never worked. His parents gave him everything," Kim said, with contempt.

"Instead of trying to figure out who he is, shouldn't we be trying to figure out what to do about him?" Mark asked, looking at Dean and Tim. "I mean, he doesn't know that we know what's in the cellar, and he doesn't know that we found

Ava at the old mansion. So, as far as he's concerned, we are clueless."

"Except for the fact that Kim thinks she saw him by the barn at the Anderson place." Ben pointed out as he stood. "I mean, he was left alone with Ava, here. How else would she have gotten there if she weren't left there by him?"

"I still say it was a ghost," Kim mumbled under her breath.

"Right. So, we'll assume he knows," Dean agreed.

"Unless he didn't see that you saw him," Mark added.

"Well, I... ah, don't know if he did. I was too busy screaming, thinking old lady Anderson was... er... um." She squirmed in her seat. "Well, you know." She didn't want to point out to the room at large that she thought he was getting the life sucked out of him by a ghost. They already thought she was nuts. She didn't need to reaffirm it with that admission.

"What I need to do is call him," Ava said, calmly.

"Like hell you are," Mark growled.

"No, not on your life," Kim said, shaking her head.

Dean pointed a finger at Ava. "That's exactly what you need to do."

Despite the squawking coming from her two roommates, she knew she had to. It was the only way to gauge his reaction. "Ben, can you give me a hand please?" Ava asked, looking up at him.

"Of course." He helped her to stand. "Where is it you want to go?" he asked, as he watched the expression on his best friend's face over the top of Ava's head. Mark was crushed. Ben decided he needed to have a chat with Mark and soon before the guy's heart broke even more.

"Outside, please. I want to talk to you alone," she said. Taking the crutches Ben held out to her, she made her way to the doors and waited for him to open them.

Once outside, Ben closed the door, and looked at her. "Out with it, Ava."

"I need you to talk to Mark. Things are..." She looked at her feet. "Developing between us."

"Okay," Ben nodded slowly, thinking to himself that it was about damn time. "About what?"

Ava looked him in the eyes. "I need you to convince him to back off where Ash is concerned. I know he's only worried about me, but I don't need him defending me. I don't want him taking matters into his own hands like you did with Raven."

"There was a reason for that."

"I know there was. He was out to kill you. Ash isn't out to kill anyone. He's just... I don't know."

Ben nodded. "I will talk to him; I'd already planned on it. But, Ava, you don't know what Ash's intentions are, because you don't even know who he is. You can't trust him. Don't trust him."

"I don't. I'm not totally convinced he's a stranger. What's the odds of two different people having a fetish for fur?" She chuckled.

He smiled and placed his hand on the doorknob. "Good point. Now, come on, let's get you back inside."

Ava made her way through the opened doorway. Not wanting to trip over the area rug on the floor at the door she watched her footing and entered the silent room. She thought it odd that no one was talking, until she looked up. Her eyes darted around the room. Mark was gone.

"Hello, Ava."

At the all too familiar voice, her breath caught in her throat as her eyes zeroed in on the person coming around the corner from the kitchen. It was Ash.

Chapter 22

Mark was pissed. After much debate, Dean and Tim had decided it was the perfect chance to see Ash in action and so they let him in the house when he came knocking. Mark had to leave. He walked past the man without a word or a glance. He had to, before he smashed his fist into Ash's smug face.

His plan was to go through to Ava's room and out the back doors onto the porch where he could meet up with her and Ben, but when he rounded the corner, he saw they were gone. Likely back into the house where Ava had to face the bastard. Mark felt an instant need to go charging in the room but knew if he did all hell would break out. No. He was better off to stay clear of it. She was safe with two cops, Ben and an aunt that would go berserk on Ash's ass if he dared say one thing out of line. Mark headed straight for the woods to Ben's house where he could wait it out at a safe distance.

He had just stepped free of the trees when his phone started ringing. He was tempted to let it go to voicemail, but one look at the screen, he knew he needed to take the call. It was Ava's brother Luke.

"Hey man, what's up."

"Not too much Mark. I got a letter here for Ava. I tried calling her, but she must be busy or something."

"Yeah, she is. Do you want me to get her to call you back?" Mark asked.

"Actually, it's not that big of a deal. I really called because I was concerned when she didn't answer. Lane and I are coming up there in a few days. I'll just bring it with me."

"Everything is fine. I'll let her know you'll be up. Ah one thing. That letter, who is it from, do you know?" Mark asked.

"Let me check the postmark. One second, I'll grab it."

Mark waited, listening to Luke's footsteps echoing through the phone. "Here it is. It's from Montreal. No forwarding address though. Say, I have to go, there's a knock at my door."

"Okay, thanks. I'll mention it to her. See you in a few days," Mark said. Hitting the end button. He glanced around the yard and shoved the phone in his pocket as he made his way to the back porch.

The way the light shone from the pole light in the yard, it was pure luck when something caught his eye. Under one of the trees that lined the yard, Mark could see fresh clumps of dirt were strewn beneath it.

What the hell is that?

He stalked over to the tree thinking it was just one of the dogs digging for a buried bone. "Son of a bitch." He hissed, looking in the hole at something white.

Grabbing a stick, he crouched down and poked at the box Ava, and he had buried at Christmas. He was surprised at how intact it was after all these months. Maneuvering the stick around he flipped the lid off and was shocked to find the coat gone.

In the dim light, he tried to focus on the inside bottom of the box. Now one would think maybe one of the dogs had dug it up and dragged the coat off into the woods. And maybe just maybe the lid righted itself when they did, but the dogs didn't have the ability to write.

Squinting, a wave of anger spread through his body as his eyes took in the words written on the bottom ... *'I've missed you'.*

Mark never did see the contents of the box when Ava had received it, but he was a betting man, and he would lay all his money on it, that there wasn't any personal message written there before. He hated to, but the only person that would know, was Ava. Sighing, he grabbed it and headed towards home. The only thing that eased his dread was the hope that Ash was still there. Mark would love to see the look on his face when he was faced with the evidence he held in his hands.

TRYING FOR A LIGHT tone, Ava, held her head high and carefully made her way to the recliner to sit down. "Hi Ash, what brings you here?" There was no way she was giving Ash the chance to sit beside her ever again.

"Ah. I was going to see if I could talk to you..." He looked around the room at the eyes staring at him, even the dogs were watching him. "Alone?"

Ben pursed his lips and shook his head. "Nah, I don't think so mate. Dean, Tim, Kim? What do you three, think?"

Tim and Dean agreed, and Kim moseyed over to the couch and plopped herself down. Patting the seat next to her, she sighed in contentment, and said, "Why don't you sit right beside me, Ashy boy?"

Ava watched as the smugness vanished and a look of pure hatred flashed on Ash's face. "Fine," he said, sitting down. His gaze fell on the coat that someone had tossed on the coffee table. Ava watched his facial expressions do a 180. "I see you got my gift." He looked at her, a smile on his face.

Ava couldn't believe how quickly he was able to jump from one emotion to the next. She frowned.

Who the hell is this guy?

Despite knowing what happened to Kurt, she still fully didn't believe he was gone. But this man wasn't him, she knew for certain. Once her ex was mad, he was in a rage until he took it out on something.

She cleared her throat. "Ah I did yes. I'm sorry but I can't accept that. You will need to take it back." Expecting him to flip out, she was shocked when he laughed.

"Well of course you can. It's a gift. I promise, no strings attached."

Kim leaned towards him. "What she means is she's allergic to fur."

"What? That's ludicrous. No one is allergic to fur!"

"Yeah, she is, she gets like these big oozie bumps all over her whenever she meets it. But only when they are made into a coat." Kim lied.

Ben joined in. "It's true. Someone sent her one for Christmas and the second she breathed in the enclosed air she got hives. It was a bloody mess."

"Is this true?" Ash looked at Ava, horrified. Likely he was calculating the cost of each of the furs in his cellar and realizing he had a useless small fortune sitting at home in the dark.

"It is." She nodded and stopped at once. It just dawned on her that the coat sitting on the table before them was the same coat that Mark, and she had buried. That could only mean one thing... Ash had been around a lot longer than he claimed to be. How else would it have gotten from the box to the table?

Tim's phone started ringing, he excused himself from the room just as the front door banged open. Ava's eyes went to Mark walking over the threshold. She was falling in love with him more every time she laid eyes on him. Realizing Ash was watching her every move, she quickly averted her gaze as Mark walked into the room. Ash already despised the fact that they were friends and roommates. No good would come of it if he guessed how she really felt about Mark.

"Look what I found." Mark announced to the room as he held the box for all to see. Sticking it under Ash's nose, he asked, "You wouldn't know anything about this, would you buddy?"

Ash snickered. "What? An empty box?"

For some reason, his reaction pissed Mark off. He pointed towards the words written on the inside. "This! What the hell is this?" He demanded, flinging the box at Ash.

Shocked, Ava covered her mouth and gasped. "Mark!" She never had seen him lose his cool. Sure, he wasn't afraid to show fear, or disgust but never had she seen him mad at another person.

"I have no idea what you're talking about," Ash answered, calmly.

Mark bobbed his head up and down. He chuckled in a mechanical way. "Right. I see what you're doing here." He rubbed his index finger along his brow then pointed it at Ash. "You're trying to play yourself off as the innocent lovesick fool," Mark said, taking a step back. He knew if he didn't, he was going to punch that sly smile off Ash's face.

Ava grabbed the box and looked at Mark. She knew exactly where he found it. Under the pine tree over at Ben's house. "Umm. Mark did you...?"

His gaze softened as it swung in her direction. He knew what she was thinking. "No Ava, I didn't dig it up." He looked pointedly at Ash. "It already was by someone else."

Kim crossed to where Ava was sitting, taking the box from her, she read the words scrawled on the bottom. She looked at Ash. "Who the hell are you?"

"Ashton Davenport," he smiled, like he was getting some enjoyment out of it.

Ava stared at him. He didn't look like Kurt but the way he acted she could swear it was him. Not at first of course. At first, he had treated her like a real man should treat a woman. It wasn't until the night he'd left her to walk alone in the dark that the real him started to appear. She had to get the hell away from him. Without a word she grabbed her crutches and stood. She narrowly missed tripping over Mouse who had been laying beside her. Thankfully, Mark was there quickly to stop her from falling to the floor. She mumbled her thanks and continued on her way. Her only thought was to get out of the room.

Mark followed her as she made her way through the kitchen to the hall to her bedroom.

"Here Ava, let me get the door for you." He reached around her to turn the knob and pushed it open. He followed her in and softly closed the door behind him.

"I'm sorry Mark. I just had to get the hell out of there... away from him."

He watched as she visibly shook. "I know. It's time I got rid of him. He isn't welcome in this house." Mark turned to do just that when Ava's soft voice stopped him.

"No. He needs to stay until I can figure out who he is." She sat heavily on the bed. "Will you stay with me?"

Mark inwardly groaned. He had been in her room plenty of times but that was before they'd kissed. He wanted nothing more than to lay her back on the pillows and make love to her, slowly and thoroughly but that would need to wait for the perfect time, and this wasn't it. Pulling the collar away from his throat, he swallowed hard.

"Sure," he squeaked. Clearing his throat, he tried again. "Yes of course." He pointed to the bay window filled with pillows. "I'll just sit over there." Flopping down on one he looked her in the eyes and asked, "What makes you think you're going to figure out who he is?"

She rubbed her forehead and sighed "He reminds me so much of Kurt it isn't funny. There must be a connection."

"A friend? One that you have never met maybe?"

She shook her head, "No. He didn't have many friends and the ones he did, I knew them."

Mark nodded. "And you already said he didn't have co-workers..."

Her mouth set to a grim line she shook her head again. "Nope. Kurt never worked. Aunt Kim was wrong, his parents didn't need to give him a cent. When his grandfather died, he left everything to him. Surprisingly, he had more money than his parents did."

"Hmm..." Mark pursed his lips. He was never any good at figuring this stuff out. Getting up, he went to the door and opened it, yelling for Kim and Ben.

"What's wrong?" Kim rushed into the room followed by Ben.

Closing the door, Mark turned and looked at them. "Nothing. We need help figuring this out."

Ben raised his brows. "Figuring what out?" he asked, taking the spot Mark had vacated. Kim settled beside him, and the two looked as confused as he felt. "Ash... and where he could know Ava from," Mark said, sitting on the floor beside the bed. Leaning back against it, he filled them in on everything that had happened since his return from Ben's.

"So that's why you flipped out over a box," Ben rubbed his jaw. "Was there writing in it when you buried it, Ava?"

"No. Nothing was in it, not even a note saying who it was from."

"Okay. So, it's obvious that Ash dug it up to get the coat and give it to Ava, right?" Kim asked, looking to everyone for confirmation.

"Yeah. But why when he has a cellar full of them?" Mark asked. "Why that one in particular?"

Ben looked at Ava. "He has to be someone who knew that Kurt gave you furs. Not necessarily the reason why he did, but that he did."

"True," Kim nodded. Feeling guilty, Kim got up and went over to Ava to hug her. "I'm so sorry he was such a monster to you Ava," she said, with tears filling her eyes.

"It's over Aunt Kim, I've forgiven him and moved on. Please don't dwell on it," she begged.

As she went back to sit beside Ben again, she said, "If ever another guy treats you that way, you promise me you will tell me."

"That won't be necessary." Mark spoke up. Leaning his head back he looked Ava in the eyes. "I will never mistreat you; I can promise you that." He took her hand in his and brought it to his lips laying a soft kiss on the back of it.

Kim jabbed Ben in the ribs, a huge grin on her face. Leaning over she whispered conspiringly as if she had a hand in it. "It's about damn time, huh?"

Ben snickered. "Yeah Kim, it's about damn time."

Happy for Mark and Ava, Kim sighed. She wondered if she would ever feel that loved by someone. Hell, she had been wondering that ever since last year, when their little family had a reunion of sorts to come and visit Abbi. Meeting Ben was the icing on the cake... Wait a minute, could it be? Kim shot up from her seat. "I got it!" She exclaimed excitedly.

"Got what?" Mark asked, as all eyes turned to her.

"Ava. Do you remember that family reunion you and Kurt went to?" she asked.

"Uh, no."

"You know!! The one where his family was coming from Alberta to visit," she said, hoping to jog her memory. "He made you wear a fur coat; it was quite the shindig." Kim searched her own memory, flinging her hand out, she said, "You didn't want to go but he insisted because his cousin was coming, and he wanted you to meet him... what the hell was his name?" She started pacing back and forth.

Ava remembered it now. It was more of a family gala than a reunion. She even said to Kurt it was only to see who had the most money in the family. That remark had earned her a smack across the head the second they had pulled away from the venue. Shaking her head to lay to rest those thoughts, she tried to recall the cousin Kurt was so eager for her to meet. He had been a strange one indeed, he'd followed her around like a lost puppy. As his face materialized in her foggy memory, a coldness seeped into her bones. It was the face of Ashton Davenport.

Chapter 23

Aknock at Ava's bedroom door had all eyes turning to it. Ben got up and opened the door a crack. Tim stood there. "Yeah?"

"I need to talk to you guys."

Ben opened the door allowing him to enter. "Where is Ash?" he asked, as he shut it.

Jerking a thumb over his shoulder he chuckled. "Being interrogated by Dean."

"Ha!" Kim barked. "Good. He needs a hard-assed cop questioning him."

"That he is. So, I got off the phone with the local OPP detachment. They are on their way here to question him about Eleanor. Doc finally convinced her to give a statement."

"Question him?" Mark hissed. "Shouldn't they be arresting him for assault at the very least?"

Tim raised a hand. "I know why you're upset Mark but it's standard procedure. They will take him into the station. Forensics found a print in her house. But nothing is showing up in the system."

"If nothing is showing up, how are you going to see if it's his?" Ava asked.

"They will question him and if they think he's guilty, he'll be arrested, his prints will be taken and a search warrant for his house will be issued. If they're a match, they have their guy. It's as simple as that," Tim told them.

"What about the pop cans I left on the counter? Can't those be checked for his prints and for whatever he used to drug Ava with?" Mark asked.

"Good point. I'll tell them to bag those up as well."

Ava leaned back against the pillows and rubbed her eyes. She was so incredibly tired, fighting to keep her eyes open, she rolled onto her side and looked at Tim. "Don't let on you know, but his name isn't Ash or even Ashton."

"You remember, don't you?" Kim asked, relieved. She had been worried for a bit, no one so young should have such a bad memory.

"Yeah," she mumbled in response. "His name is Sebastian Falconer. I'll tell you all I know about him, but later. Right now, I'd like to have a nap if that's okay?'

"Of course, it is," Mark said, looking to Tim for confirmation.

"Ahh one thing." Tim looked at each of them one at a time. "No one is to mention that Dean and I were with you two tonight at Ash's. I doubt it will come to that, but it could ruin any investigation if it does."

"Didn't someone say there were cameras?" Ben asked.

Kim nodded. "Yeah, there is. We had to get creative to avoid them."

"We saw them too, that's why we came through the back yard." Tim grinned as he made his way to the door.

Kim looked at Mark in astonishment. "Why the hell didn't we think of that?"

Mark shrugged. "Apparently, it's because we like to live dangerously," he replied dryly. Getting up, he bent towards Ava, kissing her forehead as Ben and Kim walked out of the room too.

Ava snaked her hand out to grab hold of his arm. Looking up at him, she said, "Stay with me?"

Mark sent her a soft smile. "Absolutely."

Taking the edge of the blanket, he pulled it over her like she was the filling of a pita. He crawled over and laid behind her. Pulling her into the circle of his arms he tucked her against him and held her until her soft breathing slowed down to a steady pace.

Mark peeked over her shoulder to look at her face. His heart just about stopped in his chest when his eyes took in her beauty. How he could be so blinded by his feelings for her for so long was beyond him, but he was no longer denying it. He buried his nose in her hair and inhaled the intoxicating scent of her. It was like a shot of morphine directly in his veins. Only instead of relaxing him, it went right to his groin.

Hard as a rock, Mark inwardly groaned his frustration as he slid back away from her backside. If he didn't move, Ava wouldn't be sleeping for long. Carefully he pulled his arm out from under her head and replaced it with a pillow. Dropping a soft kiss on her hair he turned and left the room. It was time to see what was happening with Ash.

Heading down the hall he stopped when he heard raised voices. Cocking his head, he strained to make out the words and who was talking. He soundlessly made his way to the kitchen and stopped. *Well, that escalated quickly*, he thought as he took in the scene before him.

Ben was talking calmly, hands out, trying to diffuse the situation and Tim and Dean were standing in cop mode, guns drawn and pointed at Ash. Mark saw him slowly backing up, holding a chair as if he were fighting off a tiger. In a way he was. Kim was jumping up and down as she jabbed a finger his way.

"Stop *lying*! Your name is Sebastian." She shouted.

Mark had the upper hand on Ash, he had no clue he was being stalked from behind. Standing directly behind him, Mark tapped him on the shoulder. Ash turned around and dropped the chair a notch. This gave Mark the perfect opportunity to strike. With all the pent-up anger and frustration, Mark's fist connected. Ash dropped like a sack of potatoes, sprawled out cold on the floor.

Ben relaxed. "Bloody hell, what took you so long to show up?"

"Holy crap!" Kim looked at Mark with admiration in her eyes. "I didn't know you had it in you Mark."

Dean whistled low. "Wowee! Man, that's some impressive shit right there. Remind me never to piss you off." He chuckled, and smacked Mark on the back.

Tim bent down and flipped Ash onto his stomach, grabbing his hands. He slapped a pair of handcuffs on his wrists just as someone pounded on the front door. Mark went to look out the side window, it was the local police.

He pulled the door open and grinned. "Come on in, the party just ended."

Within minutes Tim and Dean filled the police in, once getting the whole story they wasted no time taking a groggy Ash to an awaiting police cruiser. They collected the pop cans and assured them they would be checked for foreign substances.

Kim stood in the middle of the kitchen and clapped her hands together. "So now what do we do?"

Ben grabbed his jacket off the chair he'd tossed it on earlier and pulled it on. "I'm heading back to Abbi and Annabelle shortly." He looked at his friend, as Lucy danced around his legs, bending down he picked the little Yorkie up. "I was going to see if you could stay at the house again tonight, Mark?"

Mark nodded. "Yeah, of –"

"Ah, Ben." Tim interrupted. "Instead of Mark going, how about we go?" he gestured to Kim and Dean. He looked at the two of them. "That is if you guys want to?"

Ben shrugged, setting the dog on the floor. "Sure, if the three of you want to. It's only for the night, Doc finally gave us the all clear to come home tomorrow."

"Yeah, I'll go," Kim said. "We can clean up, so you don't have to when you get home."

"Sounds like a plan to me." Dean agreed.

"Thanks." Ben made his way to the door with Brutus and Molly following on his heels. Bending down he gave each dog a good rubdown and said to each of them, "Tomorrow guys, we will be home tomorrow." Standing up he looked at everyone in the room, "And I'll see you all tomorrow too. I gotta go, Abbi's likely wondering what happened to me." With that, he ran outside to his car.

Kim turned to Mark. "Will you and Ava be okay here alone?"

Dean snickered. "I think they can figure it out."

"It doesn't hurt to ask!"

"Stop being a mother hen and go pack a bag, lady," Dean said, pushing her towards the hall.

"Did you just call me a bag lady?"

"I don't know, did I?" Dean grinned.

She sniffed and sent him a dismissive look as she made her way to the hall.

"That woman is going to drive me nuts, isn't she?" Dean asked, looking at Tim.

Tim chuckled and nodded. "Yup. I guess you're a sucker for punishment."

Dean leaned against the counter and crossed his arms then looked at Mark. "What's up, you've been pretty quiet."

Mark rubbed the back of his neck. "Something that is just puzzling me about this Ash thing."

"What do you mean?" Tim asked, his hand on his cell phone, ready to phone any new info into the police.

"How did he know the coat was buried under the tree? He would have needed to be here to see us burying it." Mark pulled out a chair at the table and sat down. "And why that coat, what was so special about that one when he had a dozen at home?"

"Those are all questions that will be asked, I'm sure. Don't worry about it, the police will get to the bottom of it," Dean said.

"Yeah, I suppose you're right." Mark agreed as Kim came back into the room with a bag slung over her shoulder.

"I'm ready." She announced. "Let's go."

"Right, so should we take Mouse too?" Dean asked.

"Ava's pretty attached to him, I think she'll miss him when she wakes up if you do," Mark said.

"Okay, we'll see you tomorrow then." Kim went to Mark and gave him a hug. "Take care of her, will you?" She asked as she backed away.

"Jesus, woman, you're not leaving the country for crying out loud." Dean laughed.

"No, I'm not. And you can shut the hell up!" She smiled sweetly at him.

Mark chuckled. "Everything will be fine Kim," he said, getting up to walk them to the door. "Go clean." He waved them off and stood in the open doorway while they made their way across the yard, the dogs leading the way. It wasn't until they disappeared into the bush that he closed the door.

Sighing, he looked around the empty room. He glanced at the clock on the stove. It was long past dinnertime but the grumbling in his stomach told him it was time for food. Crossing the room, he went to the fridge and yanked it open. He would whip up a bacon and cheese omelet. Gathering the eggs and bacon, he decided he would toss in onions, mushrooms, and peppers too. Ava's cell phone buzzing on the counter had him glancing at it. Kim was calling.

"Hello Kim," he said, tucking it on his shoulder while he went to work.

AVA AWOKE TO HER CELL phone ringing. She searched the bed with her hand, coming up empty, she glanced towards the bedside table where it laid. Grabbing it up she stared at the screen and frowned. Kurt... Her sleep induced mind couldn't help but wonder, how did he get this number?

"What the hell do you want?" she asked in a way of a greeting.

"Ava. You're in danger."

"Ha, you would know all about that wouldn't you Kurt."

"I'm serious Ava. I'm sorry for all that I did to you. I can't take that back, but I can warn you. He's coming for you..."

"What are you talking about? The only person that would come for me is you, and you're dead."

"I know," he said, a sadness in his voice Ava had never heard before. "My cousin, Sebastian did it, he messed with my car. He knew I was coming to see you last year. To give you one last gift in hopes you'd forgive me. Not to get back together, but for you to know how sorry I was for treating you so badly."

"Like usual, your timing is wrong. But what was the gift you were bringing?"

"A Russian sable coat...."

Ava bolted upright in bed fully awake now. She knew she had been dreaming. Despite that it was Kurt that had come to her in a dream, she felt something deep in her bones. Something she hadn't felt in a long time, since before meeting him. And that something was peace. Looking around her bedroom, she softly said, "I forgive you Kurt."

Whether he truly did visit her in her dream world or not, she could honestly say she forgave him and mean it this time. Before she always said she did, but deep down she never could. Tossing the covers aside, she picked up her crutches and stood. She needed to tell Mark about her dream.

She could smell some delicious aroma coming from the kitchen. Smiling, Ava made her way to the door and down the hall, as she went, she decided it was time that Mark and she had a little heart to heart talk. She was finally free from the demons of her past and was ready to fall in love. This time she knew it was the real kind of love she just hoped Mark was in it for the long haul.

Chapter 24

Kim was cleaning the litter box in the animal's room when Dean came up to her.

"Kim."

"Yeah?" she said, looking up at him.

"What is this and where does it go?" Dean held it out for her inspection.

Taking it from him, she turned it over and looked at it. "That is a remote for one of the ceiling fans. Where did you find it?" She glanced up at him as she handed the control back.

"Believe it or not, it was on the back of a toilet." He chuckled.

"Ha! Well, I guess you go around to all the rooms and see which one it works on," she said, tying the bag of used cat litter.

"Trade you?" He held his hand out for the bag.

"Sure." She handed it to him and took the remote. She was shocked when he offered her a hand to help her stand. Taking it, she grinned and gestured towards him with the remote. "You know... you're a pretty decent guy when you want to be."

"Yeah? Well, you'll be seeing more of that side of me real soon," he drawled.

"What do you mean by that?"

Before Dean could respond, Tim came into the room with a foul look on his face. Kim raised her brows and jerked her chin towards the bag he was holding at arm's length "What's that?"

"Not sure." He shook his head. "I cleaned out the fridge and it looks like it's been in there a while. Where should I put it?"

"I'm on garbage duty. Give it to me." Dean took it from him and walked out of the room towards the kitchen. Kim followed and headed in the opposite direction to the front of the house and the living room with Tim following her.

Pointing the remote at the ceiling fan, she hit the power button. Nothing. Moving onto the dining area, she did the same thing.

"What are you doing?" he asked.

"Trying to figure out which fan this works on." She gestured with the remote. "Dean found it sitting on the back of the toilet."

"The kitchen."

She looked at him. "How do you know?"

Tim shrugged. "Because I had it in my hand when I went to the washroom. I must have left it there."

She cocked a brow at him. "Okay..."

"The battery is dead. I was looking for one."

"In the bathroom? You know what?" She shook her head and chuckled. "I don't want to know."

The two headed to the kitchen and she sat it on the counter. She glanced at Tim. "Remind me to look for batteries later, will ya?"

Dean came in from outside, stamping his feet as he slammed the door closed. "Brrrrr, it's colder than a witch's teat out there. It's June for cripes sake!"

"It's also Canada." Kim cackled. "We can have four seasons in a day, didn't you know?"

"No! Is it always like this?" he asked, rubbing his hands up and down his arms.

"No, not always. You'll get used to it." Tim grinned. "So, what are we eating?"

"Is everything cleaned up?" Kim asked. Pulling open the fridge doors she stuck her head inside.

Tim nodded. "Yeah. I vacuumed upstairs. Beds are made with fresh linen, and I cleaned Abbi's office."

Dean leaned against the wall and stuffed his hands in his pockets. "Bathrooms are all done, and I dusted the living room."

"Okay," Kim said, closing the fridge doors. "I cleaned their bedroom, checked the nursery, and cleaned the animal's room." She ticked off each task on her fingers. "I also did the laundry and the kitchen. So, everything is done." She leaned against the fridge. Jerking a thumb over her shoulder she looked at Tim. "Magnificent job on the fridge by the way. You cleaned out so much that it's damn near empty." She chuckled. "How about we go grab something from Mack's to eat and pick up some groceries while we are at it?"

"Sounds good to me," Dean said, and Tim nodded.

"Good, let's get out of here." She grabbed her keys off the counter and Abbi's sweater that was hanging on a chair.

"Wait." Dean stalked over to the coats hanging on the pegs behind the door. Taking Ben's bright yellow coat, he stuffed his arms in the sleeves and zipped it up to his chin. Reaching up on the top shelf, he snagged a woolly hat and pulled it on his head. Giving a curt nod, he said, "Okay. I'm ready."

"Are you sure?" Kim nodded, with a mischievous grin. "Do you want some mittens too?"

"You two can laugh all you want. I'm not freezing for no-body."

"Well, at least you won't get lost with that coat on." Tim laughed.

Kim let out a shrill whistle, calling the dogs to the kitchen. They all came running into the room. Excitedly, they planted their butts on the floor looking expectantly at her. "Want to go for a car ride?" She didn't have to say it twice. As soon as the door was open, all three bolted out and waited patiently by her car.

Dean ran almost as fast as the dogs. "Hurry up, woman. Get the car started and some heat going, will you?" He yanked open the passenger door and all but dove onto the front seat as the dogs piled in and over him.

Tim looked at Kim and laughed. "Should we tell him we changed our minds and decided to walk?"

Kim cackled. "You want to make him cry?" she asked, while they made their way to the car. Getting in, she started it and put it into drive. Pulling out of the driveway she set her speed to her usual 10 k/ph. As they came to her driveway she almost stopped.

Dean rocked back and forth in his seat, chanting. "Keep going, keep going."

She ignored him. "Do you think we should check up on them?" She swung her gaze to her two companions as she turned down the radio.

A resounding, "No!" came from them both causing her to jump. "Fine! We won't then." Kim scowled as she drove off towards the center of the village.

Chapter 25

Mark glanced up as Ava made her way into the kitchen. "Hey there sleepy head. I was going to bring you dinner," he said, sliding an omelet onto an awaiting plate. "I hope you're hungry. I used one too many eggs I think."

Ava pulled out a stool at the counter and sat down staring at the food. "I'd say." She picked up her fork and cut it in half. "Here, we can share this one." Pushing half onto the empty plate, she looked at him and smiled. "Come." She patted the stool beside her. "Sit with me."

A small smile tugged at the corners of his lips. He swallowed hard. What was it with this woman that made his gut twist into a knot? She had laid in his arms not more than a couple of hours ago he'd a slight problem then but nothing he couldn't control, and yet, now he felt like a teenager on his first date. Shaking his head, he came around the counter and sat next to her.

They dug into their food with silent gusto. Each lost in their own thoughts. Mark just remembered that she had no clue Ash was likely sitting in a comfy jail cell at this very moment.

"Umm, Ava –"

"I had the strangest dream –"

They spoke at the same time.

"Go ahead," he said. "Tell me about your dream."

Ava laid her fork down and turned toward him. He resisted the urge to reach out and smooth the line on her brow as she retold it and was mesmerized as he watched the emotions play on her soft skin. His breath caught in his throat when she looked him in the eyes. Before, her eyes were always guarded, as if she didn't trust anyone, but not anymore. For the first time, he saw a calmness in them. Someone who was at peace with their world.

Ava smiled. "Did you hear anything I said?" She ducked her head shyly and leaned forward, her silky hair covering her face.

"What?" Mark looked taken aback. "Me not hear anything? Of course, I did." He grinned as she looked at him. Reaching out, he tucked her hair behind her ear and lowered his hand. His thumb followed the graceful curve along her jawline to her lips.

"Do you realize how beautiful you are to me?"

Many times, Mark had told her she was beautiful but not like that. Ava held her breath waiting. Waiting for him to end it with 'in a purely platonic way,' like he had so many times before. When he didn't Ava was stunned, but not for long. She was seizing this moment before it slipped away. Grabbing his shirt in both her fists she yanked him to her and planted her lips on his before he could chicken out and run away. When she felt his arms slip around her waist, dragging her off her chair, she felt a triumphant thrill course through her veins as he pulled her close. Their lips never parting, she wrapped her legs around his waist as he hiked her closer.

Mark carried her to her bedroom, stopping only long enough to nudge the door closed with his foot. He headed straight for the bed and gently laid her down on it, pulling away only long enough to take his shirt off.

Placing his hands on either side of her, he gazed down into her eyes. He was almost too afraid to touch her. Afraid that if he did, he would wake up from the dream he was surely having.

Ava reached for him, running her hands along his muscled forearms, reveling at the feel of his veins under her palms. She wrapped her arms around his neck and pulled him down beside her. She sighed in delight when his lips sought out hers once again. To Ava, it felt like the very first time they had kissed. It left her breathless and wanting more. The funny thing was, it felt like he wasn't into it. Breaking the kiss off, she pulled away from him and searched his face.

"What's wrong?"

He shook his head. "Nothing."

"Mark..."

"Seriously, there isn't anything wrong. It's just..." He rolled on to his back and sighed.

Reaching out, she laid a hand on his face, turning it towards her. "Tell me, please."

"Fine." He sat up, his back to her. "I don't know how to treat you, okay? I'm afraid of screwing this up." He turned and looked at her. "You know I've had a shit ton of relationships... flings mostly. Nothing real... nothing serious..." When she didn't say anything, he continued. "What I'm mostly afraid of is losing you. Not having you in my life at all would crush me." *Is it too soon to tell her exactly how I feel?* To hell with it, life was about taking risks and if he didn't tell her now, he never would.

He turned on his side facing her and leaned on his arm. With his free hand he lifted her chin and kissed her softly on the lips. Leaning away, he looked her in the eyes and held his breath. "Ava, I'm in love with you. I have been since the second day I met you."

Despite being blinded by tears, she smiled. "The second day, huh?"

"Yeah," he nodded. "The first day, you beat my ass in the race along the beach." He brought her hand to his lips and laid a soft kiss on the back of it. "Took me till the next day to realize you were the one." he murmured. "And now you know why I don't want to screw this up. Why, I can't. If you're not ready, I get that, and I'll wait. But if you aren't interested in nothing more than a casual fling, I'm telling you right now, I can't and I won't take this any further."

Ava sat up and leaned into him, her lips seeking out his. She pushed against him until he was laying on the pillows and she was on top. She purred deep in her throat when she felt his hardness against her hip. Pulling her mouth away, she looked into his eyes and whispered. "I've been in love with you since the first day... when I beat your ass in that race."

"Wooohooo!" he shouted. "Buckle up baby, I'm taking you to see what heaven in the moonlight is like."

He took her in his arms and buried his face in the side of her neck as her squeals of delight echoed off the walls. They soon turned into soft moans as his lips trailed down her neck to brush against the swell of her breasts. His hands reached for the hem of her shirt as his tongue darted out, tasting the skin of her cleavage. He backed away as Ava sat up to remove her shirt.

Mark staggered back, landing square on his butt as he looked at her in amazement. She was stunning, sitting there in a black bra, her skin and hair kissed from the moonlight shining through the window. She almost appeared ethereal. Almost. But Ava wasn't a delicate flower. He knew she was tough as nails which made him want her more than he ever realized. Without thinking things through, he uttered two words he never thought he would ever say again in this lifetime.

"Marry me?"

Ava blinked in stunned silence. The only thing she could muster was, "Beg your pardon?" She watched as his Adams apple bobbed up and down. Ava knew at that moment; he was at once regretting his question. Pulling the blankets up around her neck she waited for the moment he started to backpedal his statement.

He looked at her with what he hoped was his sincerest expression and swallowed the bile that suddenly sprang to the back of his throat.

"I said marry me." He held up a hand when she started to speak. "Hear me out. We love each other, right?" He looked at her, tilted his head and raised his brows. At her nod, he continued. "I don't want to waste another second of my life waiting for the perfect moment to ask you. This is the perfect moment. I'm not saying we have to rush out tomorrow and tie the knot. *Whoa—!*"

Ava tackled him. With him flat on his back, her lips claimed his in a soul shattering kiss.

Out of breath, he pulled back, and searched her face. "Does that mean yes?"

Nodding, she grinned. "Yes, it does."

He let out a sigh of relief. "Oh, thank God! I thought I would have to beg you."

His eyes settled on her lips. Reaching up he pulled her face towards him. Kissing her ever so gently, he skillfully rolled her onto her back. His hand snaked out catching the clasp at the front of her bra. Bending down, he nipped at one perfect bud and was rewarded with a sound he'd only heard in his dreams before. A throaty moan escaped past her lips as she shoved her hands in his hair, guiding him as his tongue swirled.

When he pulled away, she cried out in pain. Pain from a burning need she'd never felt in her life. He was stirring sensations in her that she never knew existed. All she knew was that she was going over the edge at any second and it was gone. She opened her eyes, searching him out. He was undressing and she couldn't take her eyes off him. His muscles rippled under his skin, skin that felt so silky under her touch, with every move he made. Grabbing the blankets, she covered herself as she watched in stunned silence while he stood with his back to her. Ava watched as he pulled off his jeans and marveled at how he took his time. Most guys would have shucked their clothes and been back in bed in a flash. But not Mark. No. He took his sweet ole time.

She sucked in a breath and gripped the blankets tightly in her fists when he turned and stood in all his glory. Trying desperately to steady her racing heart, all she could think of was, *no wonder women were after him all the time...*

He crawled onto the bed like a cat stalking a bird and tugged on the blankets. "You're too beautiful to be hiding behind these." With a final tug, he dragged them off her and the bed.

Ava shuttered when he reached for her, and it wasn't because she was cold. No, the heat of his glance had her on fire and if he didn't put that fire out soon, she was sure she would self-combust.

Mark took her in his arms. Without a word, he laid her against the pillows. Kissing her softly, he trailed his mouth down a straight path to her belly button. As she moaned, he reached for her thong and freed her from it. Trailing his hands up her thighs, he settled himself between them, and carefully wrapped her legs around his waist.

"Is your ankle okay?" he asked.

Ava couldn't speak a word, instead she nodded.

"If it hurts you, let me know." Tenderly he kissed her eyes, her lips, and her throat as he entered her slowly, stroking her silkiness from within.

Ava felt as if she was riding a cloud in a lightning storm. With every stroke, an electrifying jolt seared her insides, turning her blood into molten fire. Mark was guiding her further and further into what felt like space. All she could see were shooting stars behind her closed eyes until they exploded into a million gleaming supernovas, lighting the heavens that lay before her. Just like he said he would.

Mark collapsed on her in spent pleasure. There had never been a time before that he had lost all sense of his being till now. He leaned over the side of the bed and pulled the blankets over them. Laying back, he pulled her close. Ava scooted towards him and laid her head on his chest, listening as his breathing returned to normal.

Mark took her chin and tilted her face, looking into her eyes he saw how tired she was. Giving her a quick peck on the tip of her nose he grinned. "All I have to say is wow."

She laughed. "Agreed. Now I can sleep. Goodnight."

"Goodnight, Ava." He trailed his fingers over the soft skin of her back.

"Mark?"

"Yeah?"

"I love you," she said quietly. Why she felt shy after what they had shared was beyond her. She felt his arms tighten around her, pulling her closer.

Mark inhaled her intoxicating scent and breathed. "I love you too."

For some reason, his thoughts went at once to Ash. If the man had played his cards right, he could be in this bed instead of him. But he didn't and Mark had finally found his one true love, his soulmate. Now he just needed to keep it that way...

Chapter 26

Ava's head was spinning like a leaf caught in a whirlwind. She was amazed at the inner peace she felt. For the first time in a long time, she was happy, almost to the point of being giddy.

It was the next morning and she and Mark had gotten up bright and early. Kim had texted the night before telling them to head over for breakfast at 9 am sharp. After being awakened by Mark's lips on her bare skin, they had showered together. Making love in the shower was a new experience for her and one that she had enjoyed thoroughly. Afterward, they headed over in his truck to Abbi and Ben's. The plan was that once the happy parents had gotten Annabelle home and settled, Mark was taking her to Springbank to buy a ring.

Walking in the back door of Ben and Abbi's, they soon discovered the house was in utter chaos. The cats were sitting in the middle of the table. The dogs were lapping up God knew what off the floor and Bird was flying around from room to room screeching at the top of his birdy lungs. Kim was cooking eggs, while Tim and Dean were blowing up balloons. There were eggshells littering the counter, bacon sizzling to a crisp in a pan and toast burning in the toaster.

"What the hell Aunt Kim." Ava coughed as a thick smoke hung in the air.

Mark walked over to the stove and turned the burners off. "Let me." He looked at Kim. "Open some windows will yeah? You can't have a baby coming into this stench."

Kim went to the windows and threw them open wide. "I got distracted from all the decorations," she mumbled.

"Here, let's move this stuff to the living room," Ava suggested, shooing the cats off the table. Gathering up the balloons and a Welcome Home sign, she looked at Mark and said, "Can you feed the beasts please?" She then made her way to the other room where Tim and Dean had gone with the rest of the decorations.

They had finished eating. Kim, Tim, and Mark were cleaning up the kitchen while Ava and Dean were finishing the decorating for the big homecoming. A knock on the front door had Kim whirling around. "Ooooh. Damnit, that's them," she squealed and waved a hand at the table. "Hurry, get this mess cleaned up. I'll get the door."

She all but ran to the front door, a big smile on her face as she flung it open. Her face fell when she saw who it was. "Oh... it's only you two," she said, stepping aside.

"Nice to see you too Aunt Kim," Lane snickered as he walked in and went to Ava.

Luke came over the threshold, stopped, and pulled her into his arms for a hug. Giving her a resounding kiss on the cheek he held her at arm's length. "You look great Aunt Kim!"

She gave him a sideways look. "Uh huh. Spit it out. What did you do?"

Luke looked at her in mock horror. "Me?! I didn't do anything." He held his hands defensively in front of him as he backed away.

Kim pointed a finger at him. "Don't you lie to me. I know when you have done something just from the way you act. Hey, don't you walk away–"

Luke ignored her and walked straight to Ava holding his arms wide. "Hey sis." He gave her a tight squeeze. "I've missed you."

Ava smiled. "I've missed you too."

"What did you do to your foot?" Lane asked.

"Long story. I twisted it bad on a run." She looked at Mark who was standing beside her then back at her brothers. "We'll tell you the rest later."

"Hey!" Kim called. "I'm not done with you Luke. Lane what did he do?" She slammed the door shut. At once a soft knock came from the other side. Kim turned and opened the door. A horrified look settled on her face when she saw who was standing there. It was Ben's parents.

"Can we come in?" A soft British accent asked.

"Oh Lord, I'm so sorry. I didn't mean to slam the door in your face," Kim said apologetically.

"Don't you worry Kim. Nancy slams the door in my face all the time," Greg smiled as he entered the house, his hands full of luggage.

Nancy giggled. "I do not!" She thought for a minute, then said, "Well there was that one time when Ben moved here, and you wouldn't allow me to follow him."

"Right! And it was a good thing too! If you'd come straight away like you wanted to, we wouldn't be here right now." Greg set the suitcases down and looked around the half-decorated room. He smacked his hands together. "Tell me what needs to be done."

All in a flurry Kim started barking orders at everyone and in no time the house was ready for baby Annabelle's homecoming. Everyone was waiting in the living room for the car to pull up when Luke got up and left the room. Within a minute he returned with an envelope and handed it to Ava.

"This went to your old business address. Julia, the new owner, thought it might be important and so she called me instead of sending it back to the sender."

Ava took the letter from him and looked at the return address. She looked at Mark and then Luke. "It's from a law firm in Montreal?"

Luke shrugged. "I have no idea, Ava."

"Open it," Mark said.

Ava carefully ripped the seal and took out the letter. Unfolding it she began to read it and stopped. "Oh my god. This is about Kurt's will." She shook her head. "I... I can't read it." She passed it to Mark.

Mark skimmed over it. It certainly was about his will and Ava was the sole beneficiary of it. A cool $30 million was left to her and her alone. It went on to say that there was a USB stick included and to please watch the video at her earliest convenience. Mark picked up the envelope and tipped it. Sure enough, a stick fell into his hand. Slipping it in his shirt pocket, he put his arm around her shoulders and kissed her on the head. "We will deal with it later."

Across the room, Lane jabbed Dean in the ribs. He jerked his chin towards his sister and Mark. "When did that happen?"

Dean rubbed the stubble on his jaw and looked at a spot on the ceiling in thought. Swinging his gaze to Lane he chuckled. "Oh, about nine months ago. Mark was just too blind to see it."

Lane smiled. "It's about damn time."

"They are here!!" Kim yelled from the front door. Nancy and she had been waiting anxiously, one on either side of the door, with their faces glued to the window. "Should we go out to greet them or hide behind the door?" She asked excitedly.

"It's not a surprise party Kim." Tim laughed. "You'll scare the shit out of them. Go."

Ava smiled as Kim and Nancy took off out the door. Truth be told, if her foot weren't still hurting, she would have beat them to the car.

Abbi walked into the house with a huge smile on her face. Ava could tell her mom was ecstatic to have her whole family under one roof again. She watched as her brothers each took their turn hugging her and meeting Annabelle for the first time. She looked at Mark who was watching the exchange as well. Ava still couldn't believe that this man by her side would soon be her husband. They had agreed not to say a word to anyone until after the excitement of the baby coming home settled down. Even then she didn't know if they should say anything. She would leave it up to Mark to decide.

"Ava honey, how is your foot doing?" Her mom asked standing before her. Ava took one look at her mother's face, and she could tell Abbi knew about her and Mark.

"Better." She looked down at her foot and remarked, "The swelling is finally going down."

"Good, I've been worried not knowing what's been going on. Ben filled me in. Shh, don't let on that I know. Kim will have a conniption if she finds out," Abbi chuckled.

Mark smiled. "We won't say a word."

"Good." Abbi nodded. "And Mark, just so you know... I approve." She winked, grinned, and walked away.

Mark whipped his gaze to Ava's. His brows shot up. "Did you tell her?"

She shook her head. "No. I imagine Ben must have said something. I think the only two people that didn't know about us before we did, were us."

He let that sink in for a second then laughed. "I think you're right." Leaning over he laid a kiss on her mouth. Her soft lips against his were intoxicating. With a groan he backed away and stood up. Something was bugging him, and it was in his shirt pocket. "Come on. We need to see what's on this stick."

Ava got up and followed him out of the room to the staircase. Without warning, Mark took her in his arms and carried her up the steps as if she weighed nothing.

"Where are we going?" She finally asked.

"To use your mom's computer," he said as they entered the office. He set her down by the desk and pulled out the chair. "Sit here." He grabbed another and put it beside her.

Sitting down, he pulled the stick from his pocket as Ava turned the computer on.

Mark looked at her while the laptop booted up. "So, have I told you lately I love you?"

She wrapped her arms around his neck and pulled him close. "No. I don't believe you have," she whispered against his lips.

Mark pulled her as close as the chairs allowed and breathed in her scent as he captured her lips with his. He wanted nothing more than to take her home but whatever was on the USB stick was bothering him too much to do so. A tightening of his jeans told him he needed to take it down a notch. Breaking the kiss off, he murmured against her parted lips, "Let's find out what's on this stick before we end up on the floor."

She grinned and nodded. He had her breathless and a little worried. Why was he so concerned about it? She didn't care. As far as she was concerned there was nothing that Kurt could have said to her that would change how she felt. But would there be something on it that would make Mark feel differently? God, she hoped not.

Mark stuck the stick into the USB slot and took the mouse in hand. Locating the file, he looked at Ava. "Ready?"

"Sure. Go ahead." She steeled herself for the inevitable feeling she knew she would experience at seeing Kurt's face after so long. Alive or dead the man still had the ability to haunt her dreams.

Ava, if you're watching this it means I've met my untimely death. I will cut to the chase and just come out with it. You were like a possession to me I guess you could say... one that I could control. I never realized how much I hurt you until you were gone. I needed that. If you hadn't left when you did, I likely would have destroyed all the good that was left in you and for that I'm terribly sorry. I never meant to hurt you like that.

Mark hit the pause button and looked over at her. She was having a hard go of it, no doubt remembering every un-called-for brutal attack. Turning the computer chair towards him, he pulled her onto his lap. "Are you okay?" Her face crumpled as the tears trickled down her cheek. He pressed his lips to her hair. "Shhh honey... We will end it here now."

Ava shook her head and sniffed. "No. It's fine." She looked up at him, a watery smile on her lips. "We will finish it."

"Okay." Mark sighed and hit the play button. If it were possible, he would have reached through the computer screen and throttled the guy.

I did genuinely love you. And because of that I leave all my money to you. The house we once lived in; I have left strict orders for my attorney that it is to be torn down. In its place, a native flower garden will be planted along with the construction of playground equipment. God knows the land is in dire need of some happy memories.

I know there is nothing of mine that you would want. Including my cars, the boat, and the house in Florida. All of that will be sold and the proceeds of that will be put to good use as well as the sale of the thirteen acres behind the house. It will be all donated.

I know your love of dogs and so it will be distributed for adoption and vetting fees at the animal shelter of your choosing. There will also be a fund set up for those who cannot cover the

*costs of their vet bills. I am including that those funds will be for
anyone that needs the help from any Veterinary clinic in Ontario. Don't worry, there will be yearly interest to give to the
fund from the twenty million I set aside for just that purpose.*

*I can't say I don't blame you for hating me. I was a monster
to you. You never deserved what I put you through and I hope
one day you can find it in your heart to somehow forgive me.
Take care of yourself, Ava. I hope that life is good to you and
that you find someone that is the total opposite of me in every
way. He will be a lucky man. I only can pray that he knows just
how lucky he is...*

Ava sat in stunned silence. She didn't know what to say.
She felt completely numb. It was like Kurt had had a pre-
monition that he had to atone for his sins. Surely to God it
wasn't from her leaving him. He would have found her and
tried to amend his way if it were. She started to wonder what
could have possibly happened when she stopped herself. It
didn't matter. She didn't want anything from him. She forgave him already; she didn't need his money either.

Mark could feel the tension radiating from her. Running
his hand down her back he said, "He got a few things right."

Ava looked at him blankly. Not understanding what he
meant. "What?"

He jerked his head towards the computer. "Kurt. He got
a few things right."

Ava's brows raised as she replayed the video in her mind.

"I am a lucky man." He pulled her close, until they were
face to face. "And I do know how lucky I am." He nipped her
bottom lip just before he captured hers in a soul shattering
kiss.

"HEY! You guys coming back downstairs?" Dean shouted from the top of the stairs. "Tim just got a call. You're gonna want to hear this." He disappeared back down the staircase.

"I guess that's our cue," Ava smiled and stood.

"I guess it is," he growled in her ear as he took her in his arms.

As he carried her over the catwalk to the staircase he said, "When Tim gets done telling us his news, should we let everyone know we are heading to Springbank to get a ring, or should we wait until after?"

"Hmm. Let's see what the news is first."

Descending the stairs, he said, "Fine by me."

Mark followed the sound of voices into the dining room. Everyone was sitting around the table looking at Tim who was talking on his phone. "Got it. Thanks Vince."

Tim looked at Ava. "That was the cop that was here yesterday taking Sebastian away. They got a warrant and searched his place. The print they found at Eleanor's matched with one they lifted from his house and the pop can. And yes, he drugged your drink. He will be charged with that. They also found a weapon stashed in his bedroom. Eleanor's rolling pin. Had her blood on it so he's charged for assault and break and enter too."

"Oh, thank God," Kim murmured.

"Also, he talked," Tim continued. "Kurt had confided in him that he was coming here to make amends with you, Ava. The police suspect he might have had something to do with the brakes failing in Kurt's car. Unfortunately, the car has since been destroyed so there is no way to tell."

"Why would the police suspect him of tampering with the brakes?" Abbi asked.

"Likely because Kurt was bringing the coat as a peace offering." Ben looked at Tim. "Is that right?"

"That's exactly right. But there was no coat at the accident scene."

"That's because it ended up being delivered here on Christmas day," Mark added. Something just clicked inside Mark's brain. "Sonofa*bitch*!"

Kim jumped. "What?!"

"I just realized, the delivery driver that brought that package was him. It was Sebastian. I gave that bastard a $100.00 tip," Mark hissed.

"That's how he knew where the box was buried. He was watching us, the creep." Ava shuddered.

"How did he get the coat though?" Greg asked.

"Sebastian was following Kurt. He was the first on scene. He called 911."

Dean rubbed his jaw. "So, he scooped the coat, threw it into his car then called the cops?"

Tim nodded.

"So, let me get this straight," Lane spoke up. "This guy has been obsessed with Ava for how long?"

"It didn't start off like that," Tim said, pulling out a chair, he finally sat down. "He might have had a case of puppy love at first. But no. What started it was when Kurt told him that he'd just finished having a will made up. What Sebastian told Vince is that Kurt told him he was coming here to ask forgiveness with the coat. Apparently, Kurt was leaving his cousin something too but didn't say what. That got the gears going in Sebastian's head, another reason why the cops think he had something to do with it. He wanted his inheritance. What he didn't know at the time was that what Kurt was leaving him was the car he was driving the day of the accident. Nothing else. Ava got everything."

"So, he comes here posing as a landscaper from Texas in hopes to sidle up to Ava. For what? The money?" Luke asked.

"Yup. He had to try to win her over though to get to the money," Tim said. "Only problem was he wasn't expecting her family and an 'overbearing friend who she constantly talked about and was in love with,' his words not mine." Tim smiled.

"Figures," Kim smacked the table and hooted. "Even an out of towner nut ball could see what you two couldn't."

Mark leaned back and stretched an arm around the back of Ava's chair. He looked at her and raised his brows. At her slight nod, he looked at everyone around the table. Finally, he said, "Yeah, well that's all changed now." Taking Ava's hand, they both got to their feet. "We are going to head to Springbank... for a few days."

Kim stood too. "What! Why?"

"We are going shopping, Aunt Kim," Ava said, holding on to the back of the chairs as she made her way over to her mother.

"For a few days?" Kim balked. "What the hell is going to take you a few days to buy?"

Bending down, Ava gave her mother a hug and whispered softly to her, "He's asked me to marry him, mom. I said yes."

Abbi stood and hugged her daughter close to her. She couldn't believe her baby girl was getting married. She leaned back and searched Ava's eyes. For the first time, longer than she could remember, Abbi saw the sparkle in her daughter's eyes. She was happy and that was all that mattered to Abbi. Tearing up, she gave Ava another tight squeeze before walking over to Mark.

"What the hell is going on?" Kim demanded as she watched Abbi glide over to Mark and Ava hug Ben.

Ignoring her sister, Abbi opened her arms wide and met Mark for a hug. "You take care of her for me," she softly mumbled as the tears started flowing.

Voice thick with emotion, he replied, "Forever Abbi. I promise you."

Mark walked over to where Ava was standing holding onto the chair. Wrapping an arm around her waist he pulled her towards him, until they were facing one another. "Kim to answer your question." He took Ava's chin in his hand and gazed into her eyes. "We are going shopping for a ring. I asked Ava to marry me, and she said yes."

Kim started hooping and hollering. Going from one person to the next she jumped and hugged them excitedly. Calming down a bit she cornered Luke. "Did you hear that!!" she asked, sitting beside him.

"I did Aunt Kim. So, um about earlier." He leaned back and reached into his jeans pocket, pulling out a set of keys he slid them in front of her.

"What's this?" She asked, turning them over.

"It's a set of keys." He folded his arms across his chest, with a smile on his face.

"I know that. What are they for?"

"For you."

Kim whipped her head up. Tears sprang to her eyes.

"I bought a Hummer. I'm giving you, my Jag. Lane drove it up here for you." He watched as her chin crinkled and her lower lip trembled. "Oh, come on now. Don't cry."

Kim flung her arms around his neck and rocked side to side. "This is the nicest thing anyone has ever done for me," she blubbered and sniveled loudly. "Thank you. I mean that."

"Come on. Let's go congratulate Ava and Mark," Luke said, pulling his aunt to her feet, they got in line.

Everyone took their turn congratulating the happy couple. When it was his turn Dean walked over and clapped Mark on the back and held out his hand for a shake. "Congrats man." Looking at Ava, he leaned down and kissed her on the cheek. "I'm happy for you Ava. You'll make a beautiful bride."

"Thank you, Dean," she reached up and hugged him.

After hugging Ava and scolding her for not telling her, Kim walked over to Mark and playfully punched him on the arm. "What am I going to do now? I'm losing my partner in crime."

Mark looked at her, his face softened when he saw her red eyes. "Have you been crying?" he asked, pulling her into a hug.

"Yeah. But not because of you," she answered. "Luke gave me his Jaguar." Stepping back, she laughed and said, "Now I'll have to drive five km under my usual speed."

"Lord help us all," he chuckled. "That was really nice of him."

"It was. But you didn't answer my question about what I'm going to do now? Without you."

"I'll still be here Kim. We will get up to some shenanigans, I'm sure."

"Yeah. I guess you're right." She now would need a place to move to. Before it was fine. But now she would just be a third wheel. Maybe she would move back to Windsor. Luke and Lane were sure to need her... wouldn't they?

"I know what you can do, Kim," Tim called out.

"You do? What do you have in mind?" she asked eagerly. She really didn't want to move back to Windsor. It never did feel like home to her. Pearl Lake was home.

Tim's eyes had a mischievous twinkle in them. "Yeah. You can help Dean. I'm sure he will need a hand."

"Yeah. I'm sure I can put you to work. Hell, how does room and board sound? I'll even feed you." Dean sent her a sly smile.

"What are you talking about?" She frowned. "You're American."

Dean leaned nonchalantly against the wall. "Was. I wasn't going to say anything. But seeing how the sale is final and my friend here can't seem to keep his mouth shut... you're all looking at the new owner of the Anderson place."

"Oh. *Hell* no!" Was all Kim managed to sputter out before she plopped into a chair. Images of the condition of that house ran through her mind. She looked over at Dean. He shot her a wink, and that damn sexy sly smile.

Call her crazy, but she was entertaining the idea.

Here is a look into The Inn at Pearl Lake

Chapter 1

[1]THERE WAS A COLD FEELING that seeped into Kim's bones when she stepped over the threshold of the old Anderson place, into the massive front foyer. You know the one. The one that infiltrates your whole being into one mind numbing thought. The only

---

thing you can think about when you're so unbearably cold. Only it wasn't the cold weather that was making her feel that way. Oh no. It was the hideous thing she had just walked into, her new home.

She rubbed her hands up and down her arms in hopes to generate some heat. It wasn't working. The fact that a massive staircase stood before her, its darkened steps summoning her to take a gander up, didn't help any.

From her vantage point, it looked like it went left and right at the top. One would think the window at the landing would allow some light in, considering it was the size of a drive-in movie screen. But no, it was dirty with dust and grime and what looked like... "Is that *batshit?!* I am *not* cleaning that," she grumbled to herself. Another thing she was certain of; she wasn't about to climb those stairs alone.

The further she walked into the cavernous manor, with its chipped paint, and plaster falling from the walls, the colder she got. As her eyes took in the sights around her, her only thought was to get the hell out of the place. It was dark and dingy, it smelled bad, and it didn't want her there as far as she was concerned.

She glanced into the living room; her eyes drawn to the fireplace where she was told old man Anderson had been shot to death. That was, according to Mark Donovan, an actor and Kim's roommate who was marrying her niece, Ava, also her roommate. He'd told her the story of the Andersons the night Ava had disappeared. When they had ended up at the house to look around, both had noticed the sold sign on the front lawn. At the time, she had thought anyone who bought the place must have had a screw loose. Little did she know she would be moving in a few months later.

Holding her breath, Kim stalked over to where she assumed the man had fallen; to see if there were any tell-tale stains. She of course was looking for blood.

"How stupid can you be?" she muttered to herself, knowing full well over 100 years had passed since the man's fate had been sealed. She swiped her foot over a pile of dead leaves, wondering if they had come down the chimney, when a rat scurried out from under them. "Gaaaahhh!" she shouted, doing a jig across the floor. With her pounding heart settling, her eyes zeroed in on the exposed floor. She moved to the other side of the large fireplace that was big enough to park a Buick in, her eyes inspecting as she went. "Nothing." Oddly, she felt disappointed.

The word was no sooner out of her mouth when she felt a vibration under her feet followed by a loud bang echoing throughout the room. She spun around at the culprit that interrupted her snooping, her gaze falling to the floor to where a suitcase laid.

"Sorry about that," Dean said, his hands full of her luggage, a bag stuffed under each arm. Brows raised, he looked at her. "Where do you want these?"

Three months ago, Kim knew she was going to be in a pickle when Ava and Mark announced their engagement. She didn't want to be a third wheel, invading their privacy, but she didn't have a place to go either. That same day, Dean had told everyone about the beautiful stately home that he'd just bought down the road that needed a little work. So, when he suggested she move with him to the manor to give the love birds some space now, instead of after the two were married, she'd jumped at it. As she looked around, she realized he just wanted free labour.

"Ah..." Her mouth worked like a fish out of water as images of bugs, and critters danced through her mind. Shuddering, she squeaked out, "I don't know, where are the bedrooms?"

"I would imagine upstairs," he set the baggage down and looked at her. "Why don't we take a tour of the place?"

Kim took a step towards him and jerked a thumb over her shoulder. "You do know someone was shot in this room, don't you?"

He placed his hands on his hips. "Yeah," he nodded. "You told me five times since we left Ava's."

"Who in their right mind would buy a house in this condition?"

Chuckling, Dean shot back, "I never claimed to be in my right mind."

Leading the way to the archway dividing the living room from the front foyer he stopped and glanced over his shoulder at her. "Which way? Left, straight ahead or upstairs?"

"The least creepiest?"

"Left it is."

Heading that way, Dean stopped and swiped at the cobwebs that blocked the entrance of a short-arched hallway.

"What is it with all these arches?" Kim asked as she gawked at what she was sure was the entrance to hell. He didn't answer. Taking a deep breath, she followed him forward into the unknown and was shocked to find the walls were made of stone like the rest of the manor. Halfway down, another arch led off to the right. Kim assumed it went right under the massive staircase. She shuddered at the thought as to what was at the end of that hall. She grabbed hold of Dean's jacket. There was no way he was getting out of her sight.

His sudden stop had her colliding with him as he let out a low whistle. "Well would you look at this."

Kim tried to look around him but at her five-foot two-inch chubby frame, to his six-foot one inch, it was impossible. She wasn't having any luck. He filled the exit of the hallway with his cop physique.

Smacking at his back, she tried to squeeze past him. "Will you get the hell out of the way?"

"Where are my manners?" Chuckling, Dean bowed out of the way for her to pass.

"Whoa..." She was gobsmacked as she took in her surroundings. It was a sunroom. No, not just a sunroom but a solarium. She counted twenty arched windows from floor to ceiling in the massive circular room. Kim looked at the ceiling where more windows were placed between honey-coloured beams of wood. "I hope those are all good. Otherwise, it's going to cost a fortune to replace them," she muttered.

Dean rubbed the back of his neck; he could already feel the tension from the mere thought of it... *What the hell was I thinking, buying this place?* "Uh huh... I'll need to get a ladder and inspect them."

Glancing around the room, Kim saw a tree growing through a crack in the floor. "Look at that," she chuckled, gesturing behind him. "You have your first plant."

Dean groaned when his eyes settled on it. All he could think of was the cost to repair the floor and likely the foundation too.

Taking notice of his reaction, Kim pointed up. "You know, if those windows need replacing on the ceiling, just take them all out." She walked over to one along the wall and ran a hand over the frame. "It would be easy enough to remove them and turn this into an open breezeway," she suggested, looking at him. She could tell the gears were moving in his mind from the way he stood there in thought.

Stepping over to her, he threw an arm around her shoulders. "You know, I think you're right. Even if they don't need replacing. We could put a door there heading into the hallway."

"Right?" she gave him a vigorous nod and smiled. "Come on. Let's finish our tour."

Together they walked back to the front foyer. "Now where?" Dean asked.

Kim glanced up the stairs. There was something about them that made her want to run for the hills. "Ahhh," she tore her gaze away from them and looked at Dean. "Kitchen?" she asked, raising her brows.

Taking her by the hand, he tugged. "Come on, I'd say it's this way." Normally she'd be the first to do the exploring, but not this time. Comforted by the feel of his skin against hers, without a word Kim let him lead the way, in case they happened upon another rat.

They stepped through an archway into what appeared to be a sitting room with a hallway off to their immediate left.

Shaking her head, she spoke first, "This isn't a kitchen."

"Nope. It's not."

Dean glanced around the room. Kim could tell he was regretting his decision. She would never understand why someone would move thousands of miles away to buy a rundown house sight unseen with the idea of turning it into an Inn. She felt bad for him.

"What are you thinking about?" she asked.

He glanced out the window at the lake. It really was a beautiful view, he thought. Clearing his throat, he said, "If I were a smart rich man, I'd tear the whole place down and rebuild. But seeing how I'm neither, I was thinking that this room would make a perfect front desk."

One hand on her hip she leaned to the side. "Not that it's any of my business, but how much money do you have?" Kim asked, frowning.

Dean pinched the bridge of his nose and sucked in a breath. "Not enough," he exhaled.

"Okay... okay, you're going to need some help. I've got a bit stashed away, but not enough to fix and furnish the place." *What the hell am I thinking?*

"No. I can't ask that of you. I'll just put it back on the market. It was a stupid idea anyway. I'll just move back to Arizona."

"Arizona? I thought you were from Tennessee?"

"I was a US Marshall. I went where they sent me. I'm from Arizona," he explained.

At his words Kim felt a sensation of panic rising in her chest. Something that momentarily shocked her from responding. She didn't want him to leave.

"You didn't ask, I'm offering. There was a reason you decided to come here. No sense in going back there. We can be partners," she suggested. "Besides, who the hell is going to buy this place?" she swept a hand around the room.

"I did. I'm sure someone else will."

"Forget it," she said, folding her arms across her chest. "You're not going anywhere. We'll become partners whether you like it or not and that's it. Now, show me where you were thinking of putting the front desk."

Dean chuckled. "Has anyone ever told you you're bossy, partner?"

A smile broke out on her face, with a twinkle in her eyes, she nodded. "All the time... partner." Laughing she held her hand out for a shake.

Instead of taking it, he leaned forward and kissed her on the cheek.

Kim could feel the blood rush to the spot his lips had touched. Was it a blush or the heat of his mouth against her skin? She had no clue, but she liked it.

Smacking his hands together Dean turned and stepped forward showing her where he imagined the desk would be. As she watched how animated his face became, she realized she had no clue what the hell he was even talking about. In her wildest dreams she never would have thought of Dean that way. But here she was entranced by this man before her. The only coherent thought she had was that she was about to become a full-fledged partner in a haunted mansion that neither of them could afford to fix. It was at that moment she realized she was crazy, or she had a serious case of puppy love for an ex-cop. Just what she needed; a man that could match her witty sarcasm like no other. Now she needed a way to keep him here and quick.

"Kim! Are you coming?"

She shook her head, clearing her thoughts, she focused on his face. "What?"

"Are you coming?" Dean asked. "I think the kitchen is this way," he motioned with a turn of his shoulders.

"Yeah, lead the way."

"Man, would you look at this wallpaper? It's in perfect condition. Should we keep it?" he asked, running a hand along the wall of the hallway.

Kim looked at the print. It was in perfect condition. The giant hibiscus stared back at her. It reminded her of a jumpsuit she had. "Uh. Sure. It will keep the cost down."

An open doorway stood to the right. Poking their heads in they saw that it was in relatively good condition, and large.

"What do you suppose this was?" she asked.

"Not sure. But we will figure out something to do with it," Dean replied, backing out of the room. "By the looks of it there are four more doors off this hallway."

"Hopefully, one is a bathroom. I've been holding it for the past half hour," Kim said.

Dean continued; each room was a repeat of the first. Except for the last, it was the coveted bathroom.

"Oh, thank you baby Jesus!" Kim slammed the door and headed straight for the toilet and grimaced in disgust. "Oh my..." Helicoptering it was, she would hover.

When she was done, she flushed the toilet and went to the sink to wash her hands. Turning the tap, the only thing that came out was a spider. She screamed at the top of her lungs when she felt the little hairy legs tap dance across the back of her hand. Flinging her hands in revulsion, she screamed even louder when the door busted in, banging loudly against the wall.

"What the hell is it?" Dean stood there, a crazed look in his eyes.

"There was a spider..." Throwing a hand towards the sink, she pointed. "That is the first thing that is going. Taps and all."

"Oh, I don't know. It looks almost brand new?"

Kim stalked into the hallway, "The hell it is, it's going."

Dean raised his hands, "Okay," he said and pointed. "The kitchen is next."

Kim headed in the direction he had shown, wanting to be as far away from the washroom as she could.

The room was large like the others had been so far. The new stainless-steel appliances that were delivered a few days ago, shone like beacons on a dismal day in the dingy kitchen, the humming of the fridge was the only sound in the silent room. Kim decided the walls needed a fresh coat or two of canary yellow paint to brighten it up. Like the rest of the house, there were windows galore, so natural lighting wouldn't be an issue. They could grow their own herbs and possibly some veggies with all the sunlight that would pour in once the windows were cleaned.

She had half expected to see a dirt floor, but instead it was brick like a cobblestoned street. It would have to go. There was no way she was scrubbing it like the Andersons maid currently was. On her hands and knees, an old bristle brush in one hand and a bucket of water alongside her. She smiled when the lady looked her way. Good lord, she felt so bad for her, it would take the woman a full day to clean it.

Wait... Kim giggled. She *was* tired from all the excitement of packing the past week. She blinked her eyes rapidly. But when that didn't help, she rubbed at them. Satisfied that that should do the trick, she cracked them open just a speck. She could feel her eyes almost pop out of their sockets. The woman was still there on all fours, scrubbing and looking straight at her.

Reaching behind her Kim grabbed a hold of Dean's pant leg and shook it. "Are you seeing what I'm seeing?" she squeaked.

"The stone fireplace? Yeah. It's awesome. It would make a perfect grilling station."

Out of the side of her mouth she muttered, "Not that..." Slowly, Kim turned around, her eyes never breaking contact, until she was facing Dean. Swinging her face towards him, she looked up and whispered, "You don't see the lady there by the window?"

Dean turned his head towards the windows. Without moving, he shifted his gaze to look back at Kim. "No?"

Kim whipped her head around. Sure, as shit the woman was gone. Eyes round, Kim said, "I'm telling you, there was a woman scrubbing the floor. She looked like a maid and had a brush and a wooden bucket."

"I believe you Kim. I just didn't see her." Glancing at his watch he said, "Why don't we grab our stuff and head upstairs. Get the bedrooms ready, then head over to Mack's for a burger?"

She rubbed her forehead. Kim didn't know if she would be able to sleep in the house after seeing that. Especially upstairs. "Can we just camp out down here in one of the rooms for now? The furthest from the kitchen preferably."

He'd never seen her so shook up before. Not even when Mark and she thought they'd met a vampire. He had to stifle a chuckle at that memory. "Sure. I'll just go get our stuff from the truck. We can figure out what to do tomorrow," Dean offered, heading towards the hallway.

"Wait for me!" she exclaimed, hoofing it after him. "I'm coming with you!".

Together, they brought in what they'd need for the night from the vehicle. Stopping briefly to pick up Kim's luggage from the living room, Dean followed her as she headed for the hallway.

"I'll take the room next to this one," he told her.

"Like hell you will mister. You got me in this mess..." She squealed as she jerked her chin in the direction of the kitchen. "After what I saw in there you're nuts if you think I'm sleeping in this room alone. Drop your shit in here so we can leave. I'm hungry," she grumbled, pointing at the floor.

Dean chuckled, shaking his head in response, he did her bidding. There was no way he was going to question her about her sanity at this point. He hadn't seen anything out of the ordinary, and he knew she was tired. The anxiety she had been feeling over the last few weeks at the thought of moving to the manor had her in a tizzy. Dean was sure that's what Kim's problem was, nothing a good night's sleep wouldn't cure. "C'mon. Let's get to Mack's before it gets busy."

Kim needed no more encouragement. "I'm driving," she said, beating him out the door to her car. She started the Jag, a gift her nephew Luke had so kindly given her and as she waited for Dean to get in, she glanced in her sideview mirror and just about pissed her pants. The second his door closed, she stomped on the gas pedal and the sleek car shot forward.

Dean darted a look in her direction, shocked that she wasn't driving her customary 10 kph. "Are you in a hurry?" he drawled.

Not wanting him to think she was crazier than he already did, she glanced at him with a nervous giggle. "What makes you think that?"

"No reason."

How would he react if she told him, she just about messed herself? It wasn't because she had to use the washroom, she'd just done that not more than twenty minutes ago. No. It was because while Dean was walking up to the car, she saw the perfect outline of a figure standing at the living room window watching him...

You can find The Inn at Pearl Lake On Amazon[2]

2.   https://mybook.to/TheInnatPL

{Pearl Lake Series}

Reading Order
Moonlit Night (Moonlit Stalker included)
Moonlit Road
Heaven in the Moonlight
The Inn at Pearl Lake
Lane's Destiny
Tim's Bar
Her Christmas Wish
You can find the Pearl Lake Series right here! [1]

{The Blood Moon Series}
The Summons
Heaven and Hell
You can find here! [2]

---

1. https://mybook.to/tKd5

2. https://mybook.to/XrHv

Made in United States
Orlando, FL
01 January 2024

41904816R00171